SHADOWSHINE

Keith Howard

TSL Publications

First published in Great Britain in 2019
By TSL Publications, Rickmansworth

ISBN / 978-1-913294-05-2

Cover image:
https://pixabay.com/illustrations/hell-purgatory-heaven-stairs-path-735995/
https://pixabay.com/photos/sunrise-sky-blue-sunlight-clouds-165094/
https://pixabay.com/illustrations/death-cute-mascot-grim-reaper-1460981/
https://pixabay.com/vectors/devil-red-demon-cartoon-satan-29973/

PROLOGUE

If the Shadowshine Reincarnation Centre exists it is merely a staging post on the way to Higher Things. A celestial sorting house with about the same efficiency (or lack of it) as any earthly administrative concern. The worst cases are sorted out while the rest move on to higher realms for spiritual assessment. But these enlightened ones are few and the ascent is merely an upward-running trickle, for Man is closely bound to the material things of life and remains basically a wilful child for his entire threescore years and ten.

And on the far-flung outskirts of Shadowshine the Clouds of Time roll in shimmering cumulus, moulded and shaped forever by the Temporal Custodian, Father Time, forever mapping out the scenario of Man's destiny in life's impromptu drama. Not for him the endless stream of wailing souls. He is but the mechanic who puts the show on the road.

But there is another realm of Shadowshine which actually impinges itself on the mortal planes of existence. Beyond the jet and gleaming broadwalk that links to its nucleus lies the Dream Zone. Here is the place the astrals of the living and the dead can meet again for a few fleeting moments in the realms of sleep. And if Shadowshine has a weak link then it is here in the Dream Zone where there is always the danger of some perceptive slumbering mortal whose astral spirit retains some memory it shouldn't do. How else are prophecies and visions born?

In the case of the Negative Zone things are far less complicated. Not for nothing is this area referred to as a 'necessary evil', resembling a fiery holiday camp.

In many guises from many spheres of life the Grim Reaper shepherds his bewildered charges through the Valley of the Shadow, neither malevolent nor benevolent. This dark servant of Eternity does not cause death – he is Death. And it is not only the Earth he has to contend with. He has other worlds in the vastness of the continuum to deal with, too. Often at the same time, and even before then.

Shadowshine is always with us, watching and waiting, missing nothing. Within its heart, where lies the crossroads of all who pass through, dwells the Soul Searcher, and entity of pure thought, untrammelled by any permanent corporeal form. He – the pronoun is but loosely used – is visible to the souls only in the guise that they would expect to see such an entity in. From his place in the centre of things he views all that occurs in Shadowshine by means of the serpentine light locks which twine and girdle around his domain, piercing through the para-dimensional planes of existence to the other realms of Shadowshine like ultra-violet-headed, infra-red-tailed worms.

Like a spider in his web, deep within the Shadowshine Auditorium, the Soul Searcher awaits the souls which bide their time in stasis cells, awaiting his summons. Then each soul is decharacterised of its former mortal identity and sent packing for another lifetime of trial and tribulation. Without ceasing, the Soul Searcher reviews the endless procession of souls with unerring accuracy. This time is it a mortal soul from Twentieth Century Earth. Hastily he resumes the white-bearded, white-robed earthly more and consults his ledger. Then in a voice that booms through the known senses and beyond, calls out his summons.

'Bring in Arthur Cramphorn!'

THE DEATH AND LIFE OF ARTHUR CRAMPHORN

Arthur Cramphorn was a clerk in a government office, but he was not very good at his job. He was married and he was not very good at that either. And one morning in March he was crossing the road and – sad to say – he was no better at that.

He died instantly and the funeral was taken care of by the Co-op, who had dealt, almost by tradition, with the past members of his family. His wife, a realistic woman in the extreme, was quite put out by her spouse's sudden demise. The kitchen was yet to be decorated and he had promised to start on it at the Easter weekend.

She wore black for what she considered to be the appropriate period of time. Then with the meagre amount left her by Arthur, she moved from their rented flat in North London and went to live with a Malagasy vegetarian in Birmingham.

But what of Arthur? For him the Great Adventure had just begun … or so he thought. His first recollection since losing the argument with the Meals on Wheels van was of sitting in pale blue nothingness on a carpet of white cloud. Glancing down, Arthur observed that his feet were encased in his favourite old carpet slippers. Odd, he thought. He had thrown them away two years ago when they had finally fallen apart. Further inspection revealed that he was also wearing his much cherished gardening trousers – condemned to a fiery fate last Guy Fawkes Night – and his dearly beloved Hawaiian beach shirt which he purchased in his bachelor days, since donated four years previously by his wife to Oxfam.

Most odd, he mused. He had a vague recollection of the van incident and although he realised that he was no longer in his mortal state, he felt no surprise only a faint air of apprehension, much the same as in the doctor's waiting room when he had 'housemaid's knee'.

He then became aware of a presence nearby. It was very strange because there had been no one in sight. But there in front of him, rooted in a sedate little pink and blue cloud, was a tall desk of silver and gold. On this desk was a magnificently bound tome, its several thousand pages gilt–edged and opened somewhere near the middle. The figure which sat on the high stool behind the desk, robed in a dazzling white toga-like robe and peering over the book at him, was most imposing. A broad brow framed by white hair that met and mingled with the curling beard gave the presence an Olympian aspect. So much so, in fact, that he exclaimed, 'By Jove!' before he realised it.

The apparition checked something in the book and looked up with a frown. 'Are you Ancient Roman?'

'Over my dead body!' Arthur retorted indignantly.

'Rather an academic statement in view of your present circumstances. Kindly answer the question properly.'

'I'm a British subject,' Arthur muttered sullenly.

'That's what it's got here,' grumbled the apparition, 'and I would be grateful if you would refrain from confusing the issue by referring to me as Jove.'

Arthur felt nettled. Typical bureaucratic pomposity. He had seen enough of it at the office. 'It's just that you look a bit like one of the Ancient Roman or Greek gods,' he replied.

'Hah!' cackled the other. 'Is that how you see me? Well you're not the only one. Several million other souls see me something like that. Others see me quite differently.'

Arthur stared around him. There was no one else in sight. In the distance, beyond the circle of white marble pillars that supported the cloudy and vaulted dome of the vast auditorium, he could hear what sounded like the heavenly choir running up the scale. 'What others?' he asked. 'There's nobody else here. And who are you anyway? Saint Peter?'

'You mortals are so egotistical,' snorted the bearded presence. 'No, I am not Saint Peter. I am the Soul Searcher and my appointed task is to sort out who goes where. And you can take my word for it that this place could be packed solid, but you wouldn't be able to see them any more than they would be able to see you. After all, you are merely an incorporeal soul.'

'But that's ridiculous,' Arthur objected, glancing down at his Hawaiian shirt, his gardening trousers, his slippers. 'I'm just as normal except for the clothes. I admit that I don't understand –'

'That's big of you,' the Soul Searcher snorted. 'You see yourself as you subconsciously wish to.'

'And how do you see me?' challenged Arthur.

'As a thought that counts ... a parting of the ways ... a shadow of doubt. Being a soul you are really quite an abstract little fellow.'

Arthur felt somewhat deflated. 'I don't think of a soul as being like that,' he murmured. 'I imagined it as a blobby little starfish thing.'

'Well you got the "little" part right – and that's about the first thing you have. You, as a soul, are so small that you wouldn't register in your own universe. A soul belongs in this one.'

Arthur's indignation vanished, to be replaced by interest. 'You mean micro universes of atoms and electrons that are really like suns' planets?'

'Right in one,' the Soul Searcher nodded approvingly. 'Just as your own universe is part of a greater existence.'

'So where does this soul universe exist in relation to the one lived in before the Meals on Wheels van hit me?'

'At that time it was part of the molecular structure of an Albanian pimp's wooden leg,' came the impatient retort. 'Now let us proceed with the business in hand.'

'But if you see so many souls as you say you do, sir, how do you have time to deal with them all?'

'We don't have time.'

'That's exactly what I mean, sir – Your Honour. If you don't have the time, then how do you manage?'

The Soul Searcher shot him a withering glance. 'You miss the point. We do not have time here – for the simple reason that here time does not exist. It's all in the Time Zone.'

Arthur mentally struggled to accept his new state of being. 'But we were right about some of the things,' he persisted. 'The long white beard and heavenly choir.'

'I am not who you think I am!' snapped the Soul Searcher testily. 'I am what you call a – a branch manager. And anyway, only you and others like you see me this way. Alpha Centaurians, Martians and Venusians all see me quite differently. Now, to business.' He marked a place on his book a long finger. 'You are Arthur Gregory Cramphorn, of Peckham, the planet Earth?'

'Well, not exactly exactly, we had just moved to Wembley –'

'Answer the question!' thundered the Soul Searcher. 'You are Arthur Cramphorn?'

'I am,' croaked Arthur, dry of throat.

'Now about your conduct sheet. Let's see how you fared with the Ten Commandments.'

'I've never coveted my neighbour's ox,' Arthur stoutly defended himself.

'And you've never returned his lawn mower. Dear me, you haven't done very well, have you, you poor soul?'

Arthur lost his temper. It was just as bad as when he had applied for a tax rebate. 'I've never killed anyone and I've never committed adultery!'

'No ... and nearly,' came the stern retort. 'Hmm you've got an X Plus grading, I'd say. Let's see how you shape up in the Seven Deadly Sins.'

Arthur quaked. He was well aware that in his mortal life he had been quite a self-indulgent fellow. 'Not very good,' rumbled the Soul Searcher. 'Not very good at all.' He closed the volume with the sound of a thunderclap. 'A Z Minus grading.'

'Does that mean I'm in for the chop?' Arthur whimpered. 'Are you going to send me to Hell?'

For the first time the Soul Searcher's austere countenance relaxed in a benign smile. A parade of seraphs marched past his desk, strumming golden harps and six chubby cherubs victory-rolled overhead and vanished into the wide blue yonder. 'Not at all, Arthur Cramphorn That Was. You would have had to incur a Double Z grading for that. By the same token you do not qualify for "higher things".'

Arthur's sudden hopes were dashed. 'Then what's going to happen to me?'

'Nothing more unusual than happens to ninety-nine percent of the other souls,' the Soul Searcher reassured him. 'You will simply be consigned to Limbo for a period of what you call time.'

'But how long will that be?' wailed Arthur. 'Weeks, months, years ... centuries?'

Soul Searcher laughed. In response a golden trumpet played something suspiciously like 'I Don't Want To Set The world On Fire', and the invisible choir warbled in chorus. 'Hardly centuries. The exact period has yet to be decided, but at the end of what you would refer to as a given time your case will come for review.

'And how do I get to this Limbo place?' Arthur enquired nervously, forcing himself to face up to the inevitable.

'Don't fret. We'll attend to the transport problem,' the Soul Searcher replied. 'You're as good as there now. Better luck next time around.'

Darkness shrouded Arthur and he felt a sense of movement. Not up or down. More like backwards and sideways. Then the darkness closed over him and was precipitated into the Gulf between All that Is and Was and is Yet to Be ...

The nurse in the little mission hospital smiled down at the plump-faced Inuit woman in the bed 'There you are, Mrs Nanook,' she said, holding up a red-faced, squalling infant, swathed in a thick shawl. 'There's nothing wrong with her lungs.'

And the fast-dispersing vestiges of the new-born child's soul which had previously been Arthur Cramphorn, realised in that fleeting moment why babies cry when they are born.

SHADOWSHINE ONE

The Soul Searcher relaxed into his natural form of a non-corporeal whorl of vacuum and passed through the light lock. There was a movement on the spectrum. Another entity was approaching. It must be Grimshaw. Yes, it was – and still in his terrestrial mode. There could be no mistaking that ragged old shroud and broken-bladed scythe that hadn't seen a whetstone in centuries.

The Soul Searcher regarded his colleague with a critical optic sensor as the Grim Reaper opened a stasis locker and carelessly tossed his scythe into it. 'Have a good trip, Grimshaw?' he asked the skeletal being who seemed to be having some difficulty disentangling his black leather Shadowshine hold-all from the frayed drawstring of his shroud.

'Fair to middling,' Grimshaw grunted, his eye-sockets drawn together in a frown. 'I've been doing the Earth sector. There's always good fishing down there.'

'That's a matter of opinion,' the Soul Searcher sternly reminded him. 'It has been noticed that on at least two occasions you have done a somewhat sloppy job as far as Earth is concerned.'

Grimshaw thrust a truculent skull from the shadowing confines of his hood. 'Oh, yeah? You just name me one instance! Go on – let's be hearing it!'

'Well, there was that Anne Boleyn woman for one, wandering about the Bloody Tower. It couldn't have been some miserable little commoner whose soul you would forget to collect – oh, no! It had to be someone of royalty, giving rise to all sorts of superstitious clap-trap!'

Grimshaw fiddled the drawstring of his shroud.

'Anyone can make a mistake, Solly –'

'Don't call me that ridiculous name!' shouted the Soul Searcher. 'And you are not just *anyone*, Grimshaw! You are supposed to be the Reaper – Death!'

'Even so, it was only the once,' Grimshaw muttered in a sulky croak.

'Don't you mumble at me, boyo!' What about that clutch of nuns haunting that burnt out old rectory in Essex? What about them, eh?'

'Oh, well, they sort of slipped my mind. I'll get them on the next trip.'

If the Soul Searcher had possessed lips he would have curled them in a sneer of mockery. 'You only go on the contract because it gives you an excuse to adopt that unsavoury skeletal mode. Why don't you change back and blend in with the surroundings?'

'I like being like this,' Grimshaw retorted, following the Soul Searcher back through the light lock and shutting the time seal behind him. 'It's dramatic.'

'It's cheap, flashy – and you know it,' snapped the Soul Searcher.

'Well, what do you expect me to do?' came the defensive reply. 'Your staff up here regard me as something a little lower than someone who cleans out the drains, but let me tell you, Solly, old golly, you would be in a right old state without me. Just think about it. If I decided to quit, every inhabited world would become overpopulated with uncollected spirits – and where would Shadowshine be then, eh? You tell me.'

'All right, Grimshaw, you've made your point, the Soul Searcher acknowledged a trifle uneasily as he positioned himself over a legless crystal table floating in the centre of the roofed Auditorium. 'Let's see what you've brought back.'

Grimshaw tipped the contents of his hold-all out onto the crystal table. 'Not bad, even if I do say so myself,' he commented.

A myriad of diamond pinpoints of light shimmered on the crystal, each glittering, but each subtly different. 'Earth souls,' murmured the Soul Searcher, automatically reverting to his white-bearded, patriarchal mode. 'Interesting quality, too.' He selected one and held it up to the celestial light. 'Not bad – not bad at all. I've just been dealing with one. Quite a nondescript entity. But if this one is anything to go by I should find the job a bit more interesting. What's this one called?'

Grimshaw consulted his tattered parchment invoice scroll. 'That one is a Horace Hapgood, third incarnation.'

The Soul Searcher replaced it with the others, swept them all back into the hold-all and handed it to Grimshaw. 'Then I might as well get things moving. Just give me the list of names and I'll have them checked out on the data files. And you can make yourself useful and mix those souls with ether to restore them.'

Grimshaw clicked his teeth in protest. 'That's not my job. Get one of the angels to do it.'

'Lazybones, muttered the Soul Searcher, glaring at the smirking skeleton. 'Anyway, you'd probably make a mess of it.' He grabbed a passing cherub by the ankle. 'Here, laddie. Want to make yourself useful?'

The chubby little winged creature puffed out its naked pink chest. 'Me, sir? Yes, sir! Certainly, sir!'

'Crawler,' Grimshaw said, but the Soul Searcher ignored him.

'Be a good little cherub and take this bag of souls along to the Transformation Department. They are to be mixed with ether until fully restored and then placed in the Limborium until I send for them.'

The cherub gathered the hold-all to him with plump little hands, his downy wings a-flutter with excitement. 'I'll attend to it at once, sir!' he chirped eagerly. Then he smartly about-turned in mid-air and fluttered off.

'And don't dawdle!' Grimshaw yelled after him, aiming an ineffectual kick with his boney foot at the fast-disappearing plump rear.

'Leave the boy alone, Grimshaw,' said the Soul Searcher. 'It's nice to find such a keen sense of duty these aeons.'

'He's a nasty little creeper!' snapped Grimshaw. 'All these cherubs are nasty little creepers. A bunch of goody-goodies!'

The Soul Searcher regarded him with a reproachful stare. 'What else would you expect to find up here? The baddy-baddies are all below in the Basement Department.'

'At least they're better conversationalists than those sissified cherubs.'

'That's a matter of opinion, Grimshaw. I'll admit they're certainly more macho – more beefcake – as opposed to … to …'

'Angel cake?' supplied Grimshaw.

The Soul Searcher groaned. 'You're the last one who should make jokes. You had best be on your way otherwise you'll frighten the poor souls to life and death again, standing around like that.'

'Can't I stay and watch?'

'No, you can't – but wait an epoch! If you pop along to the Communications Department and ask the other, er, section to send up one of their couriers for soul watch duty, I'll allow you to stay, on condition that you keep out of sight.'

Grimshaw chuckled. 'As good as done. We'll certainly need an imp on stand-by with the bag I've just delivered. There's very few sweetness and light in there.'

'Who's running this show?' the Soul Searcher shouted after the cloaked and hooded figure as it flitted through the light lock and vanished from sight. Then still grumbling to himself the white-bearded Olympian entity stumped off to the Records Department.

He was soon back with the complete dossier on this latest batch of souls clipped in his massive Records Book. Grimshaw was waiting for him, peering through the inner light lock where the souls were being placed in the Limborium. 'I say, Grimshaw,' commented the Soul Searcher, kicking the light lock's time seal into place behind him with a sandaled foot, 'I've been browsing through the files on this latest batch of yours. They're a sight more interesting than some. Did you manage to get hold of a courier from "down under"?'

They're sending one up right away – by helicopter.'

The Soul Searcher peered over the cloaked shoulder at the shifting spectrum of the dimensions which constituted the inner light lock. 'Anyone I know?'

'Young Scabwort.'

'Not Scabwort!' groaned the Soul Searcher. 'Uncouth little wretch! Couldn't they find anyone else?'

'Someone mention my name?' called out a breezy voice.

The others turned and saw a pot-bellied young demon sauntering through the light lock, leaving several colours wide open.

'Good to see you, Scab,' Grimshaw greeted him, his eye-sockets twinkling merrily.

Scabwort's snouted face adopted an expression of mock horror. 'Good to see me? That's no way to welcome an old chum from the Abyss! Bearing in mind my status "Hell-o" is much more appropriate.'

'Even so,' the Soul Searcher scathingly pointed out, 'I would appreciate it if you would observe a certain measure of courtesy while you are up here.'

Scabwort glared at him, outraged. 'Now what are you bleating about? I've only just got here. I haven't had a chance to do anything.'

'If you would be so good – or bad – as to close the light lock properly behind you. That's what 1 mean.'

'Oh, that.' Scabwort obligingly kicked the unsecured colours into place with a cloven hoof closing the time seal with a deft flick of his fork tail. 'Anything promising?' he enquired eagerly, shoving his way between the two senior entities and peering through the inner light lock.

'You'll see in good time – sorry, just time!' retorted the Soul Searcher. 'And please refrain from breathing sulphur down my neck. What have you been eating?'

'Devilled kidneys,' replied Scabwort, his piggy bloodshot eyes surveying the inmates of the Limborium. 'They look like fun. How many am I taking back?'

'If you get out of the way and allow me to continue with the proceedings I'll be able to tell you,' the Soul Searcher reprimanded him. 'Now you and Grimshaw go and stand in the lock where you won't be seen. I'm too lenient with you by half. If Head Office ever got wind of how things are run here I'd soon be back on the Styx shuttle.'

Obediently the other two moved off, leaving the Soul Searcher gazing through the Limborium's light lock. 'Yes, he murmured to himself, 'you certainly do look as if you have some interesting tales to tell, you poor, feckless little mortals ...'

Horace Hapgood sat in the threadbare, wing-backed chair and moodily studied the other occupants of the waiting room. The usual morose-looking lot, he decided, quite unconscious of the fact that his own personal appearance was far from inspiring. Plump, middle-aged and with a face that held all the force and drive of a marshmallow.

Horace glanced at his watch. It said twelve o'clock. It had said that several minutes ago. Plucking up the courage that the reserved Briton is always compelled to do in such circumstances, he turned to the person in the next chair, an even fatter version of himself, but dressed in city clothes instead of country tweeds, fair-complexioned with eyes that belied his ever-smiling, surprisingly thin lips. 'Excuse me,' ventured Horace, 'but have you the right time on you? My watch seems to have stopped.'

'Certainly,' boomed the fat man with the contradictory eyes and mouth. He produced a splendid gold pocket watch from his waistcoat pocket, studied it for a few seconds, then his mouth took on the hard scowl that lurked in his pale eyes. 'Four-fifteen,' he said. 'How odd. It was that time when I looked at it a few minutes ago.'

'Most odd,' responded Horace, glancing again at his slim digital wristwatch. 'Both watches have stopped, and both have stopped at different times. What do you make of that?'

'I don't make anything of it at all,' the other man airily dismissed the matter. 'I shall leave that to the watch-repairer tomorrow morning. All I am concerned with is how long I have to wait to see this wretched doctor. You can waste a lifetime in these squalid waiting rooms.'

Just then a voice boomed out from some unknown source.

'Eric Dodds!'

In response, a thin-faced youth with a multi–coloured punk hairstyle, got up from his chair and slouched towards the door, watched sullenly by several pairs of eyes.

'At least surgery has started,' sighed Horace. 'I wonder how long we will have to wait?'

'Like I said, dear fellow,' replied the fat man. 'Probably a lifetime.'

GHOSTING

Eric Dodds slumped into an old armchair and rubbed a far from clean hand over his weasel-like face and swore softly. It had been a hard day – and a disappointing one, too. His watery eyes roved apathetically over the gloom of his basement bed-sitter. There was certainly nothing to recommend the place. Nothing that would arouse anyone's interest – except probably the Health Inspector.

The only water that the small sash window had seen was when it had rained three weeks ago. You couldn't really count the time when that drunk had paused for vital reasons on the pavement above the stairwell the night before. Most of the furnishings – if they could be graced as such – had seen better days, and the squalid little room reeked of boiled cabbage. Eric could never figure that out. He never cooked cabbage. Anyway, he ate most of his meals at MacDonald's.

He climbed out of his chair and yawned, shrugging off his black leather studded jacket. He wore nothing else save his jeans and 'bovver' boots. At least he had got enough cash to pay the month's rent. That mean old geezer upstairs who owned the building would like to get shot of him but he was too scared to say so. Eric smirked at his unlovely reflection in the fly-specked mirror hanging by the window and stroked his punk-style crest of purple-dyed hair. Yeah, old 'Gunga Din' knew better than to cause any 'bovver'.

All the same it hadn't been a good day. Eric morosely surveyed his spoils. Fifty nicker – that was for the rent – and an old black-and-white TV set. And he was stuck with it, too. It wasn't even a colour! An old black-and-white job! He had been through a lot of trouble and risk that afternoon.

Breaking and entering was second nature to him and that stupid old biddy had left the door of her ground floor flat wide open. Eric, never one to pass up an opportunity, had nipped in and turned the place over. The fifty he had found under the mattress but there was nothing else worth taking. He had ransacked every drawer and cupboard but they were all crammed with little packets of dried weeds. At first Eric wondered if the old girl was taking pot, but the shrivelled leaves, although smelling weird, were no sort of drug that he had ever come across. They smelt spicy. Obviously, they were dried herbs. They didn't even taste good.

And the books! There seemed to be hundreds of them, lined up on shelves, on top of cupboards. Even piled up on the floor. And they were a right load of rubbish, too, as far as Eric was concerned. All about the stars, folklore ... and herbs. The old woman who lived there be some kind of nut.

Then he had noticed the television set, half-hidden on the rickety table by a stack of books. He just had time to see that it was a portable – a convenient feature – when the old lady herself came struggling in with a couple of shopping bags. For a few seconds they just stood and stared at each other. Then as the toothless mouth in the face opened to scream, Eric acted. A length of cycle chain was in his hand and arching down viciously on the grey head. The old lady seemed to shrink to the floor rather than fall. Eric gaped down at her with pale, boggling eyes. She just lay there, a dried up little old thing, who had lived through two world wars, the depression and God knows what else – to finish up like this!

But these observations spoke not in the small, grubby mind of Eric Dodds. The old bitch had asked for it! She was going to yell for help. If she had behaved herself she wouldn't have got hurt. Even without looking at her, he knew she was dead. But Eric's conscience was an easily satisfied creature. So what? She couldn't have had much more time left. He'd probably done her a favour anyway. Saved her from wasting away in some creepy geriatric ward.

Then Eric did one of those peculiar things which people often do in extreme circumstances. He hardly realised it at the time, but when he got outside and down the sheltered alley that led from the flats to a back street, he found that he was carrying the television. He dimly recalled grabbing it, and cursed himself for his stupidity. If the Fuzz had spotted him then that would have been it! But he had scuttled back to his lair unseen.

Now, he stood staring at the square, glass-fronted object wondering how he was going to get rid of it. If it had been a colour set, no trouble at all. But a black-and-white! Who wanted a bleedin' black-and-white set nowadays?

Then an idea occurred to him. Why get rid of it? He hadn't got a set, and Dolly Parton was on tonight. He'd nip down to MacDonald's, call in the off-licence for a few cans of lager and have a 'quiet, respectable' evening in front of his new telly. By nine o'clock he had done his rounds – even paid his rent – and prepared to make himself comfortable for the evening. Yeah, Dolly Parton was on at nine, followed by the news, followed by a horror film. Eric turned to the television page of *The Sun*. Looked a good film, too: *The Blood Monster of Castle Darkness*. He'd shut the news off until ten-thirty, then switched on again for the film. Nice cheap evening's entertainment, he congratulated himself. He flicked the set on, making sure it was on the right channel. Nothing happened. 'Just my luck,' he muttered, giving the side of the TV a clout. 'Ruddy thing's busted.'

Then he heard a faint hum of power coming from the set, and squinting over the back of it, he saw the worm-like glows of dull orange light flickering into life. Blimey! This was an old set and no mistake! One of those antique ones that have to 'warm up'!

Eric left the set on and opened one of his cans of lager. Just as he was washing down the remains of his carton of chicken-burger and chips he became aware of faint voices drifting through the room. He glanced at the set. The indistinct figures of two elderly women were deep in conversation on the pallid screen.

Eric snorted in disgust. Black-and-white! Grey-and-white would be more like it! Must be some soap powder commercial. Then he began to listen to what they were saying.

'Poor Mrs Fayne,' one woman was sobbing. 'I just, popped in to see if she was all right and I found her lying in a pool of blood. Stone cold dead she was. Been mugged she had. Some hooligan had bust in and turned her flat upside-down ...'

Eric nearly choked on his lager. What the hell was this? It wasn't a commercial. He shuddered. This was too much of a coincidence for comfort.

'Even took her telly they did,' sobbed the woman. 'Had it for years she had. Like a friend to her it was.'

Eric wilted back in his chair, his half-empty beer can still clutched in his hand. He must be imagining it! Surely he couldn't have heard right!

Then the advertised programme broke through the shadowy figures, and three cans of lager later Eric had put the mystery out of his mind and abandoned himself to the abundant charms of Dolly Parton. The programme finished at ten as scheduled. Eric turned the set off and looked at the tumble of beer cans around his feet. Pity he hadn't bought a few more to see him through the film. Even so, the four he had consumed had dulled his questionable wits. Eric weaved unsteadily to the door and edged his way down the unlit passage towards the toilet.

As he stumbled back five minutes later the sound of shrill, raised voices drifted down to him from the upper regions of the building. Old 'Gunga Din', the landlord, was having a row with his ten brothers. Eric groaned. They could go on all night, and judging by the energy being expended, it sounded as if they would still be at it in the morning.

Pausing only to hurl an obscenity up the uncarpeted flight of stairs, Eric slouched into his room and slammed the door shut behind him. He glanced at his watch, an insignificant disc amid the heavily-studded wrist guard. Fifteen minutes to go before the film started. A pity about the booze running out, he thought again, but at least he still had a packet of fags.

Eric spent ten minutes 'reading' page three of *The Sun* then flipped on the television. He had completely forgotten about the eerie transmission when he had first switched it on. Then voices jabbered out of the television and fiercely gesticulating figures appeared on the screen.

Eric's jaw dropped. This time there could be no doubt. It wasn't the ghosting of images he was looking at now. The man in the centre of the screen was none other than his landlord, 'Gunga Din', surrounded by his innumerable brothers! Eric even recognised the wallpaper of the upstairs room – but what did it all mean?

The weird image faded as did the voices and the usual jingle of commercials came gibbering and capering across the screen. But Eric hardly saw them. He could only find one explanation that fitted the facts. It sounded fantastic, but unless he had imagined it – and he was sure that he hadn't – then it meant that this was a very special television set. Not only could it pick up the normal transmissions, but it could also pick up the conversations of certain people in the immediate neighbourhood. But why certain people and not others?

Eric lit a cigarette and thought hard. It almost hurt. Then he remembered once reading something like this in a science fiction paperback. Highly charged emotional thoughts being picked up out of the ether like electric impulses! Yeah, that figured. Those two old girls talking about the one he'd clobbered – they had been pretty worked up. And nobody could say the same didn't apply to 'Ali Baba and the Forty Thieves' upstairs either.

Having sorted that out to his own satisfaction, Eric felt happier about things. He would be able to enjoy the film in comfort now. This cute little novelty could prove to be very entertaining. There was no telling who he'd be able to snoop on. It could have lucrative possibilities, too ...

The usual credits dripped across the screen as the horror film started. *The Blood Monster of Castle Darkness.* The letters were the usual blobby sort that all horror films used. On a colour set they would have been blood red, of course, not grey.

Eric stubbed out his cigarette on the table and lit another. On the screen he saw the usual shadowy figure moving menacingly down a gloomy passage and into a darkened chamber. Eric hunched up in his chair. This could be good for a giggle, he thought, studying the screen intently.

Grey hair straggled across the walnut-wrinkled, toothless face of the being on the screen, matted with dried blood. That face ...? It seemed to Eric that he had seen it before. The shambling horror advanced towards that of its victim – someone hunched up a chair. Then Eric's eyes nearly popped out of his skull. That punk hair-style of the huddled form in the chair – it was himself!

Eric Dodds involuntarily glanced over his shoulder, and just had time to scream.

SHADOWSHINE TWO

Perched at his cloud–rooted tall white and gold desk, the Soul Searcher glared down thunderously at the quaking soul of Eric Dodds. 'You haven't shown up in a very good light, have you, my little man?' he rumbled. 'A nasty little reptile. We get plenty of weak, misguided or just plain rotten souls up here – but you must have been taking lessons in your particular field of unsociable behaviour.'

Eric Dodds cowered away from the white-robed entity. 'I dunno what you mean,' he whined, his purple, punk-style coxcomb almost wilting. 'I ain't done nuffink.'

An uncontrolled thunderbolt leapt from the Soul Searcher's upraised fist, nearly zapping a cherub flying overhead. 'You ain't done nuffink!' he bellowed, lapsing into his victim's vernacular. 'You croaked that old biddy and nicked her telly! Is that plain enough for you?'

'Well she was so old as to make no difference,' Eric protested, even managing to instil a measure of righteous indignation into his voice.

The Soul Searcher pounded his fist on the Record Book with such violence that the lock went into the Doppler Effect and out again. 'Don't you tell me when she was due for the chop, laddie! What do you think I'm here for – to collect tickets? I've got a team of specialists up here whose job it is to decide such things. Where would they be if you mortals were allowed to run the show? On the scrap heap!'

'What's goin' to 'appen to me?' wailed Eric.

'You're going to Hell where you belong!' snapped the Soul Searcher, losing his temper. 'Scabwort – here's your first customer!'

'Great!' crowed the young demon, bouncing jauntily through the light lock, waving his pitchfork triumphantly. 'Come on, squire, shift it.' He jabbed Eric in the seat of his jeans. 'We're going to teach you a new trade – pitchfork-grinding.'

'No!' shrieked Eric, collapsing to the cloudy floor.

'Suit yourself,' retorted Scabwort, hauling him to his feet. 'Cloven hoof re-treading or fork tail sharpening or talon manicuring – oh, there's plenty of trades to choose from.'

But Eric's prolonged and agonised wails proclaimed that he did not seem at all impressed by this particular range of job opportunities, and ever considerate, Scabwort tried a fresh approach. 'Yeah, see what you mean,' he commented, throwing a friendly arm around Eric's trembling shoulders. 'Not macho enough. How about a military career? Oh, believe me, it's a fine sight on Parade Day when all the Cadets are doing the Skulking of the Colour and Sergeant Major Azrael – we call him "Brimstone Guts" – is putting them through their drill. Mind you, he's a tough one. I can hear him now, bawling out blood-curdling niceties and telling than that they were too good for the place, and unless they didn't degenerate pretty holy quick he would pack them all off upstairs where they would spend eternity as a bunch of fourth-rate harp grinders. But it's a spectacle once seen never forgotten. The rhythmic stamp of marching cloven hooves and fork tails nourished in salute as they parade across the molten tarmac. I only wish I had been able to join up, but failed the medical. Asthma, y'know ...'

I don't want to go to Hell!' screeched Eric as Scabwort proceeded to drag him by the scruff of his neck towards the fireproof escalator.

'Of course you don't,' the Soul Searcher murmured unconcernedly. 'Nobody does.'

But this did not appear to be of much consolation to Eric, who had begun to froth and gibber. Scabwort paused and stared at him in admiration. 'He's convincing, isn't he? I thought I'd seen the best when we handled the Sodom and Gomorrah contract with all that wailing and gnashing of teeth, but this boy's performance puts a sense of meaning into the job.'

'Don't take on so, Dodds,' the Soul Searcher complained. 'There is no need to be so noisy. You're giving me a headache. And after all, you've got to learn your lesson.'

Eric twisted around in his demoniac escort's grasp, a glimmer of hope showing in his bloodshot eyes. 'You – you mean I won't be there for ever?'

'Of course not, you stupid mortal,' the Soul Searcher replied reassuringly. 'It will only seem like it. Wheel him off, Scabwort.'

Dragging the screeching, threshing Eric Dodds behind him, Scabwort hopped nimbly onto the asbestos treads of the escalator and disappeared downwards.

'Hang on!' The skeletal cloaked figure of the Grim Reaper emerged from the light lock. 'What's been going on here? I don't remember bringing him up. What's it all about?'

'Grimshaw, I told you to stay out of sight,' the Soul Searcher sternly admonished him.

'I don't care what you told me!' snapped Grimshaw, turning his scowling skull towards the now vacant escalator. 'I want to know how that soul got here!'

'The old duck he bumped off is one of down-under's field agents, retorted the Soul Searcher, riffling through some memos on his desk. 'Ah, here we are. Minnie Fayne, registered as Agent Z93. Secret Witch – Licensed to Curse. When young Dodds "put the boot in" so to speak, her astral spirit went after him and brought him here.'

Grimshaw stamped a boney foot. 'Well that's bloody nice I must say! Blackleg labour. I've half a mind to take this further and down shrouds!'

'Now don't be childish, Grimshaw,' the Soul Searcher reproved him. 'After all, it isn't as if you haven't got enough work on your talons.'

Grimshaw favoured the patriarchal entity with a sullen glance. 'I hope this sort of thing isn't going to become a habit,' he muttered. 'I've got a deading to earn.'

'Just a one-off, Grimshaw, don't worry so. All the rest were brought up here by you … or most of them were.'

'What's that supposed to mean? Come on, Solly, don't hold out on me.'

'You'll see,' responded the Soul Searcher, turning once again to the inner light lock portal. 'In the fullness of time, to use a perfectly fatuous mortal expression. Yow who shall we have next …?'

'Funny sort of coincidence, both our watches stopping,' remarked Horace Hapgood, speaking more to himself than his companion-in-waiting, Hubert Square. He glanced around at the other occupants of the gloomy waiting room. A decrepit old man in what looked like evening dress, a genial old buffer in tweeds and a spotted bow tie, a large and muscular lady traffic warden, a dark-skinned gentleman wrapped snugly in his tribal blanket and snoring gently, and a young, athletic-looking man with auburn hair, quite at ease and reading a back number of *Reader's Digest*. And there was someone else, large and shadowy, sitting on the far side of the waiting room, obscured by a large and wilting rubber plant. Horace couldn't make him out from where he was sitting, but he could just discern a diminutive figure next to the shadowy hulk, wearing what appeared to be industrial overalls and suffering from what looked like chronic acne.

Quite a mixed bunch, he reflected, hoping that there was nothing contagious within striking distance.

He had just got around to scrutinizing the African gentleman in the blanket again, having come to the decision that he was the same chap he had seen in the new delicatessen when the fat man sitting next to him, Hubert Square, said, 'I beg your pardon?'

Hapgood repeated his comment about watches.

'Life's full of coincidences,' Square dismissed the matter. 'It would have been stranger still if they had both stopped at the same time. I was just looking at the chappie near the potted plant, Hapgood. He doesn't look at all well. I hope it isn't catching.'

'I can't make him out well from here,' murmured Horace. 'It could be acne.'

'Indeed it could. He looks terrible. His skin is all red and his eyes are puffed up. I shouldn't be at all surprised if it isn't some form of dermatitis. The fellow next to the African.'

Horace peered through the gloom, trying not to make it too obvious. 'Sorry. I can't make him out very well from here. Which side of the African do you mean? The old man in tails?'

'No,' retorted Square, a shade impatiently. 'I mean the Martian.'

Just then the Voice boomed out again.

'Dennis Strangles!'

And in response the creaky-looking old man in tails arose from his chair and tottered towards the door ...

TIME EXPOSURE

It was in the Summer of 1896 that a scientific miracle was discovered – and lost the same day. Sir Hector Troy, a wealthy gentleman of eccentric tastes and inquiring disposition, announced the birth of his invention to society in a veritable snowstorm of invitation cards. Some fell upon stony ground. Many retired generals and should-be-retired politicians, merely studied their invitations through a trellis of bloodshot eyes, grunted, then forgot about them and ordered another glass of the club's brandy.

Others were more happily received. This latter group consisted of a varied cross-section of society, for Sir Hector, being a visionary, spread his news far and wide, though not, of course, to *trades people*. Men of science, elderly and learned professors, arrived that Saturday afternoon at Sir Hector's splendid residence at Richmond. Financiers and various assorted men were invited, too, for Sir

Hector, inheriting his title and wealth, was sensible to the hard facts of life. Certain 'gentlemen of the Press' were also included – but only from the more respectable newspapers.

The sun enhanced the expectant scene with its warmth as the carriages trundled up the drive to Troy Manor, rising up a sea of rhododendrons like some druidic monolith, to be greeted on the steps of the Manor by old Strangles, the butler.

Dear, faithful old Strangles, the epitome of butlerdom, anticipating everyone's wishes and carrying out his instructions with creaking dignity. Jolly old Strangles, with his merry, bright blue eyes, apple-red cheeks and serenely toothless smile, steering the guests through to the vast library where they would pick at seed cake, sip Indian Tea – and wish that they were somewhere else that was at least within sniffing distance of a bottle of brandy or within reach of a well-turned ankle.

For the female ankles present – the ladies having, of course, accompanied their gentlemen, may well have been 'well-turned', but they were also well-hidden beneath billowing gowns and dresses of such abundance as was demanded by propriety.

There is, however, always one exception, this to be none other than Sir Hector's wife, the beautiful Lady Eglantine Troy. 'A blonde abundance of femininity,' one society gallant had commented with a twirl of his military whiskers. But no one could fault her on the sheer decorum and charm with which she conducted herself. True it may be that many women present hated her to death, inwardly praying for this paragon of virtue to make some social faux pas, but they had always been disappointed. 'A woman with such a – er, profusion of femininity has no right to be so respectable!' hissed one lady guest to her equally tight-lipped neighbour. 'It just isn't respectable for her to be so – so respectable!'

Oblivious to these murky undercurrents Lady Eglantine sailed gracefully through the motley gathering like the figurehead of a sailing ship, dispensing a kind word here, a caraway seed cake there, while staunch and stoic old Strangles poured the Indian Tea – some of it even managing to get into the cups.

The murmurs of anticipation welled as the throng slowly coagulated into little groups. Then through the open French windows bounded Nostril, a black and white bull terrier, followed by his master, Sir Hector Troy, who beamed around at the gathering. 'Ladies and gentlemen – welcome. My thanks for your presence here, and my apologies for not being here to receive you on your arrival. I have been setting up my new apparatus for the demonstration in the Azalea Bower. What you will see this afternoon is something which will push back the boundaries of science and open new vistas of discovery. In short, it will enable us to recapture and bring back times past.'

'Doesn't sound feasible to me,' grunted one member of the listening throng, a round-faced man, sporting a luxuriant moustache. 'You night be able to visit other times, but I can't for the life of me see how other times can visit you.'

'Be quiet, Wells, there's a good fella,' admonished a saffron skinned veteran of the Indian Army. 'You just listen and you might learn something.'

Sir Hector smiled brightly behind the light brown thicket which was the only memorable feature of his nondescript face. Indeed, his head seemed no more than an extended neck, crowned by a scant and mediocre thatch of brown hair. The moustache and a monocle were the only details worth mentioning about his uninspiring and chinless visage. 'Allow me, ladies and gentlemen, to put an end to your speculations and doubts. I suggest that you all accompany me to the Azalea Bower and permit the apparatus to perform its own explanations.'

This was greeted with approval. After all, it was what they had all given up their Saturday afternoons for. So with an assortment of creaks, grunts and other sundry noises, the whole company followed Sir Hector out onto the spacious lawns. Lady Eglantine twirled a salmon-coloured parasol as she walked in the van with her husband. Though, perhaps 'walked' would be an inadequate word. But as things were in 1896 it would have to suffice. A more suitable word was yet to be coined. Nostril bounded joyfully at their heels, a four-legged dumpling of a dog. A colonel trod on him and Nostril's romping suddenly developed a painful list to starboard. Strangles followed in their train, having left the maids to remove the crockery and portions of caraway seed cake hidden behind cushions.

Five minutes later the company were gathered around the Azalea Bower, a secluded little nook, comprising of a domed, Grecian-style temple with a marble seat, nestling within a dense semicircle of colourful azalea shrubs. Several feet away from the domed and pillared building stood an ungainly object resembling a tin box with lightning conductors strapped to each side and a conglomeration of wires tangled around an electrode poking out of the front. The whole thing was supported on a camera tripod.

'It's a magic lantern!' squeaked one lady.

'Something a little more complex, madam,' Sir Hector smiled. 'I call it, a Temporal Particle Recaller. In layman's terms it emits an invisible ray from the electrode which is focused on the interior of the summer house. This ray reacts on certain etheric vibrations in the precise area and causes them to become visible to the naked eye.'

'What are these ethereal articles, Sir Hector?' queried an old lady.

Nostril bit her to demonstrate his opinion of her stupidity.

Sir Hector smiled his most patronizing smile. 'Just as an object dropped into water causes ripples, so objects cause invisible disturbances in the ether. My apparatus can be finely tuned to record a visible display of any person or object that was in the chosen area previously.'

The old lady paused from rubbing her ankle and swearing at Nostril to say, 'you mean like the echo of a sound?'

Again the patronizing smile. 'Precisely, madam. Quite an acceptable comparison if may say so. Strangles, look after Nostril, there's a good man. Now if you would all watch the seat in the summer house I will show you visible proof of what 1 have told you. I picked up this particular subject while I was testing the device a few minutes ago.'

Lady Eglantine's wifely bosom heaved with pride as she beamed radiantly at the onlookers. The onlookers beamed radiantly back at her – the men did anyway. The ladies merely curled their lips and sniffed. Strangles gathered Nostril in his arms and gibbered soothingly to the animal, which growled ominously in reply.

Meanwhile Sir Hector was busy twiddling with various knobs on the machine. A humming sound accompanied by a sudden flicker of electronic light – and a fat black cat appeared on the seat.

'My Wiffles!' shrieked Lady Eglantine. 'He's come back to me!'

'My wife's cat,' explained Sir Hector. 'It was run over by a Danish Doctor of Divinity on a penny-farthing bicycle three weeks ago.'

Cries of 'Good Grief! Great Scott!' and 'Merciful Heavens!' greeted this revelation, while the ladies present blanched or blushed, each according to own her constitution, at these crude outbursts of strong language and profanity. Nostril growled as he recognised his old enemy, and it was with great difficulty that Strangles succeeded in restraining him.

'Is it a ghost?' quavered one timorous old gentleman. 'Has this singularly remarkable device of yours, Sir Hector, conjured the animal's spirit back to haunt, us?'

Sir Hector uttered what he fondly imagined to be a merry laugh. Everyone else thought it was the projected cat. 'Not at all, sir. I shall now tune the machine to a more recent setting – fifteen minutes ago, to be precise.'

As he adjusted the knobs the image of the cat vanished, to be replaced by the facsimile of his garishly-checked coat, mercifully reproduced in black and white. More cries wonder and surprise greeted this latest miracle. Sir Hector stood back from the wonderful machine while Lady Eglantine simpered and preened herself in his reflected glory.

'Now let us attempt something a little more ambitious, declared the aristocratic young genius. 'I shall adjust the timer to something like five weeks ago and see what we can find.'

All eyes riveted on the interior of the summer house as Sir Hector operated his invention. 'Aha!' he exclaimed as something began to form on the marble seat. 'What have we here?'

His audience stared with eyes agog as the apparition took on definite form. Then Sir Hector's smug smile froze beneath his moustache and his Adam's apple death-dived into his wing collar, for before the assembled multitude was none other than his wife, Lady Eglantine. And she was not alone. In fact, she was most definitely not alone!

The lady – if one could still use the term – was disporting herself in the most abandoned and profligate manner with great enthusiasm and gusto, in the arms of none other than Strangles, the family butler! Devoted old Strangles! Most obliging old Strangles!

Chaos reigned. The ladies screamed, but their gleaming eyes drank in the spectacle with malicious glee. The gentlemen ''pon my souled!' and had adjusted pince nez monocles for better focus. The shock was too much Strangles, and dropping the indignant Nostril, he clutched at his heart and fell flat on his back on the lawn, his legs in the air and his socks flashing in death!

'You scarlet woman!' cried Sir Hector. 'You have cuckolded me in the Azalea Bower.'

Lady Eglantine decided that the best thing to do in the circumstances was to swoon, so she swooned. Nostril leapt into the milling throng of scandalised socialites. Sensing the general air of excitement he entered into the spirit of the thing, biting people right, left and centre, regardless of creed or political persuasion, until a sharp swipe from the Vicar's wife's duck-head-handled umbrella caught him on the muzzle and sent him yelping on a collision course with the Temporal Particle Recaller.

The apparatus crashed to the ground and shattered into a thousand pieces. Thus was the wonderful device lost to Mankind on the same day as it appeared.

Sir Hector retired from society, a broken man and rumour has it that he went to Russia and joined a subversive Bolshevist movement. Needless to say, he took his secret with him to the grave.

Lady Eglantine's fall from grace and society was inevitable, but she made a fairly good landing. She moved to Penge and embraced a new life of charitable self-sacrifice, doing good work at a home for retired military gentlemen.

And Nostril the dog? Now we come to the final and most mysterious part of the entire story. Three weeks after the scandal at Troy Manor, he was run over – by a touring Turkish taxidermist ... on a penny-farthing bicycle!

SHADOWSHINE THREE

'That was very naughty of you, Dennis,' the Soul Searcher gently reproved the aged butler who stood – or rather crouched – before the tall desk. 'I am well aware that Lady Eglantine possessed great mortal charms, but there is no excuse.'

Old Strangles plucked at a drooping lower lip with a rheumy finger. What suspiciously sounded like a snigger creaked somewhere within the dewlap between the crisp white triangles of his collar. 'Indeed, sir, you are quite correct in what you say,' he croaked. 'I really don't know what came over me. Maybe it was the weather or the rhododendrons. They always have a telling effect an me.'

'Well, your, er, actions appear to have been without any malicious intention,' the Soul Searcher mused, scanning the Records Book before him. 'And when all is said and done, you were the only fatal casualty when your, er, sanguine behaviour was revealed by Sir Hector's device. Tell me, Dennis, did you hurt yourself when you fell over and died?'

A little brave little smile fractured across the butler's wrinkled apple-cheeked face. 'Not so you would have noticed, sir, but thank you for enquiring. As it happened, I did twist my ankle rather painfully, but as I died almost immediately it did not trouble me for long.'

The Soul Searcher smiled. 'I'm very pleased to hear it. Now, Dennis, we are going to give you another chance –'

'You mean ... Lady Eglantine ...?

'No, I most certainly do not mean Lady Eglantine! I am referring to your next reincarnation.'

The ancient retainer's watery eyes widened in mild surprise.

'Reincarnation, you say? Do you know, I've never really believed in reincarnation.'

'Whatever you believe or don't believe, Dennis, I can assure you that it is quite the usual practice. Most souls who come up are reincarnated again. Those that aren't have either done their quota and are ready to "move up the ladder" so to speak, or else they have been unusually wicked and are sent, to "the other place" for a period of severe correction.'

'How very interesting. Tell me, sir, do I have any chance to voice a preference in regard to my next reincarnation?'

'Not really, Dennis. It doesn't quite work like that ...'

Scabwort peeped out of the light lock. 'They're still nattering, Grim. I wish he'd get on with it. I could be at Ghengis Khan's barbecue party for all the use I am up here.'

Grimshaw cracked his knucklebones sympathetically. I know just what you mean. Those two old fogeys could go on for an epoch. And by the way it's shaping up it doesn't look as if he'll be a client for you either. I wouldn't be surprised at all if Solly sends the old fool down to Earth again.'

'Well I'm blessed if I'm standing in this draughty light lock much longer,' muttered Scabwort. 'I get this terrible catarrh right up my sinuses so bad that makes my horns tingle.'

Grimshaw hugged his shroud closely about him. 'I suppose it is a bit on the nippy side for a hot-blooded little devil like you, Scab. Why don't you stand in the infra-red? It's a bit warmer there.'

'Solly would see me then,' Scabwort grumpily objected, 'and you know what an old fusspot he is about protocol. Nothing must spoil the image of "sweetness and light".'

'Tell you what,' he added as idea occurred to him. 'Those two, are going to be nattering for ages, so why don't we just slip away to the Time Zone and see what's when?'

Grimshaw stroked his jawbone doubtfully. 'I don't know about that, Scab. He'd raise Cain if he ever found out.'

'Raise Cain?' echoed Scabwort indignantly. 'I'd like to see him try! Cain is a very important soul "downstairs". Besides, he's kept very busy with his new gymnasium, teaching the other promising doomed souls unarmed combat.'

'I didn't mean that!' snapped Grimshaw impatiently. 'I meant that Solly would be annoyed if we went AWOL.'

Scabwort curled his lip. 'Solly is always annoyed, so where's the difference? Come on, Grim. If we sneak off now we can have a quick look around the Time Zone and be back before we're missed. Unless, of course, you're chicken?'

The Grim Reaper bridled angrily. 'Nobody's ever called me chicken! Come on, I'll race you to the ultra-violet.'

Grimshaw got there first despite Scabwort's efforts to trip him up with his pitchfork and both entities emerged from the light lock into the silent black and vast emptiness that was the Time Zone. Scabwort peered at the surrounding nothingness. 'Big ain't it?' he remarked.

'The biggest thing going,' Grimshaw agreed, straightening his shroud. 'When you think about it time's got to be the biggest thing – even bigger than space. Just look at it all!'

The entire Time Zone was ringed by an endless cloud of semi-luminous stuff that looked like cotton wool with highlights. 'The Clouds of Time,' murmured Scabwort in an unusually reverent voice. 'Let's get down there and have a peek.'

A few cherubs were ambling about the place, some drifting towards the adjoining recreation centre where a goodminton match was in progress. Some paused and stared at the two new-comers in surprise then fluttered swiftly on their way. Grimshaw gazed upon the scene and sighed nostalgically. 'Y'know, Scab, I used to come down here and play when I was a skeletot, playing hide-and-seek among the shunting engines as they were being loaded up with crates of good old days and hard times. They sure were happy days.'

'You two!' bellowed a voice. 'What are you doing here? Be off with you at once. You're trespassing.'

They stared at the robed, bent and bearded figure hobbling towards them, an ancient-looking scythe slung over his shoulder and a digital hour-glass strapped to his left wrist. 'It's Father Time,' groaned Scabwort, 'Now we're for it.'

'Don't panic,' whispered Grimshaw. 'Just leave the talking to me.'

'Are you deaf?' shouted Father Time, shuffling across the gleaming black Time Walk towards then. 'Clear off or I'll set the Seraphic Security Guards on you!'

'Hello, Uncle,' called out Grimshaw. 'Don't you recognise me? It's your nephew, Grimshaw.'

'Oh, it's you, is it?' Father Time's greeting was anything but avuncular. 'What are you doing here?'

'I just wanted show my best chum, Scabwort around some of the old haunts, Uncle,' Grimshaw replied innocently. 'That's if you don't mind, of course?'

'Well make sure you don't start meddling with anything, Nephew,' Father Time grunted, favouring his kin with a suspicious glance. 'The Time Zone can be a dangerous place, and there's a troublesome blight of Black Holes around here that need weeding out.'

'Maybe I can give you a hand with them, Nunky?' offered Grimshaw in his best toadying voice.

'You keep your sticky little claws away from them if you know what's good for you, Nephew, or you'll have me to answer for,' snapped Father Time. 'Now you mind what I say!'

And with that he shuffled off, muttering about young hooligans trampling all over the Parsley and Time beds.

'C'mon, Scab, let's have a look at these Black Holes,' said Grimshaw. 'The only ones I've ever seen are in graveyards.'

'I didn't know Father Time was your uncle,' remarked Scabwort, closely following on Grimshaw's boney heels as he scuttled along the edge of the Time Clouds.

'Well he is and I'd rather not discuss it,' Grimshaw retorted over his collar bone. 'You can choose your friends but not your relatives. Now, I wonder just what these Black Holes look like.'

'Would that be them?' Scabwort pointed a gnarled talon at a clump of black discs sprouting from a seething patch of Time Immemorial. 'They sorta look as if they shouldn't be there.'

'Yeah, that's them, sure enough,' nodded Grimshaw, pausing before the offending Black Holes and squaring his shoulder blades. 'I'll soon get rid of them.'

'Hang about, Grim,' Scabwort nervously cautioned him 'I've heard about these things. They can be real tricky. I think you oughta leave them alone.'

'I'll soon get rid of them,' sneered Grimshaw. 'Just give room and I'll show you.'

Still muttering nervously, Scabwort moved back a couple of paces. Grimshaw tightened the drawstring of his shroud and took a running kick at the nearest Black Hole, intending to send it soaring across to the far side of the Time Zone. At least that was his intention but the Black Hole had other ideas, for the next moment Grimshaw was threshing about on one leg while his left one vanished within the Black Hole.

'Help me, Scabwort!' he screeched, his skull white with fright. 'It's dragging me into it!'

Scabwort grabbed Grimshaw with both his arms around the rib cage and tugged hard. There was a crisp and very final-sounding click followed by another screech from Grimshaw and then the two meddlers were threshing around on the hard unyielding blackness of the Time Walk.

'Blimey, that was a close thing,' puffed Scabwort, scrambling to his cloven hooves. 'It nearly had you then, Grim.'

'Waddya mean – "nearly"?' yelled Grimshaw, writhing about like an eel. 'It got my leg! Pulled it clean off and gobbled it up!'

Scabwort gaped at his friend in amazement and dismay as he helped him to his foot – his right one – for his left, with femur and tibia in attendance, had disappeared into the Black Hole. 'I suppose that's what they mean when they someone has put his foot in it,' he murmured reflectively.

'Don't talk tripe,' Grimshaw screamed hysterically, trying to balance on his leg. 'I'm ruined! I'll be the laughing stock of the Charnel Club. I'll never be able to hold up my skull again.'

'Get a grip on yourself, Grim,' Scabwort told him. 'Grab hold of my batwings to steady yourself and calm down.'

'Talk's cheap! It's not your bloody leg!'

'Now you're working up into a state of neurosis. You must keep things in perspective, or you'll became, er, unbalanced.'

Grimshaw thrashed his boney arms about in a fine old fury while Scabwort, ducking down out of the danger zone, loyally held him in a more or less upright position. 'I'm finished – washed up!' Grimshaw raved. 'How can I do grim reaping with only one leg? A fine twit I'll look – hopping around the graveyards like this!'

Scabwort stoically tried to rationalise the situation. 'Don't take on so, Grim. Maybe it's not as bad as you think. Remember Long John Silver in *Treasure Island*. He had one leg, too.'

'What d'you mean – "one leg two"? That makes three! And I'm not hopping about with a messy parrot perched on my collar bone either!'

Several cherubs had paused in mid-ether to watch and giggle amongst themselves at poor Grimshaw's predicament. Scabwort shook his fist at them, shooing then away, but in so doing, lost his grip on his semi-legless companion who clattered despairingly to the black concrete Time Walk. 'Watch out!' Grimshaw shouted. 'You'll chip me!'

'I still say you're over-reacting, Grimshaw,' Scabwort said as he helped the very Grim Reaper up again. 'After all, it doesn't show under your long shroud. I'm sure no one would notice.'

A shrill whistling sound blotted a particularly obscene and venomous observation uttered by Grimshaw, and glancing up, seeking the cause of this alarming sound, they saw, up in the Time Zone, a vibrating disc of glowing white light. 'It's a White Hole, Grimmo baby!' cheered Scabwort, waving his big fork tail gleefully in the air. 'Your luck's in – look!'

Dead on cue the errant leg popped out of the White Hole like a guided missile, scattering the loitering Cherubs and arcing through the void. 'My leg – my leg!' gibbered Grimshaw, flailing around like a mad thing. 'Quick, Scab – help me up! I must see where it comes down!'

Clutching hold of Scabwort's batwings for support, Grimshaw hopped and hobbled his way along the Time Walk. Suddenly a bellow of rage disturbed the eternal tranquillity of the Time Zone and Father Time reeled into view from behind a freshly harvested stack of seconds, rubbing his bald head with one hand and clutching Grim Reaper's missing leg in the other.

Grimshaw covered his eye-sockets and groaned in despair. 'Oh, no! Of all the people – it had to hit him!'

'Then get out of sight before he sees us, hissed the more practical and realistic Scabwort, pulling his friend into the concealing shadows afforded by a crate of dark times.

'People dumping their junk through the Spacetime Continuum!' shouted Father Time. 'It's disgraceful – utterly disgraceful!'

And with that he hurled the leg across the Time Walk so that it came to rest only a short distance from where Grimshaw and Scabwort crouched.

'Grab it!' Grimshaw yammered in an ecstasy of dread. 'Grab it before anything else happens to it!'

Waiting until a very irate and sore-headed Father Time had moved out of view, Scabwort darted out of cover and retrieved the wandering limb. He paused for a moment, testing the joints and listening to the patella click. 'Seems okay to me,' he finally decided.

'Then bring here!' snapped Grimshaw, reaching out a boney claw. 'Hurry up! Someone might come along and see me!'

Scabwort dutifully handed him the leg. 'Be careful,' he warned. 'It's still a bit hot from going through that time warp.'

Grimshaw rudely snatched the leg from Scabwort and thrust it up under his shroud. 'I think I am quite capable of managing my own leg, thanks very – yeeow!'

'I told you it was still hot,' said Scabwort reproachfully. 'Are you sure you don't need any help?'

'I can manage,' muttered Grimshaw, poking his leg his up his shroud again. There was a faint click. 'Ah,' he sighed thankfully, 'that's got it.'

'And about time, too,' sniffed Scabwort who had become thoroughly bored and fed up with the whole business. 'Let's get away from this place. It's dreary.'

Grimshaw scrambled up, intending to follow Scabwort along the Time Walk, but next moment he corkscrewed to the ground swearing. Scabwort turned and glared down at him irritably.

'Now what?'

'I – I seem to have put my leg on back to front,' came the sheepish reply. 'The foot's facing the wrong way.'

'You twerp!' jeered Scabwort. 'Here – let me sort it out.'

He tried to manipulate the backward-facing limb but Grimshaw fussily slapped his hands away. 'Leave me alone!' he shrilled indignantly as he straightened out his disarranged shroud. 'You know I don't like to be manhandled!'

Scabwort turned his back on the fretful skeleton in disgust. 'Oh, get on with it then. I wish I'd stayed in the light lock. You're not fit to be let out on your own.'

Grimshaw stood up again, flexed his leg and found it satisfactory. 'That's better,' he sighed happily, his good humour restored along with his leg. 'Where shall we go now, Scab?'

'Might, as well get back and see if Solly's still nattering,' retorted the young demon, heading towards the light lock entrance. 'I don't want to miss out on a doomed soul.'

Grimshaw had at least the tact and common sense to refrain from any flippant remark and they were soon back at their appointed station, just inside the orange zone of the light lock. 'Are they still at it?' he asked, craning his skull forward to peer over Scabwort's leathery batwings.

'They haven't budged,' grumbled Scabwort. 'I reckon you're right about this ruddy butler. Him and Solly are still yapping. They'll be bringing on the port and cigars soon. And just when we could do with some new blood "downstairs".'

'Never mind,' said Grimshaw. 'Tell you what. Let's have a look in your Lost, Stolen or Strayed Property Department. The missus was on at me the other day about the kids. The eldest lad has joined up with a comprehensive haunting class and could do with a new skulking jacket.'

'Might as well,' sighed Scabwort, casting one last, disapproving glance at the Soul Searcher and Strangles the butler, still deep in genial conversation. 'It will give me something else to think about.'

'Things aren't so hot in Hell, eh?'

'You can say that again, Grim. It's real quiet down there.'

'But we did have one bit of excitement.'

Grimshaw looked astounded. 'Only one? You surprise me, Scab. What was it?'

Scabwort glanced over his shoulder to make sure that no Cherubs were eavesdropping. 'You ain't gonna believe this, Grim, but we had a new arrival – and he wasn't even dead! Straight in as bold as brass – and still breathing!'

Grimshaw stared hard at Scabwort. 'Are you having me on? I've had my leg pulled once today and don't fancy having it done again. A bodied soul would have to go through the normal channels – and that means facing up to Solly. And whatever his faults, Solly's a stickler for doing things properly.'

Scabwort glanced over his shoulder again. Two Cherubs hovered nearby, pretending to watch the Seraphic Gold Band marching along Shadowshine Mall, beyond the marble colonnades of the Auditorium. 'Let's move away from here, Grim. There's too many big ears flapping.'

'We hadn't better be too long if I'm going to do my shopping as well,' Grimshaw reminded him. 'What if the next soul is a mixture of Hitler and Attila the Hun? There would be merry He –, er, the deuce of a lot of trouble.'

Scabwort nodded towards the top of the fireproof escalator where a thin and spotty young demon lounged against a fire extinguisher, smoking and blowing fire rings. 'My mate, Rubbish-Legs, will cover for us,' he whispered. 'Come on and I'll tell you the whole sad and sorry story ...'

HELL HATH NO FURY

His Satanic Majesty, Lucifer the First and Last, had just had a tasty snack of smoked cheese and tomartyr sandwiches in his private grotto when the small chamber was lit by a soundless explosion of green light, streaked through with orange and yellow dots and dashes. 'Heaven's Harps!' he swore as a figure materialised out of thin air from the fading glow. 'Get thee behind me, Saint!'

But the newcomer showed no inclination whatsoever to get behind him. Clad in a bulky pressure suit of luminous metal, he just stood in front of Lucifer, his bespectacled eyes blinking through the transparent visor of his massively domed helmet. 'Guess not where I hoped I'd be,' he murmured with an embarrassed grin.

Lucifer had recovered his composure, and smoothing out his black cape and scarlet hose, demanded, 'and where might that be, puny mortling?'

The round freckled face beamed back. 'North-northeast of the Crab Nebula – Third Millenia. Er, my name's Elmer Glumwood of the Temporal Space Expeditionary Force – that's the bunch who handle time travelling.' He glanced down at a metal box strapped across his chest and began to fiddle with the many dials and buttons that studded it. 'If you would be so kind, sir, as to tell me just where I am, I can feed in the new coordinates and be on my way.'

Lucifer drew himself up to his full height, his forked beard bristling with outrage. 'You, sir, are in Hell. I am Lucifer, Prince of Darkness, this is supposed to be day my off. Just what do you mean by bursting into my grotto uninvited?'

Elmer glanced around helplessly and shrugged inside his unyielding protective suit. 'Aw, gee. Looks like I made another boo-boo.'

Lucifer's eloquence knew no bounds as he enquired just what the intruder was about.

'Shucks, I should have known something like this would happen on the last time warp,' Elmer apologised. 'My spatial trajectory was intercepted by a Black Hole.'

'Miserable wretch!' thundered Lucifer. 'Are you not in terror? Know you not that your mortal soul is in peril of eternal damnation? Can't you get through your thick skull that you are in Hell?'

Elmer smiled nervously. 'Well, the training course officers always told us freshmen to be prepared for anything, anywhere, at any time,' he admitted. 'I guess this is one of those situations. If it hadn't been for that Black Hole ...'

Lucifer's terrifying demeanour suddenly disappeared. He slumped down into his iron chair and poured himself a jigger of brimstone. 'It had to happen one day,' he muttered. 'Sooner or later the human race would become so wrapped up in science that they would cease to believe in us – forget us altogether.'

He fixed Elmer with one glittering eye. 'The question is what am I to do you?'

'You could help me get back to where I should be,' Elmer suggested. 'I'd hate to be in the way.'

'I have it!' exclaimed Lucifer, thumping down his goblet on his desk built from the bones of dead vicars. 'If I agree, will you give me a really terrifying, fiendish write-up?'

Elmer looked baffled. 'How d'you mean, sir?'

'Well, it's obvious, isn't it? What time are you from?'

'The year 3027 AD, sir.'

Lucifer looked down his nose. 'Young man, down here we don't mention AD. Not regarded as proper form. But never mind. What I mean is that in your particular era Mankind has ceased to believe in the powers of Evil and Good.'

'Now that's just not so, Mister Lucifer, sir!' protested Elmer. 'We abide by a strict code of ethics –'

Lucifer waved a talon for him to be silent. 'I know all that!' he snapped. 'I refer to the religious angle. Are you aware of what the initials AD stand for?'

'Er, After Darwin?'

Lucifer sneered. 'And when was the last time you went to church?'

'What's a church, sir?'

'Precisely. And when was the last time you participated in a Black Mass?'

'A black mass of what, sir?'

'Hah! You haven't the foggiest idea what I'm talking about!' Lucifer cackled triumphantly. 'In return for sending you back to your own time, I want you to take back a report about Hell and make then all realise the terrors that await them – or most of them – when they die. Is it agreed?'

'It sure is,' Elmer enthused, his eyes shining as he withdrew a flat plastic box from his suit. I can record it on my telecorder. Gee, what a story this will make!'

Lucifer pulled a bell rope and the cracked, doom-laden peal of an iron bell tolled out somewhere. 'I will be unable to accompany you on your sightseeing tour, Mr Glumwood,' he said, 'as I am somewhat indisposed. I'll have one of my deputies to escort you.'

Elmer looked concerned. 'I'm sorry, sir. Nothing serious, I hope?'

'Just the usual common hot. Nothing that a short rest in Limbo won't cure. Ah, here is your guide.'

A cloud of sulphurous yellow smoke exploded out of thin air in the middle of the grotto and a small, pot-bellied red demon with a pitchfork under his arm, stood before Lucifer.

'You're late, Scabwort,' accused Lucifer. 'What kept you?'

'Sorry about that, skipper,' Scabwort replied. 'Had a bit of bother in pit 17. Those two politicians and that male ballet dancer were having a punch-up –'

'Never mind the excuses. Mr Glumwood, this is Scabwort.'

'Pleased to meet you, sir,' said Elmer, holding out a metal-gloved hand.

But Scabwort ignored it, and rubbing one of his stubby horns in bafflement, turned his round red face to his master. 'I don't get it, skipper. He ain't even dead.'

Lucifer snorted in exasperation and tersely explained the circumstances. When he had done, Scabwort thumbed his lip doubtfully. 'Are you sure that's a good idea, skipper?' he murmured.

'Of course it is!' bellowed Lucifer. 'I thought of it so it must be. And stop calling me by that disrespectful title!'

'Sorry, chief.' Scabwort gave his charge a critical glance. 'Come on then, squire. Let's be moving.'

'I'll see you later then, Mr Glumwood,' said Lucifer, sitting down and pouring himself another slug of brimstone. 'Enjoy yourself.'

'Enjoy yourself!' snorted Scabwort as he led the way down a passage from the grotto. 'That's the last thing mortals are supposed to do here.'

Elmer followed dutifully after the stumpy little demon until they emerged into a colossal cavern, lit by the flames erupting from bottomless sulphur pits. 'Golly gosh!' he exclaimed in wonder. 'I sure have never seen anything like this! It's hotter than the sun-side of Mercury!'

'Hot as Hell,' Scabwart sniggered. He cast a glance of cynical pride over the scene before them. 'Things ain't what they used to be, though.'

The whole landscape was dotted with all manner of weird contraptions. Iron wheels suspended on frames, torture racks, fiendish devices that all had one thing in common – spiked points. But they had fallen into disuse, many were broken and covered in rust. A few pale souls were in evidence. Elmer observed that they didn't seem particularly bothered about anything. Some were just sitting on the ground, warming themselves by the sulphur pits, while others merely sauntered around, chatting.

'I remember when it really was merry Hell,' Scabwort grunted. 'We had an image to live up to. Some painter called Brueghel did us a few advertising posters. You ever see 'em? No? The old torture wheel spinning like a top – all the lost souls yelling their heads off. Yes, they were happy days. A bit different from now.'

Elmer, who had been busy with his telecorder, made a polite noise of sympathy. He dimly recalled the old legends and from what he recalled, Hell was a lot more livelier than this place. It looked more like some sleepy resort. The only real activity in view was a couple of demons having a fight, just to break the monotony.

'C'mon, squire,' said Scabwort. 'Let's have a look over the estate.'

Off they trotted, Scabwort picking the way between the sulphur craters and Elmer cautiously following. It struck him as a very dull dreary place. Not much going on at all. 'I would have thought that there would be folk around,' he remarked. 'If all the sinners from the year dot are here –'

'Oh, they're here,' Scabwort told him without pausing in his stride. 'They're all in the Grand Cavern, watching the Seven Deadly Sins Olympics.' His scaly red chest puffed with pride. 'I was coach to Plook, the Saturnian, at the last SDS Olympics. He gotta Medal for Lust.'

Elmer's ears pricked up. 'A Saturnian? You mean there are alien souls here as well as Earth souls?'

Scabwort glared at him indignantly. 'Of course there are! D'you think you humans have got sole rights to the place? What are you – some kind of racist?'

Elmer hastened to assure him that he was not. 'Is there any chance of me getting in to see the Olympics?' he ventured. 'Just a quick peep.'

Scabwort shook his head. 'Man, you've as much chance as a cinder in Heaven. Members only. Belial's very strict on that.'

'Who's Belial?'

'Don't you know anything? He's on our Board of Directors. Top exec to Lucifer himself. He's done a lot for the old establishment. Won the Ignoble Prize for Demoniac Literature.'

They had come to a ledge overlooking the next pit which appeared a bit more promising. Demons skipped around jabbing their pitchforks at thin-looking souls who struggled along carrying great bundles of what looked like silver wire. But on closer inspection it could be observed that more than a few quips and ribald pleasantries were bandied back and forth between the demons and the damned. An almost party spirit pervaded.

'What's that metal stuff those guys are carrying,' asked Elmer, pointing his telecorder at the scene below.

'Wire wool for bondage knitwear,' Scabwort explained. 'That's about all those poor old souls are fit for. I know all the publicity handouts make a big thing out of "the wailing and gnashing of teeth", but by the time some of the souls pass over they haven't got any teeth left to gnash.'

They trekked on. A few demons waved up at them and Elmer waved back. It took several minutes of hard climbing before they arrived at the next pit. At the edge of the crag Scabwort paused and folded his arms across his chest. 'Just listen to that,' he murmured. 'Doesn't it bring a lump to your throat?'

Elmer peered at the scene below. Thousands of souls and demons were sitting cross-legged in a vast semi-circle before an elderly batwinged demon who conducted their cacophonous singing with his pitchfork.

Scabwort chuckled affectionately. 'Old Astoroth taking choir practice. *The Hellilujah Chorus*.' He wiped a tear from his eye. 'Never heard it sung better.'

Elmer tried to shut his ears to the hideous din while he recorded sight and sound on his telecorder. He half-expected the machine to blow up in disgust. But it was better than anything he could have picked up in the Crab Nebula anyway. This reminded him of a question he intended put to Lucifer, but perhaps his guide would be able to help. 'Where abouts is Hell?' he asked.

'It's here, you fool! Where d'you think?'

'No, I mean where is located in relation to my own world?'

'Oh, I see what you mean. Well, it's all around it, sort of. Physics isn't really my line, but you know that the atoms and electrons which exist in your own universe are like microscopic stars with planets orbiting them? Well, the stars and planets of your own universe are the atomic structure of Hell … sometimes.'

Elmer's eyes gleaned with scientific greed. 'Gee whiz! Move over, Einstein – Glumwood's on his way! And where is, er …?'

Scabwort favoured him with a leery sort of look. 'The "Other Place"? Just a couple of blocks along the way … sort of. Now don't stand there with your mouth open, chummy. I want you to see where the real work is done. About the only place left – though it shames me to admit.'

Moving awkwardly in his pressurised suit, Elmer followed the rotund little demon along a pumic ridge. 'Where to now?' he puffed.

'You wait and see,' came the retort. 'Lucifer's first and finest racket since he set up shop here. No future at all for his go-getting sort of enterprise in the Other Place. I know all your philosophers say he was kicked out but that's just so much propaganda.'

Elmer caught hold of Scabwort's forked tail and hauled himself up the last difficult bit of the climb. 'I'd be glad if you would tell me about it, Mister Scabwort, sir,' he asked as they set off along the black pumice crest. 'The folks back home seem to have mislaid all the old records on early religion.'

'Fair enough, squire,' Scabwort responded in a more civil tone. 'The official bulletin stated that Lucifer was a fallen angel who tried a takeover bid for the Other Place. But the truth of it is the skipper's no more a fallen angel than I'm a risen demon.'

'You mean he was pushed?'

'Dunderhead!' snapped Scabwort, flapping, his stunted batwings angrily. 'Of course not! He opted out of his own free will.'

'But why did he do that?'

'On account of all those Elysian Fields. When the angels got to mowing them, it brought on big hay fever something awful.'

'Aha! Here we are – the Mines of Hell. Now this is something the old priests did manage to get right. The only place in Hell that still keeps the old flag flying. What we'd do if this place folded, I hate to think. Sit around like your gurus, contemplating our navels – only we haven't got navels to contemplate. You get your eyeballs peeled for the finest sight in Hell. It's just the other side of the next rock. All the souls of the damned screaming in anguish as they toil endlessly in the mines. All the demons sticking 'em with their pitchforks and having no end of fun. Oh, yeah, there's wailing and gnashing of teeth there, sure enough.'

Elmer hurried after the scuttling figure and collided with it force-fully as Scabwort stopped dead in his cloven hoof tracks. 'What's wrong?' he asked.

'It-it's closed down,' whimpered Scabwort. 'The mines ... the mortal souls ... the demons. Wait here. I'll be back soon.'

Elmer stood helplessly on the rock crest overlooking the silent and gloomy pit. He was at a loss to understand what had hap-pened. It wasn't as if the place was deserted. He could dimly see clusters of thin and grimy souls, and even a few sullen-faced demons among their ranks. Elmer hoped that Scabwort wouldn't be too long. Hell was bad enough to be in when you were dead, but when you were still alive ... It just didn't bear thinking about.

Scabwort came hurrying back a couple of minutes later. Elmer had meanwhile noticed a crowd of souls – millions of them, in fact – thronging an adjacent valley. 'Say, Mister Scabwort, sir,' he called out. 'What's with all those guys in the next valley?'

'Spanish souls,' Scabwort puffed, hustling Elmer along ahead of him. 'Get moving – back to Lucifer's grotto as fast as you can.'

Elmer stumbled along bemusedly. 'Spanish souls?' he echoed. 'Why are they all around like that?'

'The Spanish section is still being built, stupid.' 1 thought you would have guessed that. Now shift it or you'll be in mighty big trouble.'

'Okay, okay. Quit shoving,' retorted Elmer, picking his way between the rocks. 'But why the rush?'

'There's something called a picket line back there!' snapped the demon guide. 'Some twit from Twentieth Century Earth has called all the souls out on strike and closed the mines down. Even some of the demon overseers have come out in sympathy. When Lucifer hears about this there'll be trouble, so if you want to get back home then we had best get to Lucifer before he finds out. He'll only take it out on you for being an Earthling.'

They scrambled back past Astoroth's massed Glee Club, past the steel wool gatherers until they finally arrived at the desert plain outside the grotto. Scabwort paused to compose himself and Elmer took this opportunity to ask just one more question. 'Why are you so concerned about my welfare, Mister Scabwort, sir?'

Scabwort blew his snout noisily on his loincloth of Irish linen. 'Because you remind me of my favourite uncle,' he mumbled. 'Now not one word about what's happened. Just leave all the talking to me.'

'You're back early,' remarked Lucifer, glancing up from his copy of *Witch Magazine*. 'Everything okay?'

'Just fine, skipper,' grinned Scabwort. 'Glumwood ran outa video film so we didn't see any sense in hanging about.'

Lucifer fingered his spiky fork beard. 'I see. Just make sure you give me a good press coverage, Glumwood.'

'Oh, I'll do that, sir, never you fear,' Elmer beamed.

'I don't,' retorted Lucifer in a flat voice. 'And now I suppose you want to get to your own time. I can transfer you as far as the Dawn of Creation. From there you turn left at the Second Exploding Universe Theory, then third right until the first Red Shift. From there straight on until you come to Halley's Comet. Reckon you can find your way from there?'

'Kindergarten stuff,' smirked Elmer.

'Now don't get, cocky,' Lucifer admonished him. 'Ready?'

'Fire away, sir,' grinned Elmer as Lucifer made some mystical gestures with his hands, 'and thanks for everything. Goodbye Your Highness, sir. Goodbye, Mister Scabwort, sir.'

And as Elmer was swallowed up in the interlocking dimensions of time and space in an explosion of crimson energy, Lucifer murmured, '*Au revoir*, Mr Glumwood. *Au revoir* ...'

SHADOWSHINE FOUR

The Grim Reaper's jawbone hung open in astonishment. 'You're having me on, Scab,' he said. 'You must be.'

Scabwort looked up from his scrutiny of two Cherubs hula-hooping with their haloes. 'Cross my horns and hope to live, Grim, the truth – every word of it.'

Grimshaw gazed down at the Time Zone far below the lofty and luxurious Paradise Bar where they took their ease amid the stumbled angels and derelict demons who were disporting themselves on the small dance floor. 'I still think you're sending me up,' he retorted, munching on a misfortune cookie.

'It's hardly the sort of thing I'd brag about!' Scabwort snapped in a fine old huff. 'After all, it doesn't put my firm in a favourable light. And if word of this ever got out I'd be on a fizzer, with the gaffer as sure as eggs are eggs.'

'Well if you say it's true then who am I to contradict,' Grimshaw hastily replied. 'It' s just incredible – well, it shakes one's faith to hear things like that.'

Scabwort snapped his talons and ordered two more brimstone and brandy cocktails from a passing topless, headless waitress. 'It's what they call a recession, Grim. Things have come to a pretty pass when the doomed souls start answering back and holding demonstrations.'

'You mean they really do that?'

'Too blessed right they do,' Scabwort threshed his fork tail angrily. 'Only last week they held a demonstration outside Purgatory Cathedral, waving placards that said, "Keep Hell Merry" and "Cave the Caveless". Why – they've even started smiling!'

'What about this Elmer Glumwood character?' asked Grimshaw, cunningly switching the conversation away from its depressing trend. 'How did he do as a canvasser for your people?'

'Lousy,' growled Scabwort, taking a swig from his tall and fuming glass. 'Far from striking fear and dread into the galaxy he caused just the opposite effect to what we wanted. Everyone from Earth to Epsilon Ceti has become so rotten good it's sickening. They've even made him Pope of Jupiter. Just imagine Pope Elmer I of Jupiter! It's sickening!'

Grimshaw downed his drink and nudged Scabwort, 'Care for another? One for the road?'

'It's your turn to pay,' Scabwort reminded him.

'Oh, so it is. Well perhaps we ought to get a move on if I'm going to do that shopping for the kids. Solly won't be pleased if we're late back.'

'I've told you Rubbish-Legs is covering for us,' Scabwort assured him as they edged their way between the hopping, gyring and gimbling entities. 'Anyway, what's this shopping you keep on about? Y'know, we have got time for another drink.'

'Oh, I really don't think we have,' Scab, replied primly. 'It is getting rather late.'

The stumpy little demon glared up at the gloom-shrouded skeleton. 'Heel-tapper,' he sneered.

'It's the new skulking jackets for the kids,' Grimshaw told him. 'I promised the wife I'd get them.'

'I didn't know you had a family,' mused Scabwort as they floated down from the Paradise Bar towards a very busy-looking cloud, all lit up with neon advertisements. 'How many are there?'

'There's Demise, she's the eldest, then Charnely and Edeath – they're twins – and the youngest boy, baby Hellary.'

Scabwort cast him an odd and rather leery glance. 'Are you sure?'

'Of course I'm sure!' hooted Grimshaw indignantly. 'I'm their daddy aren't I?'

Scabwort looked somewhat embarrassed. 'Well that's just it. If they're your kids and they, er, take after their daddy who is – how can I say? – rather high on calcium, how do you, er, tell the girls from the boys?'

Grimshaw favoured his companion a withering eye-socket. 'How d'you think? The girls' mouths are always open, of course.'

They both alighted on the shopping cloud's soft and busy thoroughfare. Off-duty Seraphs, Angels and Cherubs thronged the floatways, mingling with Demons, Imp Cadets and asbestos-robed Low Priests of the Luciferian Order. Horned and hooded Red Friars were plentiful, too, as were Red Roasters and Red Boilers. A jolly procession of cherubic drum majorettes paraded by, zinging their haloes high into the ether and catching them while their gold-jackbooted cheerleaders chanted their slogan in shrill young voices. 'Good is good! Good is good – G-O-O-D – Good is good!'

Grimshaw peered about uncertainly. 'I never feel at ease in these new shopping precincts. Where would be the best place to get the kids' new jackets, Scab?'

'Henry's place,' Scabwort promptly told him, 'and it's just past the next cumulus.'

'Henry?' echoed Grimshaw, 'Who's he?'

'Henry the Wongle. He runs the best rag-and-bone shop in this precinct. Just right for you, Grim.'

Taking the sleeve of Grimshaw's shroud in his claw, Scabwort hustled his bemused companion through the of late-millenia shoppers until they got to a gloomy-looking hole in the cloud with 'Desperate Measures – Bespoke or Off-the-peg' painted on the fascia in merry-coloured mud. 'Henry the Wongle?' frowned Grimshaw. 'I don't think I've heard of him. And what's a Wongle when it's home, anyway?'

'You appear to be disappointingly thick today, Grimmo baby,' Scabwort retorted scathingly. 'A Wongle is a familiar spirit of suburban bedrooms, mainly in the Twickenham area. They're quite malevolent spirits really.'

Grimshaw's teeth clicked nervously. 'A malevolent bedroom spirit?' he squeaked. 'Just how malevolent, are they?'

Scabwort shoved him through the shadowy portals into the emporium's equally shadowy interior. 'They turn peoples' underwear inside-out at night and make them late for work in the morning. Now just get on with your shopping.'

A fat and oily-looking entity with transparent green skin, bald head and ginger beard and fishnet tights under his black morning jacket, approached them. 'Hi there, punters,' he greeted them. 'How can you waste my time?'

'I want four skulking jackets,' Grimshaw replied stiffly. 'A size six, a size three and two size fours, if you please.'

Henry stroked his beard and leered at Grimshaw. 'Well it won't send me into ecstasies of mirth but it might just please me.' He pointed a blue-striped finger towards a disconnected electric chair. 'You just park your pelvis there, Boney, and I'll see what I can dig up.'

Grimshaw collapsed into the electric chair with a surprised clatter and glanced at Scabwort. 'I say,' he whispered. 'He's a bit familiar, isn't he?'

'Like I told you,' Scabwort whispered back. 'He's a familiar spirit.'

Meanwhile Henry was rummaging through a fusty, musty rack of old rags, all hanging inside-out. 'Here we are,' his muffled voice triumphantly emerged from the jumble. 'Four skulking jackets – a size six, a size three and two size fours. Only one previous owner each,' he added, flourishing the mouldy garments before Grimshaw.

'Are they under guarantee?' Grimshaw asked. 'I don't want any foreign rubbish.'

'Of course they're under guarantee,' Henry sneered. 'Just look at the labels inside. "Buried in Britain". Now you can't do better than that. And about the weave? You must admit it. They're just right for the little clatterers.'

'Herringbone,' observed Grimshaw, studying the fabric closely. 'Yes, they should suit the kids down to the ground and under. You're sure they're hard-wearing? The kids are very tough on their clothes.'

The Wongle cast a rolling boiling-egg-of-an-eye at Scabwort. 'Your skinny friend is very hard to please. Is he always like this?'

'He's had a very worrying time lately,' Scabwort excused his companion. 'Quite overworked, y'know. Hasn't had a holiday for centuries.'

'At least he doesn't get any complaints from his sort of customers,' cackled Henry. 'Now come on, squire. Are you having them or not?'

'Oh, very well,' muttered Grimshaw, fidgeting uneasily on the electric chair. 'And I'd better have a pair of swearing rompers for the baby while you're at it.'

Henry scuttled off into the gloomy depths of his emporium, still sniggering to himself. 'I'll be glad to get out of here, Scab,' said Grimshaw. 'He makes me quite nervous, and anyway, I hate shopping.'

Scabwort curled a lip in true bachelor scorn. 'Henpecked – that's what you are, Grim. You should have started as you meant to go on.'

'Talk's cheap! Just you wait until it's your turn!'

'Hah! That'll be the day,' Scabwort responded complacently.

'You mark my words,' Grimshaw cautioned him, 'you'll get landed one of these fine centuries. That Banshee from Fifth Dimensional Dublin and those two Night Hags from the City of Ur – they're all after you. And once you're caught it'll be "Scabby, do the washing up – Scabby, have you wiped your cloven hooves – Scabby, have you put the cat out –".'

'Oh, shut up!' snapped the young demon. 'Just because your old woman has got you under her thumb doesn't give you the right to get stroppy with me!'

'Kindly refrain from referring to Millidew by that common and revolting term!' Grimshaw angrily objected. 'She is a fine spectress – not one of your good-time ghouls –'

Further argument was terminated by the reappearance of the grotesque little Wongle with two neatly-folded swearing rompers. 'Is that everything or do you require a little something for the wife?' he asked.

Grimshaw started nervously, invoking a mocking snigger from Scabwort. 'Yes, I'd better get something for her,' he nodded. 'what do you suggest?'

'How about a nice mink hangman's noose to keep the cold in?' suggested Henry. 'They're very fashionable, y'know.'

'Yes, that will do fine,' said Grimshaw. 'Just wrap them all up and I'll settle the bill. Now you're quite sure those skulking jackets are okay?'

'Is he always like this?' declared the Wongle, casting an appealing eye at Scabwort. 'Listen, Skinless, you won't find anything better. The labels inside tell you that they are genuine Transylvanian Tweed, woven by Vampires by the light of the Full Moon. Is that good enough for you?'

'It'll have to be,' muttered Grimshaw in a sulky voice. 'Do you take Darklycards?'

'Like they were free double scotches,' retorted Henry, snatching the plastic card with a green and rubbery claw and deftly running it through the imprinter. 'There you are, duckie,' he added, handing the card and Darklycard chitty to Grimshaw 'Will that be all? How about for yourself?' We've gotta new line in jump-suit shrouds just come –'

'No thanks,' Grimshaw replied hastily as he scrambled to his metatarsals. 'I've got the marsh gas bill to pay yet.' Pausing only to sign the chitty and snatch up his parcel of purchases, he quickly followed Scabwort towards the door.

'Suit yourself,' Henry shrugged. 'See you around, Boney. Goodbye, Scabwort.'

'Badbye, Henry,' Scabwort called back over his batwinged shoulder as he followed Grimshaw out of the shop.

'Thank badness I'm out of that place,' Grimshaw sighed thankfully as he stood on the cloud walk, clutching his parcel of purchases. 'We really ought to be getting back. Solly will be furious if he finds out we've skipped off.'

'If you say so,' Scabwort muttered resignedly. 'But I still think you're worrying too much. He'll still be gassing with that apology for Jeeves.'

'I wish I could be as certain,' Grimshaw murmured. 'He can turn very nasty when he's crossed.'

Still arguing, the two entities made their way back towards the Time Zone and the light lock that would return them to the Shadowshine Clearing House Auditorium.

The Soul Searcher ambled his leisurely way back through the light lock after seeing Dennis Strangles the butler off on his new incarnation. He quite enjoyed the session with the elderly and venerable mortal. How he would adjust to finding himself born as the heir of a supermarket millionaire he wasn't quite sure. Those early Twentieth Century mortals had peculiar ideas about class, especially 'trade'. Probably it was just as well that his previous existence been erased from his soul memory.

The Soul Searcher chuckled at a sudden thought. The old butler's previous incarnation had been just as unlikely, too. Nell Gwynn. Ah, well. Variety is the spice of lives.

Still pondering on butlerdom and its various fascinations, the Soul Searcher drifted out of the light lock and sauntered across the cloudy floor, one hand raised as if carrying a small tray. 'Lord and Lady Ratpacket wish to know if you are at home today, Milord,' he announced in nasal falsetto. 'No, sir?'

'Very good, sir. I shall bang the gong when your slippers are adequately warmed in the oven, sir. Will that be all, sir? Very good, sir. Thank you, sir.'

He pulled himself together with some embarrassment to find a Messenger Seraph standing in front of him, complete with goggles and white leather flying suit. 'Top priority message from the Sorting Office, sir,' he announced, handing a slip of paper to the Soul Searcher. 'There's no reply.'

The Soul Searcher nervously watched the Messenger Seraph soar aloft and vanish into the clouds. A top priority message from the Sorting Office? Now what had gone wrong? He glanced around the silent Auditorium, looking for Grimshaw and Scabwort but they were nowhere to be seen. Probably lolling about sulking in one of the rainbow corridors that bisected the light lock at intervals. They always got like that when they hadn't had a really exciting doomed soul to mortalhandle. Very touchy they were, especially Grimshaw.

His thoughts reluctantly turned to the message. Was he on the carpet with Upstairs? Had he spent too much time with Strangles and missed a deceased warlock being rushed through on a Grade One priority? Surely not!

'Unexpected continuum warp in the area of Mars,' he read aloud. 'Time period 1056/6 – Alpha on the Temporal Martian scale.' With a nasty sinking feeling he suspected that to be the equivalent of Earth's Twentieth Century, and after a hurried mental calculation his fears were confirmed. He rapidly scanned through the rest of the message.

'A Martian mortal has penetrated a small Black Hole in the area of Phobos, one of the Martian moons. In doing so, this entity has terminated his mortal existence and by-passed the normal fatality

collection channels. This has also resulted in a short-circuit of ...'
He skimmed through the rest of the usual official gobbledygook
which didn't concern him.

Honestly! he thought. The bumf they wasted in Admin! Then he
got to the nitty-gritty. '... therefore this unforeseen penetration of
the dimensions has resulted in an extra soul in your Limborium.
Details of the subject's case history are also enclosed. If you have
not already done so, please adjust your ledger accordingly. Your
eternal servant, H. Evans.'

So that was it! A Martian! A rotten Martian cuckoo in the nest!
The Soul Searcher stared about for some sign of his helpers, but in
vain. Oh, well, it wasn't his fault. Then he noticed a postscript to
the directive. 'We would be obliged if you would deal with this
aberration promptly.'

The impudence! Typical of those white-haloed quill-pushers Upstairs! Well he was blowed if he was going to bow and scrape to
some jumped-up little pip-squeak, still downy between the shoulder blades! Who was running this Clearing House anyway?

His mind made up, the Soul Searcher stumped over to his desk,
climbed on his stool and glared at the Recorder Book open before
him. Just to prove who was boss he would deal with the next listed
– and the Martian 'aberration' could wait until after or take a jump
into another Black Hole. His eye ran down the list of names. Now
who was next? 'Oho,' he chortled with inappropriate wickedness.
'That one, eh? I'm just in the mood for him.'

The chunky-looking woman in the Traffic Warden uniform glared
at Hubert Square. 'You'll pardon me for saying this,' she began in
a tone which held more of a declaration of war than a note of
contrition, 'but I find your comments most repugnant.'

Hubert studied the woman with plump aloofness. 'The name is
Square, madam – Hubert Square. I'm afraid you have me at a
disadvantage, Mrs, er, Miss ...'

'Elvira Spratt – Ms Elvira Spratt, of DAD.'

Hubert's flesh-buttressed face took on a perplexed look. 'Dad?' he
echoed.

'Discrimination Against Discrimination. I am the society Chair-
person for the South London Area. We are concerned about all
forms of discrimination, be it against creed, colour or inanimate
objects.'

'Inanimate objects?' objected Horace with a squeak of amazement. 'You mean things?'

'I mean things!' thundered Ms Spratt. 'All manner of persons, places and things, be they decorative or practical. All things from a flawless diamond down to the lowliest form of used appliance. And in that spectrum, I include our unfortunate red-skinned little kinsperson sitting yonder.'

'But dammit all, woman!' exclaimed Horace in a loud whisper. 'That fellow's a Martian!'

Elvira glanced at the metal-garbed figure in the shadows on the far side of the waiting room. 'I suppose he could be,' she conceded. 'I'll bet he's not European. But what of it? If the poor person is sick then he has as much right to see a doctor as you have, Mr ...?'

'Hapgood,' supplied Horace bemusedly wondering why he himself had not questioned the presence of a Martian in the doctor's waiting room before. And why should he assume the being to be a Martian? Why not a Venusian? Or for that matter a Saturnian? 'I suppose you do have a point,' he finished lamely.

'I'm sure I have,' retorted Elvira with the confidence of single-mindedness. 'And if you really do want something outside your own miserably narrow existence to worry about, Mr Hapgood – and the same goes for you, too, Mr Square – then you should be more concerned about the floor. I'm not at all sure that it is safe. It most certainly doesn't feel very solid.'

Both men glanced down at the gently-undulating carpet of grey-blue-patterned cloud under their feet. 'I assumed it to be some new type of cushioned-surfaced floor covering,' murmured Hubert, staring down at the rippling surface from which the legs of his wooden chair appeared to be sprouting. 'But since you mention it –'

'Hubert Square!' boomed out the disembodied Voice.

With a squeak of fright Hubert leapt into the air, all traces of urbanity shot to ribbons. Then composing himself, he nodded stiffly to Elvira, managed a frosty smile in Horace's direction, and made his way towards the waiting room door with a heavy, almost steady tread.

THE FORTUNES OF WAR

Portly, middle-aged Hubert Square stood between his two suitcases in the saloon bar of The Compass. 'I've always liked Copton,' he gushed. 'Used to come here quite a lot before the war. Nice, quiet sort of place. Such a change from London.'

Mr Rivett, the proprietor, and his wife, stood behind the bar. 'I'm sure we're very pleased to have you stay,' beamed Mrs Rivett. 'Just the one week, is it?'

'Unfortunately yes, just the one week.' Hubert Square's pink moon-face expressed contrition. I'd like to stay longer. The East Anglia coast is so clean and refreshing. You can keep all those noisy, commercialised places. Give me Anglia any day – Copton in particular.'

'I'll take your bags up to your room,' Mr Rivett said. 'You want a meal yet?' His tone was indifferent, almost cool.

Hubert Square's chubby hands fluttered fussily. 'No, thank you. I think I'll go and have a look at the sea. Get the feel of the place, eh – what?'

The Rivetts watched his massive form depart and amble down the Coast Road. Patronising lump,' muttered Mr Rivett hefting the two suitcases in his strong, sinewy hands. 'These *townies* are all the same. Say a few pretty words an' they think they're doin' us a favour. Ruddy civil servant, I'll be bound.'

Mrs Rivett sniffed. 'You're glad enough to take his money, Tom. I thought he was a nice polite gentleman.'

'You would,' snarled the landlord, and trudged upstairs with the suitcases.

Hubert Square waddled down the Coast Road towards the cliff path. He remembered it well from six years previous, just before the outbreak of the war. The old cottage should be just beyond that clump of trees. His mind went back to six years ago – his first and only visit to Copton. Hardly a holiday! An overnight stop was more like it, but now he was a respectable citizen, recently demobbed from His Majesty's Armed Forces.

Pete Sharkey had been with him in the old days. Times to remember indeed! Shotguns were easy to come by before the war. It all should have been so simple. Armed and masked, they had forced their way into the little Post Office in the neighbouring village of Horton just as it was closing. The old fool behind the counter had been rash enough to try and prevent them getting away. Well, you can't argue with a shotgun, and he became part of the interior decorations within a second. Sharkey had been close to panic, but Hubert Square – always the cool one – had hustled him away with a satchel crammed full of crisp white fivers. There must have been hundreds there – a devil of a lot of money for a small village Post Office! They drove off in their hired car, well aware that the police would be setting up checkpoints. They had to hide the money and the guns.

Copton supplied the answer. Under cover of darkness they found the empty old cottage at the end of the cliff path. The oilskin satchel containing the incriminating evidence they placed in a tool box from the boot of the car and buried it under the stone flags in the kitchen, intending to return for it when the hue and cry had died down.

But their plan had misfired. The war came along and they were both swept up in it. As there was a nationwide search for the two killers it was as good a way as any to get out of the country. Sharkey had died on the Normandy beaches, but Hubert Square had been more fortunate. He had wrangled himself an administrative job, partly due to his age and partly to his medical grading.

And now, six years later, he returned to Copton to harvest his ill-gotten gains. On reaching the edge of the trees Hubert Square stopped and stared, his eyes mouth-round with dismay. The cottage was no longer there! Where it had stood were the jagged lines of the cliff, overlooking the wide sea and softened by clumps of weeds. Erosion! The East Coast was notorious for it. During the past six years that part of the cliff had given away and crashed down to the beach, taking the cottage with it.

Hubert Square cursed, almost in tears of rage and frustration. Mastering himself he gingerly approached the precipice and peered down. It was not a sheer drop. In fact it looked quite negotiable. The jagged surface consisted of sandy boulders and earthy outcrops on which wild flowers flourished. And there at the foot of the cliff lay the sprawling jumble of brickwork and stone, washed clean of the loose plaster and timber by the Spring Tides.

All was not yet lost! The oilskin bag of money was in a strong metal box. Hubert Square's devious mind calculated the possibilities. It would have stood up to the battering and was certainly much too heavy to have been washed out to sea. The weight of the two shotguns would have made it even heavier.

Five minutes later found him, sweating and dishevelled, clawing with his bare hands amongst the debris. The beach lacking in commercial amenities, was both beautiful and deserted, the only sound being the never-ending, gentle roar of the surf frothing over the smooth sand and the wheeling and screaming gulls. His torn and gritty hands caught on a metal corner hidden from view by a large section of brickwork. Hubert Square could hardly credit his luck as he wrenched the metal box out into the open.

If he had bothered to use the steps that led down to the beach he would doubtless have seen the notice that warned of unexploded mines. As it was, he hadn't …

SHADOWSHINE FIVE

'That old village Post Office was hit by a bomb only six months after I, er, visited it.' Hubert Square desperately defended himself. 'I was but a tool of circumstance.'

The Soul Searcher studied his latest client with smug satisfaction. This one was trying to make a verbal fight of it. At least it would provide something of a diversion. At best it could develop into a most invigorating slanging match. 'What do you mean – "a tool of circumstance"?' he enquired with such honeyed sweetness that had Hubert been diabetic he would have collapsed on the spot.

The latter appeared more than a little uncomfortable, mangling the astral form of his grey homburg hat between his sausagey fingers. 'The man I, er, helped on his way to higher things – he would have died in the bombing. Everyone else there did.'

'That's just where you're wrong!' the Soul Searcher crowed triumphantly. 'He was destined to be in hospital having his varicose veins done during that bombing raid. Oh, no, Mr Square. I've got you well truly by the ectoplasm now! You are guilty of murder! Guilty as Hell! And that's where you're going!'

'I most strongly protest!' Hubert's face registered fear, outrage, disgust and despair simultaneously. He had a very large face with enough surplus flesh to accommodate this trick. 'I demand to see my lawyer! I have a right for someone to represent my defence.'

The Soul Searcher stroked his long white beard complacently. 'But you've already been represented – by me.'

'You?' Hubert nearly burst. 'Heaven help me! If you represent, my defence then what can I expect from the prosecution?!'

'Heaven has tried to help you on several occasions,' replied the Soul Searcher. 'And as for any prosecution council – well, you, by your mortal acts, have been your own prosecution.'

'But – but haven't I the right of appeal?'

The Soul Searcher smirked but it was hidden by his beard. 'I don't find you in the least appealing, Hubert. Now don't take on so,' he added as the defendant began to tear at the few strands of hair that defiantly flourished atop his pink bald head. 'You won't be the first and you most certainly won't be the last. Your old pal, Peter Sharkey, is down there. Maybe Scabwort can arrange things so that you're both on the same furnace duties. It's not so bad if there's someone you know. After all, a trouble shared is a trouble halved.'

But Hubert Square had ceased to offer anything constructive to the argument. He seemed to be fully occupied with tearing at his hairs, shrieking and babbling. The Soul Searcher glanced towards the light lock. 'He's all yours, Scabwort. Wheel him away.'

A demon blundered out of the light lock, tripping over his pitchfork. Hubert's screams waxed ultrasonic at the spectacle as the uncouth and scruffy-looking demon scrambled to his cloven hooves and lunged at him with his pitchfork.

'You're not Scabwort!' bellowed the Soul Searcher. 'And look what you've done to the light lock! You've busted it! The place is awash with rainbows!'

'Sorry about that, brother,' came the off-hand reply as the demon tentatively poked Hubert in the stomach with his pitchfork. 'I'm

Rubbish-Legs. Scab and Grim have just slipped out for a while, so I'm standing in for them until they get back.'

'Don't you "brother" me! They've no right to leave without permission. And what do you think you're doing with that pitchfork? He's dead already, or are you trying to turn him into a sieve?'

Rubbish-Legs paused in the act of doing something uniquely fiendish with his pitchfork and glared indignantly at the Soul Searcher. 'Give us a chance, Guv. This is my first doomed soul and I want to make something of it to impress Belial and the other talent scouts.'

Hubert took advantage of the brief exchange to hide under a gurgling torrent of indigo bubbling forth from the damaged lock. 'Gotcha!' shouted Rubbish-Legs, jabbing at the seat of his pants. 'On your feet, chum, and on your way!' A blob of sulphurous bubble gum swelled from his hoary lips like a molten fireball, causing Hubert to break from cover, bleating hysterically.

'Kindly desist from that unseemly behaviour!' roared the Soul Searcher, pounding his white and gold desk with a clenched fist. 'Save it for down below. You are quite lowering the tone of Shadowshine.'

Rubbish-Legs seized Hubert by the scruff of his natty grey suit and waded with him through the swirling colours towards the fireproof escalator. 'Sorry about the mess, Guv,' he called back over his batwings. 'Got a bit carried away, I did. It won't happen again.'

'It had damn well better not!' the Soul Searcher yelled after him. 'When you've got shot of him you can find Scabwort and get him back here. If he was taken short he at least should have had the courtesy to ask to be excused instead of slinking off!'

'He's out at the Time Walk with Grim, getting a breath of fresh ether,' the voice of Rubbish-Legs floated back as he booted his very first doomed soul down the fireproof escalator. 'He'll be back soon.'

The Soul Searcher was having difficulty in maintaining his earthly mode, and covered his face with semi-vaporous hands. 'Why, oh why did I give up my job as Botanical Consultant at the Garden of Eden?' he moaned. 'I could have made a go of the place. For one thing I could have got rid of that damn serpent.'

'Your milk and honey, sir,' piped up a voice.

The soul Searcher uncovered his eyes and saw a little, earnest-faced Cherub hovering by his desk, holding out a silver dish.

'Thank you, laddie, he murmured, taking the dish and placing it on the desk before him. 'It's so nice to see that some folk around here still have a sense of responsibility. You're new here, aren't you?'

'Yes, sir,' sighed the Cherub. 'I was a junior trainee guardian angel on Earth, but it didn't work out very well.'

The Soul Searcher wiped a blob of honey from his beard with the sleeve of his white robe. 'It didn't? Where were you based?'

'Atlantis, sir.'

The Soul Searcher nodded sympathetically. 'Well you can just put all that behind you now, my boy. Just keep your wings preened and your halo gilded and you'll be all right. Now be off with you while I finish my high tea.'

'Good eternity to you, sir,' announced a new voice. 'I see you've got a spot of bother with your light lock.'

Two Seraphs stood before the Soul Searcher's desk. They wore peaked haloes and shimmering white overalls with 'Sweetness and Light Lock Maintenance' emblazoned on the front in blue and gold.

The Soul Searcher glared across the colour-drenched Auditorium at the twinkling, creaking light lock. 'A spot of bother is putting it mildly,' he snorted. 'Do you think you can fix it? I've got a grading session on at the moment and I can't afford delays. Apart from a stray Martian on a top priority I'm expecting an influx of casualties in from the Saturn-Jupiter Space Wars at any century now.'

The two Seraphs paddled through the gouts of light adjusting their black anti-glare goggles. 'Looks worse than it really is, sir,' commented one of them. 'Seems to have jammed on the infra-red. We'll have to use a spark hammer to get it back on the right frequency.'

The Soul Searcher gestured at the flood of colours staining the cloudy floor. 'But what about all this mess? I can't have the mortal souls seeing the place like this. It would be quite disillusioning for them.'

The other Seraph fished in his white shoulder bag concealed behind his wings. 'I'll have that attended to in a brace of shakes, sir,' he replied, withdrawing a round disc of black nothingness. 'This Black Hole will soon suck up all the waste light.'

'Good enough,' grunted the Soul Searcher, settling himself down at his desk. 'Just as long as you know what you're doing. I'll bone up on my next client.'

While the Soul Searcher made a few necessary amendments in the Recorder Book concerning the errant Martian client, a cluster of wide-eyed Cherubs hovered watching the two maintenance Seraphs with interest. But the constant flutter of their wings was so distracting that the Soul Searcher shooed them away. 'How the Heaven am I expected to concentrate with them breathing down my neck?' he muttered.

'Looks like we'll have to cut away some of the red and tighten up the bands of purple, sir,' one of the Seraphs called across to him. 'When was this light lock last serviced?'

'Just after the Flood.'

The Seraph whistled. 'As long as that, eh? Could be the guarantee has expired by now. We'll try to keep the costs down as best we can, sir. Hand me the torch, Ambrose, and I'll weld a patch on this section of ultra-violet to hold the colour frequency chromo stat in place.'

The Soul Searcher winced and shielded his eyes. 'Could you possibly work a little less brightly?' he pleaded. 'I find all this quite blinding.'

'Nearly done, Guv'nor,' sang Ambrose. 'We'll be finished in a twinkling.'

'Thank goodness for that,' muttered the Soul Searcher, returning to his Recorder Book. 'Now let's get the show on the road again.'

Horace Hapgood felt lonely. A waiting room had to be the loneliest of places and he had only struck up a casual acquaintance with Hubert Square for a few minutes, he missed the social contact. He studied the other occupants of the room with lacklustre eyes. The lady traffic warden, the old buffer in tweeds, the Martian – yes, it certainly must be a Martian – the African, the relaxed young man engrossed in his *Reader's Digest* back-numbers, and a big, bearded fellow sitting in the gloom of the far side of the shadowy waiting room, partially obscured by the wilting rubber plant. He gave the general impression of being quite a disreputable character, what could be seen of him at any rate. Smelly, too. A fishy odour. There was really no excuse for such a flagrant disregard of hygiene in this

62

day and age. Probably some vagrant from the docks. Horace
hoped that he had nothing contagious.

'They do seem to take rather a long time, don't they?' remarked
the elderly man in tweeds.

Horace nearly jumped out of his skin. 'Y-yes, they do,' he stuttered. 'Have you any idea who's next?'

'None whatsoever,' replied the other man. 'But I've always found
that I'm never in the doctor's surgery as long as other patients.'

Horace smiled, grateful for this friendly overture. 'Just one of
those strange facts of life, Mr, er ..?'

'Doyle – Professor Desmond Doyle. And you are Mr Hapgood,
I believe, from what I overheard of your discussion with the
recently departed Mr Square.'

For some unaccountable reason Horace shivered. 'You make as
if he's dead. He's only in the doctor's surgery, doubtless being told
to ease up on the brandy.'

Desmond Doyle puffed reflectively on his pipe, invoking a disapproving glance from Ms Spratt the lady traffic warden. 'I suppose
he is,' he murmured. 'Yet I have the oddest feeling about this place.'

'Kugg, of Mars,' boomed the summoning Voice.

In response, the Martian slithered from his chair, clumped across
the cloud-covered floor of the waiting room, and disappeared
through the door.

INCIDENT AT KRUTT CORNER

Mr Kugg left the vac-tube station and ambled slowly along the
stone-blossomed lane that led to his home at Krutt Corner. He
wondered what his wife would be cooking for supper. A nice
tender wuggler and a glass of heavy water was what he fancied, but
it would probably be moonbugs again. She really had no imagina-
tion when it came to cooking. Even the ultra-violet grill he had
bought her had failed to stimulate any real initiative.

High above, the cloudless pink sky was already darkening to
purple and the two Martian moons scudded serenely overhead. Mr

Kugg was worried because his departmental chief and his wife were coming to dinner tomorrow and he dreaded to think what muck Mrs Kugg would serve up. It could well affect his career in the Crater. Just because she was expecting an egg was no excuse.

He strolled up the path to the sedate little metal dome that was his residence. Each side were similar sedate little metal domes. Krutt Corner was a very select neighbourhood in the heart of the Red Belt where the most important domestic occupation was 'keeping up with the Jovians'.

The silica garden would need attending to, he mused. He would have to borrow back his laser-powered glass mower from that scrounger, Mr Jikk, next door, before his visitors arrived.

The circular door opened, responding to his tail print, and he stepped wearily indoors. Mrs Kugg was in the hall, a cheerful black apron tied around her pear-shaped body. A woman of her years should wear less frivolous colours, thought Mr Kugg disapprovingly, but he wisely kept such thoughts to himself, saying instead, 'Hello, dearest. What's for dinner? I've had the most hectic day at the Crater –'

'And I've had a hell of a day!' complained Mrs Kugg, her green, button-like eyes dilating violently. 'I'll be glad when I've had this damned egg! All the time I worry in case I crack the shell. It's a pity you males don't lay eggs. You'd soon learn to be more considerate. Sometimes I wish I'd never been hatched!'

Mr Kugg gave her the customary spit on the mandibles and sauntered past her into the parlour where he slumped down into his rest pit. 'What's for dinner, dearest?' he repeated, a hard edge creeping into his voice as he picked up the evening video and scanned the headlines.

Mrs Kugg stood over him, tentacles akimbo. 'Moonbug pie,' she retorted, and waddled off to the kitchen, slamming the door behind her.

Mr Kugg sighed. Just the same as last night and the night before. He caught sight of himself in the triangular ceiling mirror and shuddered. His once glossy red skin looked pink and tired around the eyes, and his domed hairless skull was beginning to flatten on top. Oh, well. No one can hold back the years, he sighed again.

He put down the video and dialled the kitchen extension on the house visiphone. Instantly his wife's harassed red face appeared on the hexagonal screen. Clouds of purple billowed around her from the oven, and her hairs were awry. 'What?' she demanded.

Not the best psychological moment, Mr Kugg reflected, but the die was cast. 'Dearest, you haven't forgotten that Mr and Mrs Rumm-Tumm are dining with us tomorrow evening?'

The response was almost deafening, becoming almost obscene towards the end. 'And the trouble I've had with the plants!' she concluded shrilly. 'Why we couldn't have proper pedigrees like everyone else in Krutt corner, I'll never know! But you have to get a pair of untrained, cross-pollinated mongrels that have been in and out of the house all day, leaving muddy rootprints everywhere! Why don't you do something useful like taking them out for a walk while I'm getting the dinner?'

Not a bad idea, thought Mr Kugg as he switched off the visiphone. She might be in a better mood by the time I get back, especially as her favourite programme, *Constellation Street*, is on the televisor tonight.

He strolled out onto the patio and clicked softly. In response the plants came scampering out of their kennel pots and romped playfully around him, pawing at his spindly red legs with their tendrils as he fastened on their thin leads and patted their buds. Leading the plants to the garage, he hustled them aboard his sports hoverplat, switched on the motor and cruised down the drive, out into the silent avenue.

All the little domed houses were peaceful, their blinds drawn. Everyone was settled indoors for the night, watching the Mathematic Olympics on their 4D televisors. Mr Kugg drove down the lane to the heath and, cutting the motor, gazed about him. It was a fine night and the pumice craters glittered coldly in all their pastoral splendour. The plants nuzzled him impatiently, hissing and snapping their petalled jaws. They wanted 'walkies'.

Mr Kugg led them out of the hoverplat, and up the low rise. A few moments drinking in the tranquillity of the night and then he would stop off at The Alien's Arms for a more robust drink before returning home. He unclipped the plants' leads and they bounded off, squeaking with glee. Mr Kugg took his atomic pipe from the pocket of his silvery tunic and, igniting it, placed the metal stem in his lipless mouth, savouring the metallic aroma. A Martian with his pipe and two faithful plants. What more could a man want?

The stars twinkled icily in the purple dome overhead as Mr Kugg sought out the most conspicuous. A green star with a smaller white companion. Some said that intelligent life flourished there but most people doubted it. All that oxygen and water vapour! How could anything remotely intelligent live in that sort of environment? Possibly a few mammals crawled around in the slime, but that, was all?

And then he saw the point arching down from the sky. His gaze followed its descent with astonishment. It was travelling too slowly for a meteor and it looked as if it would come down near, too. As it approached he was able to make out details. A stumpy metal cylinder with four spidery hydraulic legs extended. On the side of the cylinder was a colossal panel with some sort of emblem consisting of red, white and blue stripes and dots. From the base of the cylinder a pillar of fire roared, acting as a break.

Suddenly things seemed to go wrong. The column of fire flickered out and the craft lurched drunkenly in mid-air and crunched down among the rocks some distance away. Fire gushed from somewhere, then a hatch was thrown open and something emerged to fall heavily to the ground.

Mr Kugg nervously edged away into the shelter of a scented shrubbery of boulders, clicking loudly for the excited plants to heel. The thing that leapt from the cylinder was staggering away among the rocks, an ungainly, alien shape. Then with a soft, billowing roar that carried faintly through the thin Martian air, the craft exploded in a most spectacular fashion, hurling debris in all directions.

The plants were racing about, showering pollen everywhere, and Mr Kugg lost sight of them in the clouds of black smoke. Then he saw them scampering around the thing which had jumped of the machine. It lay motionless on the ground, its white rubbery-looking limbs outstretched. Mr Krugg clicked urgently to the plants. 'Root!' he commanded them. Despite what his wife said, they were quite well-trained plants, and they obediently rooted, but their stamens still hung out, quivering with excitement.

Mr Kugg cautiously approached the prone form. It was obviously dead, caught in the blast of the explosion. He wondered what sort of creature it could be. It was vaguely Martianoid in form, possessing two arms and legs, but it was soft-looking with an odd hump on its back, almost like a metal box or container. Possibly some spinal protuberance. It was most likely mammalian, and that round, shiny head did not look large enough to house a brain of any consequence. Probably its brain was located in that spinal hump. It seemed to be faceless as well, for the front of its head was just a plain optic organ, almost like glass.

Mr Krugg stared up at the green star that was Earth. Could it have come from the sister planet? There had been rumours in the Imperial Lavender Dome concerning space probes from Earth, but a security gag had been placed on all data by no less than His Royal Bigness himself.

Whatever it was, it had made the very devil of a mess, he reflected, staring in distaste at the wreckage scattered everywhere. What would Mr and Mrs Rumm-Tum think if they saw all this junk? It would create a bad impression. He would have to get his house robots to clear the place up.

Mr Kugg swore. No time for a drink now if he was to make this place presentable. And he had yet to mow the glass. Then an idea occurred to him and, clicking to the plants, he hustled them aboard the hoverplat and headed for home.

The dinner of the following evening was an unqualified success. The guests relaxed in their pits, replete and basking in the glow of the uranium isotope that blazed merrily in the metal grate. Mr Rumm-Tumm, his plum-coloured head mushroom-shaped by an over-indulgence of expense account luncheons, had expanded verbally as well as physically, and Mr Kugg's future career in the Crater seemed well assured.

Mrs Runm-Tumm also regarded her host with an approving eye, showing more tentacle than modesty decreed and fluttering her antennae demurely. Mr Kugg hoped that his wife had not noticed, but she was busy clearing away the dinner things. The house robots had worn themselves to fuse wire clearing the rubbish at the end of Krutt Corner and were being recharged in the garage. Even the garden had been cut and polished so that it glittered all colours of the rainbow.

'Let me help with the dishes,' offered Mrs Rumm-Tumm, uncoiling herself from her pit and following her hostess into the kitchen. 'Really, you shouldn't have gone to all that trouble, dear. Certainly not in your condition.'

Somewhat mollified, Mrs Kugg let her help with the drinks trolley. 'I'll just get rid of these odds and ends,' she said, moving over to the disposal chute.

'That meal was divine,' cooed Mrs Rumm-Tumm. 'You must let me have the recipe, darling. What on Mars was it?'

Mrs Kugg smiled modestly. 'You'll have to ask my husband. It was his surprise. I'll just get rid of these skins.' She opened the disposal chute and tipped down a dented space helmet and the shredded remains of a spacesuit.

'That's all cleared up,' she smiled brightly. 'Now does your husband take one or two lumps of plutonium in his sulphuric acid?'

SHADOWSHINE SIX

'Do you think we've been missed,' murmured Scabwort as he and the Grim Reaper slunk back through the newly-repaired light lock. 'I didn't realise we had stayed away so long.'

Grimshaw shrugged his boney shoulders, affecting nonchalance. 'I couldn't care less. Fat lot of use me being here if he's going to have blackleg transport for souls like that psychotic little mortal, Dodds. He's only got to say one word out of place to me. Just one!'

'Hang about, Grim,' Scabwort warned him, placing a cautionary talon on his companion's ulna. 'He's not there. The place is empty!'

'Of course he's there!' snapped Grimshaw. 'He's always there. Out of my way and let, me have a look.'

Still lurking in the dimension shrouding, the upper regions of the spectrum, Grimshaw and Scabwort peered into the vast, cloud-ridden Auditorium. True, no one sat at the imposingly lofty desk of white and gold, but the hall was not completely empty. A figure stood before the desk. A little red-skinned and tentacled form, clad in a close-fitting metallic suit. 'It's a Martian – a bloody Martian!' hissed Grimshaw. 'I didn't bring him up! What's the old fool playing at? He keeps on like this I'll be out of a job!'

Scabwort nervously pulled him back into the recesses of the light lock. 'Shut up, you idiot! More to the point – where is Solly anyway?'

'That's the least of my worries, you silly devil! This is terrible. I could be made redundant at the drop of a coffin!'

'Don't take on so, Grim,' Scabwort tried to calm him down. 'Things are never as black as they're painted. Remember the old saying – "never say die".'

'Don't say that! You'll bring on my calcium deficiency!'

'Oh, well – sorry. How about "while there's life there's hope"?'

But Grimshaw's eye-sockets had noticed something that he had not seen at first glance. 'What's that brown pot thing on Solly's desk? It wasn't there before.'

Scabwort peered past him. 'Probably his dinner things. Let me have a look.' Then he recoiled in alarm as the brown pot began to hop up and down on the desk.

Grimshaw snapped his fingerbones as the light dawned on him. 'It's a Boggo-Vup!' he exclaimed.

Scabwort stared up at the excited skeleton as if he had gone mad. 'Bog-who?'

'Boggo-Vup – the Soul Searcher's Martian mode! Great galloping ghouls, this does change things! He's in session with that Martian soul and I'm still in my Earth mode! Give me room, Scab. I've got to change my image.'

Grimshaw's panic was infectious. 'Change your image?' squawked Scabwort. 'What the angel are you talking about, Grim?'

I must assume the mode of Plap-Quirk, the Martian equivalent of the Grim Reaper, Grimshaw hastily told him, 'and unless you want to be on the carpet I suggest that you get a squad of Martian demons up here pronto in case they're needed – at the double!'

Scabwort gaped in amazement as Grimshaw, his dark shroud billowing around his skeletal figure, executed a couple of graceful and mystic pirouettes – and changed into a diminutive object resembling a bright green tin can, poised on a single bird-like claw. Scabwort gaped for a few more seconds, then gathering his wits, scampered off to the asbestos escalator and disappeared from sight, to drum up a couple of Martian demons, as fast as his hooves would carry him.

The Soul Searcher – now Boggo-Vup, the Martian equivalent – wobbled with a dignified gait along the edge of his desk. 'You have displayed a most unattractive side to your nature, Mr Kugg,' he admonished the humbled figure of the Martian. 'Such behaviour cannot be allowed to go unpunished.'

'But the astronaut was quite dead when I found him, O Exalted Pot,' replied Mr Kugg with a throwaway gesture of his tentacles. 'Surely it is only logical that even in extinction he should serve some useful purpose? And he did make an excellent dinner.'

'Do not procrastinate!' thundered the Pot. He had already observed Grimshaw in his Martian mode of Plap-Quirk, hopping furtively out of the light lock. Keeping a wary optic sensor trained on the errant entity, he saw him scuttle across the cloud-carpeted Auditorium. The wretch was skulking behind a stack of halo crates, hoping it would be thought he had been on Soulwatch Duty all the time. This only served to put the Soul Searcher in an even fouler mood.

'You are guilty of a crime far more serious crime eating an Earthman,' Mr Kugg, he telepathed loudly at the Martian. 'I refer to your lascivious behaviour concerning Mrs Rumm-Tumm, your employer's wife.'

'That was a misunderstanding,' the Martian protested, his scales paling visibly.

'She understood all right!' yelled the Pot. 'You deserted your poor, long-suffering spouse who, might I add, was eggnant, and took up with that flashy slut – one of the Flying Saucies Set! Not content with that you contrived to do away with Mr Rum-Tumm, her lawful wedded husband, by luring him into the Martian badlands – to be savaged to death by wild flowers!'

Mr Kugg held himself erect, his eye-stalks fixed unflinchingly on the bouncing pot that was Boggo-Vup. 'What you say is true, O Peerless Pot, and it is only logical that I should endure the fitting corrective treatment. I shall abide by your decision in this matter.'

The Pot nearly lost its mode control and exploded in fury. This damnably little smug Martian! They were all alike – so logical and complacent. It quite took all the fun out of the proceedings. 'Let me tell you, Kugg, you haven't got any choice but to "abide by my decision"! You must be punished for your repugnant behaviour!'

Mr Kugg's stoic calm persisted, even to the point of serenity. 'The system must run its course,' he sighed in what sounded preposterously like a bored voice. 'It is only logical in the ordered state of things. But it is, after all, only for a limited period and I shall be reincarnated again. Am I not right?'

If the Pot had possessed teeth it would have ground them. Vicarious vindictiveness was almost brimming over as it grimly thought to itself, 'fair enough, clever-clogs'. We'll see who has the last laugh. Aloud, it called out, 'let this sinful Martian be borne away to the seemingly-eternal miseries of the Martian hell!'

In response two demons stepped briskly from the fireproof escalator and converged on the thunderstruck Mr Kugg. They were humanoid in form, wearing bowler hats and pin-stripe suits, and each carried a copy of *The Financial Times* and a rolled umbrella.

Mr Kugg screeched in horror as they seized him and dragged him, protesting, towards the escalator. 'They're Earthlings! Inferior beings from the third planet! I demand to know the meaning of this!'

'I'll tell you the meaning, you lecherous bug-eyed monster!' the Pot screamed triumphantly as it hopped gleefully up and down on the desk. 'Martian demons are humanoid – just as the Martian hell is the planet Earth! And that's where you're going, Mr Kugg – straight down to the hell that is so feared by your scientifically superior species! Earth – where you will find more unscientific muddling, lack of logic and crass stupidity than anywhere else in all the universes put together! I relish the thought of your rotten, evil soul in torment as you languish at bus stops, waiting for buses which never arrive, get pushed and shoved around on the London Underground and short-changed in shops! You will surely learn what it is to wail and thrash your tentacles in travail!

'Attaboy, Boggo!' crowed the bright green tin can, hopping about on its bird's leg. 'You tell him!'

The Pot bounced angrily to the edge of the desk. 'And you can shut up for a start! Where were you and that twit Scabwort when you were supposed to be on Soulwatch Duty? Skulking around the Time Zone, eh? Re-dying old memories? Well we won't go into the details. Just keep out of the way.'

Quivering with anger Plap-Quirk returned to the sanctuary afforded by the halo crates where it sulked and hooted to itself. The bowler-hatted demons had each secured an effective hold on their victim by the simple method off hooking their umbrella handles around his scrawny neck and dragging him along the cloudy floor.

'Get him out of my sight,' the Pot roared after them. 'He quite disgusts me!'

The two nattily-dressed demons and their squawking charge descended from sight down the fireproof escalator and the customary serene silence returned to the vast Auditorium. A few nervous cherubs peeped out from behind the soaring pillars and the Pot – Boggo-Vup, the Martian Soul Searcher – resumed his human form. 'I hate that Martian mode,' he grumbled to himself. 'It always makes me cough.'

Grimshaw quietly emerged from hiding, having also resumed his favourite skeletal mode of the cloaked and cowled Grim Reaper. He affected a nonchalant whistle in the hope that the Soul Searcher's mood had improved along with his appearance. He was to be disappointed.

'Watch it, Grimshaw! the Soul Searcher snapped at him. 'You're not above being corrected in a most humiliating fashion.'

This only served to spark off resentment. 'I've a bone to pick with you, Solly!' he snapped back, clattering up to the desk and thrusting his skull forward aggressively. 'What's going on here? Are you trying to make me redundant?'

'Don't you raise your voice to me, you – you refugee from a glue factory!'

'I'll damn well raise my voice if I like! What was that Martian doing here? I didn't bring him up. I've been on Earth duties. Are you sub-contracting the work out to some bunch of cowboys?'

'Don't talk rubbish,' growled the Soul Searcher. 'If you must know, that Martian soul arrived here by pure fluke. His space car fell into a Black Hole when he was fleeing from the law. He was killed, of course, but by some freak of metaphysics his soul was projected directly here at the speed of thought. It made a frightful hole in the firmament and the decorators have only just finished patching it up.'

'Well if that's what happened, I'll say no more,' muttered Grimshaw. 'But I hope you're on the level with me because if you're not and there are other souls here which I didn't bring up, I'm going to raise merry Heaven!'

The Soul Searcher averted his gaze, unable to meet the other's accusing eye-sockets. 'Well, since you mention it, there does happen to be –'

'I knew it!' screeched Grimshaw, wringing his fingerbones in a fine old fury. 'I just knew it! As soon as my spinal column is turned you get up to these sort of tricks! What about my deadlihood? How am I supposed to make a deading if this sort of gazumping goes on? The wife wants a new patio on the tomb and I promised the kids a Wendy Grave for Halloween! And how am I going to afford all that if you keep my commission?'

'It's not my fault if you are dying above your means,' the Soul Searcher retorted. 'Anyway, it's not like that at all, Grimshaw. I promise you that every case will be credited to your tally.'

'How can they if I haven't brought them here?'

'But you're on Soulwatch Duty – or supposed to be – and that pays special overtime rates. In fact, I've done you a favour, even if you don't deserve it.'

Grimshaw folded his arms and snorted. 'Well, can't see it for the death of me.'

The Soul Searcher clutched at his brow despairingly. 'Bonehead! You will be getting paid for all the cases which come before me while you are officially clocked on for Soulwatch Duties. All of them, whether you collected them or not. Is that plain enough now?'

Grimshaw's skull lit up with happy understanding. 'I'm with you now. Oh, well, that does put a different complexion on things. Sorry if I was a bit bolshie with you just then.'

'Think nothing of it. We all have to let off a little steam every now and then, and we could both do with a break.'

'You're right there, Solly,' sighed Grimshaw, flicking a piece of loose cloud from his tibia. 'I did promise the wife a holiday, too.'

'Oh, yes? Anywhere in particular?'

'The Dead Sea. We went there for our honeymoon. Had a rattling good time.'

'We'll have to see what we can fix up,' nodded the Soul Searcher, turning to his Recorder Book. 'In the meantime we had best get on with the rest of the souls. I only hope that I won't have as much trouble with them as some of the earlier ones.'

Grimshaw looked interested. 'What happened then, Solly?'

'That relief demon Scabwort sent up – he broke the light lock. You can imagine the mess here. These fitted clouds are very difficult to replace when they've been cleaned.'

'Someone mention my name?' called out Scabwort, hopping out of the light lock.

'So you're back then,' sniffed the Soul Searcher without much enthusiasm. 'At least you're a bit more reliable than that dunderhead, Rubbish-legs.'

'I've been looking for him,' said Scabwort. 'Where is he?'

'He's just got back from making a delivery – his first, and it shows,' the Soul Searcher answered. 'I think he's in the music room, watching the Cherubs cloud-surfing.'

'I'd better get him out of there,' Scabwort declared, trotting off towards a shaft of light with handrails. 'He's very impressionable. He might get into good ways.'

'And don't be long,' the Soul Searcher called after the squat disappearing form. 'I want you back here at the double – and keep out of the light lock until you're wanted.'

'These kids,' chuckled Grimshaw, his good humour now fully restored. 'I suppose I was much the same when I was a skeleteenager. 'Who's next for the chop, Solly?'

The Soul Searcher flinched but refrained from making any comment on his colleague's flippancy. Then his whole being tensed as he noted the next name in his Recorder Book. 'Him? I don't believe it! Heavens alongside!' he exclaimed. 'It can't be!'

Grimshaw glared at him. 'Who's "him"?'

The Soul Searcher glared owlishly back. 'But surely you must have noticed when you collected him? Number 4783 on your delivery invoice.'

'Oh, that one,' said Grimshaw. 'Now you come to mention it but I did notice him at the time. Funny sort of soul – a bit lumpier than the others. What about it anyway? Who is it?'

The Soul Searcher hopped off his stool, and taking Grimshaw by the sleeve of his tattered shroud, led him towards the inner light lock portal. 'You know – him,' he muttered, a trifle nervously.

Grimshaw snatched his arm away. 'Stop that! You know I don't like to be handled. It makes me nervous. Who are you talking about?'

They paused before the swirling colours of the portal and peered into the depths of elsewhere … into the Limborium. 'Him,' whispered the Soul Searcher in a hushed whisper.

'I've had an interesting life,' said the old gentleman with the polka dot bow tie. 'Professor of physics and all that. I used to be a science teacher at one of our oldest public schools. Retired now, of course.'

He paused, seeming embarrassed by his own overtures. 'I know it's not the done thing in England to speak to your neighbours in a doctor's waiting room, but this place is so oppressive I feel it wouldn't hurt to break one small tradition.'

Horace Hapgood returned the genial smile. For some odd reason he felt more than a little nervous. 'They are pretty deadly places, Professor Doyle,' he responded.

'Oh, please don't call me Professor,' Doyle smiled modestly 'When all is said and done it's just an empty title.'

'I suppose the same goes for names as well,' Horace nodded, surprising himself with his own philosophical observation. 'They are just labels, after all.'

Professor Doyle beamed at him. 'Very good. Not many people realise that.'

'If you two gentlemen insist on talking I would be grateful if you would moderate your voices!'

The guilty parties glanced around the waiting room to see who had spoken. The African, wrapped snugly in his tribal blanket, had gone to sleep, and there was no indication of life from the still and giant figure that lurked in the outer limits beyond the 'rubbery shrubbery'. Only the stunning odour reminiscent of Billingsgate Fish Market gave any sign that he was still there. The young red-haired man was increasing his word power with the dog-eared *Reader's Digest*, but the fourth occupant of the waiting room was glaring at the two men with beetle-browed indignation. It was Elvira Spratt, the lady traffic warden.

'I'm trying to add my summonses,' she complained. 'It's difficult enough by the light of this pathetic little forty-watt bulb, and your continuous chatter doesn't help either.'

Professor Doyle said, 'I beg your pardon, madam,' and was favoured with a malevolent stare.

Horace Hapgood said, 'Get knotted,' and Elvira merely glared and returned to her mathematics. She was obviously more used to, and at ease with, the latter response.

'We seem to have been here ages,' whispered Horace, casting a wary glance at the black-uniformed lady. 'You wouldn't happen to have the right time on you, would you?'

Doyle took an ornate gold pocket watch from his heather-coloured waistcoat.

'Sorry,' he murmured. 'It's stopped.'

Horace squeaked with alarm and Elvira glared hard at him as if hoping to find that he was sitting on double-yellow-lined-patterned-linoleum. 'But that's terrible! My watch has stopped, too, and so had the big man's – whatsisname – Square. And if yours has stopped – well, what, can it all mean?'

Professor Doyle returned the watch to his pocket and looked gently at the podgy, frightened, rabbity face of his companion.

'I wouldn't let it worry you, Hapgood. After all, I'm sure I remember that I forgot to wind my watch this morning ... I think.'

Horace's stuttered response was drowned by the abrupt, stentorian voice issuing from some hidden source.

'Neptune!' it summoned.

To Horace it smelt as if he were inside a prawn cocktail as the shadows on the far side of the waiting room stirred. Then the hulking, and scaly figure arose from its chair and plodded awkwardly across the floor on large webbed feet, pausing only to collect a seaweed-mantled trident from the umbrella stand.

A DEATH AT SEA

Malcolm Thornton handed the pint mug of ale to the old man and sat down opposite him at the round, beer-puddled table. His own glass of scotch sat almost primly beside the massive, man-size tankard.

'Thanks,' acknowledged the older man, raising the tankard in a little salute appreciation. 'This'll help to wash the taste away – if not the smell.'

Thornton grinned ruefully. 'That's what I'm here about, Mr Rivett. The barman said you might be able to help, seeing as you've lived in this village all your life. I'm a freelance journalist and want to do a story about the pollution issue. Something for one of the big newspapers about the trouble you've been having with oil pollution.'

Rivett's brick-red face with its jutting buttress of a nose, moulded into frown. 'An' I can tell you plenty, Mr Thornton. I've lived in

Flaxport all my life an' it's been a life, too. The fishin' were good here, an' like my father an' his father before, I been a fisherman until I had to pack up a coupla year ago. Arthritis, y'see. But I done my fair share an' no mistake.'

Thornton was already mentally sketching his article. The personal viewpoint would put it over well. Generations of fishermen – and now their livelihood ruined because of this oil pollution. 'It's all up the coast, isn't it Mr Rivett?'

'The oilslick? That it is. Right from Claviston to Copton. You never seen anythin' like it. The beach is thick with the muck! Damn foreign tankers bustin' themselves in half an' poisonin' everythin'!'

He quaffed his ale in brooding silence, staring at, yet not seeing, the other occupants of the bar who sat singly or in small groups, each with their own lifetime of hopes and fears. Thornton downed his scotch decisively. 'Tell you what. I know it's late, but how about taking me down to the beach to see things for myself?'

Rivett considered the question doubtfully. 'It's getting dark now. You wouldn't see much. Best wait until the mornin'. You stayin' in the village?'

'Yes, at The Sextant, but this sort of thing can't wait. There'll be any number of reporters flocking here by tomorrow. I'm surprised there's not more here already. If I leave it too late, I'll be trampled underfoot. Just a quick look to give me a true idea,' he concluded artfully, 'then we can both come back here for a nightcap.'

Rivett drained his tankard and thumped down onto the wet tabletop. 'Done!' he responded. 'But we'll have to look sharpish. The light's goin' fast –'

'I've got a torch with me.'

Rivett chuckled throatily as he stood up. 'Have you now? There's no flies on you, young feller. Wish I could say the same about the beach,' he added in a tone of disgust.

Thornton followed him from the snug and smokey comfort of the inn and out into the windswept, gloom. 'We'll cut down Dock Lane,' said Rivett, leading the way along the narrow road with its random scattering of villas and cottages flanking each side. Thornton studied them wistfully. The warm yellow rectangles, cosily shrouded by tasselled curtains, looked so inviting. But he had a job to do. Time enough to relax when he had seen the beach. Smelt it, too, if his senses were anything to go by.

Five minutes later the two men were plodding through the twilight, their boots clinking on the shingle. The air was rank with the stench of oil and the shore was thick with tarry deposits. A strong north-easterly wind had got up, chilling the men through their tightly-wrapped coats. And with it came another smell. The smell of decay. For once Thornton envied Rivett his fuming pipe. Its smoke was certainly more preferable than the sickly sweet smell that wafted in from the sea.

'Fish,' grunted Rivett as they trudged diagonally across the beach towards the foaming surf, now virtually invisible in the failing light. 'Any amount of 'em. Killed by the oil an' rottin'. Seagulls, too.'

He paused at a seaweed-draped groyne and pointed down mutely. Thornton directed his torch and saw the pathetic bundles of claws and feathers, matted together into unrecognisable little mounds by thick black oil.

'We don't need no nuclear war to finish us off, muttered Rivett. 'They're doin' it just fine, them big businessmen. Killin' off fish an' fowl to make their fortunes.'

Olympian rumbles echoed through the infinite black vault of the night sky. The darkness intensified as storm clouds, massing together as if for attack, loosed off a salvo of jagged lightning fingers. 'Reckon we're in for a real bad storm,' the old fisherman commented. 'If you seen all you want to see, Mr Thornton, I think we had best be getting back. I reckon there's as much water up there in them there clouds as there is in the sea, an' we don't want to be out here when it comes down.'

And then the storm broke in all its elemental fury. Like the gusting breath of some invisible giant the wind fairly blasted across the shore, the cliffs and the village. Thunder boomed its demented drumming and the clouds gave vent in a teeming deluge. Soaked to the skin within seconds, Thornton slapped the older man on the shoulder and pointed with his torch back to the cliff path. Then it seemed as if the foaming darkness of the sea became darker in one vast area and an unspeakable, cloying odour of death assailed the nostrils of the two men.

'They've killed everything,' roared the old man, standing defiant and erect. 'Them clever scientists and fine rich men! Somethin' big has died out there an' there won't be a mortal thing left alive in the seas anywhere if this goes on!'

'What d'you mean – "something big"?' Thornton shouted to make himself heard over the tumult of the storm.

'I dunno. Could be a whale or probably a shoal of fish. But it's somethin'.'

'There's no whales on this coastline,' Thornton objected, catching hold of Rivett's sleeve. 'This is the East Coast.'

Anger and grief coloured the other man's words. 'Don't you tell me what damn coast it is! I been fishin' it all my workin' life! But that there oil slick has poisoned half the North Sea, an' maybe further. Who can tell how far that muck has spread?'

Then Thornton stumbled over something hard that barked his shins, and plunged headlong the reeking shallows. The torch flew from his hand and shattered on the pebbles. Rivett grabbed at the floundering figure and helped him to his feet. 'You be all right?' he asked.

Thornton swore as he rubbed his injured shins. 'Tripped over something. It felt like a metal bar. He winced painfully as he stood. 'I've lost the torch, too, so we might as well be getting back. There's no sense in staying down here any longer.'

'You got what you wanted then?'

'That – and more.' Thornton limped off in the direction of where he judged the cliff path to be. 'Come on. I'll buy you that drink I promised. I think we both need it.'

The following morning Thornton had just booked out of The Sextant, and was on his way to fetch his car from the back of the inn, when he heard someone calling him. It was Rivett, still clad in his anorak and boots despite the change in the weather that had followed the storm of the previous night.

'Mr Thornton! There's somethin' on the beach you should see!'

Wondering what had so excited the old man, Thornton followed after him. His bruised legs were stiff and sore and he felt that he had had enough of this place. The weather, the stench and the mess were more than he could bear. But after all, he told himself, it was such things that he had come to see for himself and report on.

At last they arrived at the end of Dock Lane, overlooking the dismal, oil-stained sands. Even the waves seemed to be sluggish with the stuff and the clouds hung low overhead as if in mourning. 'Well, what is it?' Thornton demanded irritably. Then he checked his words. Rivett was clearly agitated. Very much so, in fact. Tears welled from his eyes and trickled down the weather beaten fissures of a face that had confronted the sea in a lifetime of love and hate.

'Are you blind, man?' he choked. 'Don't you see?'

'What am supposed to see? Your "whale" of last night?'

'T'weren't no whale, Thornton. It were dead all right, but t'weren't no whale. Oh, no.'

His words faded away in a sobbing chuckle as he pointed down to the shore. Thornton saw the gleam of metal jutting out across the sands from the sea and he realised all too clearly his painful encounter of last night.

'The sea took back her dead last night,' muttered Rivett softly. 'He's lying in the deeps now, but he left that behind.'

Then Thornton stared again at the length of metal, dappled with filigrees of seaweed. It was no metal spar left over from some old wrecked pier that he had stumbled over in the dark. Fifty feet of it he could see resting on the beach, and God knows how much more lay hidden in the turgid waves. But, at the end which lay across the beach, the metal spar terminated in the three colossal prongs of a strong gigantic trident ...

SHADOWSHINE SEVEN

The Shadowshine Auditorium literally stank to high Heaven. So was the reek. There was hardly enough room for an embarrassed silence to pervade, but somehow it managed to squeeze itself in. The Soul Searcher's austere countenance had taken on a greenish hue, and he envied the Grim Reaper his fleshless visage. Even so, Grimshaw seemed to be all too well aware of the piscean stench that wafted around the hall. Clutching at the bone cartilage where his nose would have been situated was not one of his usual nervous characteristics.

The subject of their discomfort loomed over them to a towering height of some twenty feet, dripping seaweed and shrimps from his scaly body. Neptune, the King of the Sea. And judging by the state of the place he appeared to have brought most of it with him, too. Especially the bilge water.

'I find this whole affair most embarrassing,' he rumbled through his matted beard. 'That Limborium isn't big enough to swing a catfish in. I had to reduce my size intolerably to fit into it. And those mortal souls weren't much company either – talking and muttering amongst themselves.

The Soul Searcher brushed a baby squid from the Recorder Book. 'I agree with you, sir. Nothing like this has ever happened before – quite an unprecedented incident. When I saw your name down here I just couldn't believe it. Poseidon alias Neptune. I don't quite know how we are going to deal with this. I suppose you are the person named?' he concluded hopefully.

'Of course I am!' thundered Neptune. 'If your records are in nick, they will show that I relinquished my Greek citizenship and applied for a visa with the Ancient Romans when the Greeks started discovering angles and the hypotenuse. I also changed my name to Neptune when the visa came through. That lasted for a few centuries but then the Romans had a religious reshuffle, got rid of me and my kind and threw in with your lot. But when they started calling themselves Italians and went on to discover ice cream and macaroni, I left them to it. A fine kettle of fish, I must say!'

'The problem is,' began the Soul Searcher nervously, 'you don't really come into Shadowshine's jurisdiction. It would appear that you are a stateless person –'

Neptune stamped a webbed foot on the floor, causing more fishy eddies to permeate the air. 'This is too bad! To think that I – Neptune – who has rubbed dorsals with superior mortals such as the Argonaughts – to say nothing of family connections with Olympus – should be described as a "stateless person"!'

Grimshaw was becoming thoroughly fed up, what with all the shouting and the smell. For once he sympathised with the Cherubs tailspinning about overhead, fluttering their downy wings and gagging. 'At least you've a planet named after you, which is more than most of us have,' he muttered.

Neptune glared down at the cloaked figure of the skeleton. 'Don't you mumble at me, boy! If you've got anything to say to me – then say it!'

'I said at least you've had a planet named after you, which is more than most of us have!' Grimshaw yelled back, oblivious to the Soul

Searcher's agonised warning glances. 'Don't blame us if you've got yourself in a mess!'

Instead of flying into yet another rage, Neptune became almost maudlin. 'To think that this should happen to me,' he sighed. 'It used to be so different in the old days when Ulysses and his crowd were around. I got a bit of respect then. And how do I finish up? Choked to death on diesel oil just off some obscure East Anglian seaside village! How can you compare the Suffolk coastline with the Aegean Sea?'

The fishy aroma was fast becoming quite unbearable, much to the distress of the Cherubs overhead. The Soul Searcher glared up at them. 'If you must be ill,' he snapped, 'kindly do it at floor level!'

'Better still,' added Grimshaw, 'clear off.'

The Cherubs happily followed this advice and winged their unsteady way between the pillars and colonnades to more fragrant climes. Grimshaw watched their departure sourly. His ill-humour was not lessened by a glimpse of Scabwort skulking in the light lock, sniggering. 'Where's the rest of your crowd then?' he asked the Sea God. 'Venus, Jupiter and the rest. Surely they managed to come to terms with a changing world?'

'Oh, they still have a lot of pull,' Neptune replied evasively, 'but that's classified information. They meet every other Friday – not that I'm ever invited,' he concluded sulkily.

'Oh, and why is that?' the Soul Searcher enquired.

'Because they're a bunch of jumped-up snobs – that's why! As your thin friend here pointed out, I've had a planet named after me, but that wasn't good enough. It wasn't one of the original planets known to the ancient mortals. It was just some gas giant discovered during Earth's Eighteenth Century by some frog astronomer who used mathematics to find it. Mathematics! The selfsame thing that drove me out of Greece! Oh, yes, I can still hear them laughing at me! That drunken lout, Jupiter, utterly legless as always, with that blonde slut, Venus, and that yobbo, Mars – not to mention his thieving crony, Mercury – never did trust that one! The Planet Club, they call themselves – and damned snotty they are about it, too!'

For once, Grimshaw was almost lost for words. 'I wouldn't let it get to you,' he said at last. 'After all, it's only the four of them.'

'Oh, there's more!' snapped Neptune. 'Don't forget Jupiter's good-time-girls, Io, Europa and Callisto! He made sure to have them in tow once they had been immortalised by the discovery of the Galilean Moons – not to mention that simpering little poofter, Ganymede! But, for me and the others it's "pull up the ladder," boys. Jupe's all right.'

'Others?' prompted the Soul Searcher warily. 'What others?'

'Why, Uranus and Pluto, of course. They suffered the same mathematical disgrace as I did. It's not so bad for Pluto. He's got an agreement of sorts with the set-up Downstairs. But it's poor Uranus I feel sorry for. He's not much good for anything after that ungrateful brat of his got at him with a sickle.'

'I'm quite sure you're right,' the Soul Searcher interrupted him, 'but we seem to have digressed from the immediate problem. This department of Shadowshine is not equipped to deal with your problem as you aren't on our Mortal Rota. Really you should take your case down to the, er, other department. It's more in their line, you being a pagan – er, deity – no offence meant.' he added hastily.

Neptune glared at the Soul Searcher, huddled at his desk, irritably brushing shrimps from his toga. I may be amoral but definitely not immoral – and there's a hell of a difference,' he retorted. 'And that lot in what you call "the other place" are downright evil.'

'Well you certainly can't consider the, er, alternative zone,' came the prim response. 'The moral standard there is exquisite.'

'Why not send him back to Earth?' suggested Grimshaw. 'That's the most obvious solution. I'm surprised you didn't think of it, Solly.'

The Soul Searcher looked shocked at the idea. 'What ... you mean reincarnate him? But we've never done any one like that before.'

Grimshaw tossed his skull in a mocking gesture. 'Only because none of these heathen gods have been stupid enough to guzzle their own weight in polluted sea water before. Think about it, Solly. It's the only logical thing to do.'

'I'm not used to people talking over my head,' Neptune complained, casting an angry glance down at the diminutive figures before him. 'I am – when all is said and done – the god of the Sea.'

'Oh, do shut up,' snorted Grimshaw. 'We're not talking over your head. Between your knees would be more like it.'

'A great idea!' the Soul Searcher exclaimed. 'I like it – I definitely like it! We could send him back through the Time Zone to the point just before he hit the oil slick just off the Suffolk Coast.'

Neptune beat his finny fists against his barnacled brow, letting his astral trident fall to the cloudy floor with a thunderous plop. 'Will someone please tell me what is going on? Never before have I been so rudely ignored! I demand that my presence is duly acknowledged!'

'Calm down now,' the soul Searcher told him. 'All is under control. Where were you just before you got yourself caught up in all that oil pollution?'

'Just dawdling around the North Sea off the coast of Scotland, watching the Russian trawlers.'

'That's all we need to know. Now all you have to do is trot along to the Time Zone Terminus, find the right date and climb aboard. You will have the knowledge, and the sense, too, I hope, to avoid the coastal areas of Britain in future.'

'You mean it's as simple as that?' Neptune gasped as he retrieved his trident. 'All will be as it was and I shall rule my marine domain once more?'

'If you so wish,' the Soul Searcher replied off-handedly. He had begun to lose interest in the matter and was secretly rather piqued that Grimshaw should have thought of the answer to the problem instead of himself. 'Just go through the light lock and follow the signs marked "Now".'

Grimshaw escorted the aqueous titan towards the swirling vortex of the light lock. 'And steer clear of the Med,' he advised the departing deity, 'otherwise you'll be back here even before you've left.'

Neptune paused at the threshold of dazzling colours and stared down at Grimshaw. 'The Med?' he echoed. 'What's that?'

'The Mediterranean Sea, of course, you big nit-wit! The place is a veritable cesspit.'

'But those are my ancestral waters,' wailed Neptune in despair. 'Where else can I get the respect that is my due?'

'You'll have to make a fresh start in cleaner waters,' Grimshaw advised him, watching the huge, seaweed-draped form squeeze through the light lock, causing the spectrum to pale as it expanded to accommodate him. 'Try Baffin Island now, in breaking new ground – or water in your case. And give my regards to the penguins.'

The Soul Searcher sat back in his chair and eyed Grimshaw thoughtfully. 'You know, I'm not at all sure if there are any penguins at Baffin Island.'

Grimshaw strutted back from the light lock, petulantly drawing his shroud about him. 'Well, puffins then. Ornithology is a bit out of my province. I'm only grateful that we've got rid of the big booby. The place smells like Great Yarmouth in a heat wave.'

'I'm inclined to agree with you,' the Soul Searcher sighed, casting a thankful glance at the timely arrival of a V formation of Cherubs zooming overhead, armed with ether fresheners. 'I shudder to think what our other clients in the Limborium made of him.'

'You get all sorts in doctors' waiting rooms, Solly,' Grimshaw replied, breathing in the myrrh-scented air. 'Ah, that's better,' he crooned, stroking his finger bones aver his rib cage with xylophonic effect. 'It makes one glad to be undead.'

A loud thump followed by a grunt of pain heralded Scabwort's emergence from the light lock. 'You could have warned me about that big lout blundering through,' he complained. 'He nearly flattened me with his size twenty-four webbed feet. I'm putting in for danger money.'

The Soul Searcher waved him to silence. 'The status quo has now been restored. All is as it should be. I think I handled that business rather well.'

Grimshaw turned his scowling skull away in a huff. 'Desk wallahs are all the same,' he muttered. 'Always taking the credit.'

'I'll have you know that you're only here on sufferance,' the Soul Searcher sternly admonished him. 'By rights you shouldn't be here at all. Your part of the job is completed when you deliver the de-etherised souls.'

'But mine isn't,' chipped in Scabwort. 'And all I've had so far in this session is that miserable little squirt, Eric Dodds.'

'And you've only yourself to blame,' the Soul Searcher loftily pointed out. 'You were skiving when Hubert Square came through, and that young fellow with the boils on his neck – Rubbish-Legs – had to deal him. Nearly wrecked the place, too. The other was a Martian sinner which doesn't come under your jurisdiction.'

'Even so, things had better improve or I'm slinging this job in,' growled Scabwort, and he joined Grimshaw in a mutual huff.

The Soul Searcher climbed down from his desk and wearily made his way towards the inner light lock portal that looked into the Limborium. 'We could all do with a holiday,' he sighed. 'The pressure is getting to us. If only the mortal souls were immortal, we might be able to have a break. I'll whistle up the next soul and see if we can get things back to normal.'

'I'm sure none of us have anything to worry about,' said Professor Doyle. 'I agree, Hapgood, that things do seem a bit strange, but I feel equally sure that everything is under control.'

The red-haired young man glanced up from mentally digesting his *Reader's Digest*. 'But whose control?' he ventured with a wink at the glowering lady traffic warden, still struggling with her tally of parking offences. 'Or what control, even?'

Attracted by the note of quizzical humour in the young man's voice, Professor Doyle glanced across at him. Hapgood had proved to be singularly devoid of humour, also lacking in the flexibility of argument to make an interesting conversationalist. The dusky gentleman still slumbered on, and 'the scourge of the hatch-backs' was utterly unapproachable. 'A good point, Mr ... er. I didn't catch the name, sir ...'

'– Peter, commercial artist.'

'Ah, well, Mr, what, do you make of the situation?'

'Predicament more likely,' muttered Horace Hapgood, glancing down suspiciously at the undulating pale blue linoleum that formed the floor of the shadow-filled waiting room. 'Just look at this floor for instance. And what about those other two patients – the Martian and the big, scaly nudist! They never came off the new estate, I'll wager!'

'But surely you must appreciate the intriguing question they raise?' the Professor asked. 'After all, where there is cause there is effect. Just as in this case, where there is circumstance there must be reason. Nothing is without purpose.'

'I'll go along with that, Professor,' agreed Peter.

'Furthermore, there must be a common factor involved.'

Professor Doyle beamed at him. 'Sound reasoning, sir.'

'Thank you. Now with regard to this common factor. Why are we all here?'

Horace looked at him blankly. 'To see the doctor, of course.'

'Precisely. And what if it is for the same reason? Now wouldn't that hold a clue?'

Horace nodded slowly and then looked embarrassed. 'I suppose it would, but you're not going to believe this. I can't remember what's wrong with me.'

Professor Doyle scratched his head. 'Now you come to mention it,' he murmured sheepishly, 'I'm not at all sure why I came here either.'

Peter smiled the smile of one whose theory has just been proved. 'And the same goes for me, too. It could be anything from a broken leg to black water fever for all I can recall.'

Horace snapped his fingers excitedly. 'I see what you mean! We're all suffering from amnesia!'

Peter laughed as he selected a new old magazine from the little table in the centre of the room. 'No, you miss the point, old man. I think we are all here because we are dead.'

The mouse-like squeak that issued from Horace was drowned by the portentous voice summoning the next patient.

'Desmond Doyle!'

Doyle rose from his chair and smiled at his two companions. 'It has been most pleasant talking to you, gentlemen. And now to see the Great Doctor and learn his diagnosis of my ailments – be they physical or spiritual.'

AD INFINITUM

'Most kind you to allow me to share your moment of triumph,' murmured the tall grey-haired stick of a man, folding himself slowly into the high-backed chair. 'Quite a breakthrough for you, eh, Frank?'

Dr Franklin Raven perched himself on the edge of his desk and raised his glass of sherry in salutation. 'More than you could ever realise, Desmond. The greatest thing that's ever happened to radio astronomy. Most fortunate that you chose today to drop in. You'll be able to see the first transmissions for yourself without having to wait for garbled reports to filter through the media.'

Professor Desmond Doyle smiled, nursing his sherry glass in one knobbly, blue-veined hand. 'I happened to be in the North for a few days holiday and thought I would look you up. I little expected such a treat as this, though.'

'My life's work realised,' Raven smiled back, speaking as much to himself as his guest. 'It's been many years since the ways parted for us.'

Doyle sipped his sherry and nodded. 'Since we were at school together, you mean? Why it's longer than I would care to reckon up.'

He studied his host quietly for some moments from beneath grey and tufted eyebrows. Time and fortune had been kind to Frank Raven. Apart from the distinguished grey 'wings' at each temple and the subtle lines that were only just beginning to etch their mark each side of his nose, he hadn't really changed all that much. Still the dashing 'lady-killer', too. A couple of broken marriages had left him apparently unscarred. Indeed, it was even rumoured that he was contemplating marrying again. This time to an actress in her mid-twenties, some forty years his junior. Some said that Frank Raven had turned radio astronomy into a 'three-ring circus'. Rather harsh criticism, Doyle reflected. After all, he had simply made the subject more presentable to the layman, dressing it up with a bit of harmless – what was the word? – razzmatazz. What a dated expression that was, to be sure! But nonetheless it was true, and what was more to the point, it had worked. Three television series spoke for themselves, even if Dr Frank Raven hosted and dominated each one of them, taking care to present his best profile to the cameras.

Doyle mused wryly on his life. How different it had been for him while Frank was peering into the macrocosm through his telescopes, he – Desmond Doyle – had been squinting at the microcosm through microscopes. Not for him the glamour of the universe, expensive parties and equally expensive women. He had held a steady if monotonous teaching post at a little-known college, lecturing adolescent cynics on the habits of the amoeba. After Alice had died he retired from teaching, taking a little cottage in the Cotswolds. They had never had children but he and Alice had been very happy together. No one could ask for more than that. Happiness and contentment.

'You and I couldn't have gone to greater extremes, Desmond,' declared Raven, setting his empty sherry glass down on the desk. It was almost as though he had read the other man's thoughts. 'I don't know how you stuck it all those years, dabbling around with those mucky little germs.'

Doyle smiled and shook his head. 'They're all God's creatures, Frank, no matter how large or small.'

Raven's finely-chiselled lips twitched into the start of a sneer, then moulded into a patronising smile. 'Afraid I can't share your views, Desmond. There's no heavenly choir of angels up there. The voyager probes would have spotted them for sure if there was.'

His dark eyes glowed as he leaned forward slightly. 'This is just the beginning. So far we have had to depend on space probes crawling around the solar system. Not anymore. It's all out there waiting for us. Waiting for Mankind to stake its claim. No longer will the universe be one great boundless vacuum of mystery! With the new galactoscope in orbit we will be able to penetrate the very limits of the cosmos. And then we shall see what we are dealing with!'

Doyle rose and placed his empty glass on the desk. The small gesture also helped to mask the faint expression of disapproval at his old friend's boastful words. 'You speak with confidence and ambition, Frank,' he commented mildly. 'After all, we are but mortal men.'

'There's nothing wrong with confidence and ambition,' Raven chaffed him, rising from the edge of the desk. 'Think what those qualities have bestowed on civilization over the last century. Air travel, radio, television, space flight –'

'– the atom bomb,' added Doyle quietly.

But Raven was not to be baited. 'You've been staring at too many glass slides of mud, Desmond.' He took Doyle by the arm. 'Come on. The first transmissions will be coming through soon. I'll take you over to the control centre, then we'll hear what you have to say.'

Computers definitely had a smell of their own. A sort of plastic, electric smell. The thought struck Doyle as Raven ushered him into the control centre which seemed to be full of despairingly complicated control consoles, manned by keen-faced young men in crisp white coats.

Doyle felt conspicuously out of place. The only thing he felt he had in common with any of them was the little yellow plastic card that someone had pinned on the lapel of his worn and baggy tweed jacket. Doyle thought that at first glance it looked like a credit card. 'That will do nicely,' he had quipped as it was being pinned on. But the homely little jest had fallen on deaf ears. These people seemed to be above and beyond humour. It was like being in 'The Hall of the Mountain Kings'.

'Transmission due through in thirty seconds, Dr Raven,' announced one of the keen-faced men. 'It may be a bit foggy at first but computer enhancement will soon rectify any distortion.'

Raven and Doyle sat down in two seats at the back of the semi-darkened room. On the opposite wall was a glass screen that flickered with scientific lightning. 'It's like being at the pictures,' Doyle remarked.

One or two keen faces deigned to project cool contempt in his direction.

'Now watch that screen carefully, Desmond,' Raven whispered in a voice that was low with excitement. 'Obviously can't go through the technical details. Security, y'know. But very soon now you'll be seeing the edge of the universe.'

'But surely,' Doyle gently interjected, 'it takes light an unthinkable time to travel the vast distances you speak of. I may not know a great deal of these matters, Frank, but I do know that the speed of light is –'

Raven chuckled. 'You miss the point altogether, Desmond. The galactoscope – now orbiting by remote control – is an utterly new conception of radio astronomy, based on a new development with lasers. What it sees, it sees instantly. The only time lag involved will be the transmission from it to our receivers here. And as it is only two thousand miles out in space the time lag will be infinitesimal. What we will be looking at will always have been there.'

'First images coming through,' announced someone as the screen began to brighten. 'Am cutting in automatic computer enhancement.'

Raven gripped Doyle's arm tightly. 'This is it, Desmond! This is it! Doesn't it make you feel good? We are on the threshold of learning the secrets of the cosmos. Mankind will be able to grasp its rightful heritage!'

Doyle gazed sadly at the flickering screen. 'And the meek shall inherit the Earth,' he quoted, more to himself.

Raven's response was almost fanatical in its intensity. 'And the mighty shall inherit the universe! Look at the screen, man! Look and learn!'

They looked. The tense-faced scientist, full of his dreams of achievement and glory. The quiet, tired professor for whom the universe had shrunk when Alice had gone away. The keen young clones in their white coats ... they all waited.

Then the image from the end of beyond clarified and focused on the screen.

Gasps drifted through the air. Raven choked in disbelief mingled with anger. Doyle began to laugh softly to himself as strange, unbidden tears stung his pale eyes. 'What's your answer to that, Frank?' he asked. 'I've often wondered what it felt like to be at the other end.'

For staring at them on the screen, transmitted across a distance of endless light-years, was a vast, compassionate eye.

An eye that had wept for a millennia at the pride and folly of the human race ...

SHADOWSHINE EIGHT

'Looks like you've drawn another blank, Scab,' murmured Grimshaw, peeping from the infra-red edging of the light lock at the scene in the Auditorium. I wasn't aware that there were so many good people on Earth.'

Scabwort lashed his fork tail viciously. 'Wash your mouth out, Grimmo baby,' he snorted. 'Un-bad is a far more acceptable term. There's no need to resort to swearing.'

The Grim Reaper's skull flushed with embarrassment. 'No need to get snotty with me. It's not my fault. I only deliver the goods.'

'You've said it again!' Scabwort hissed angrily. 'That word! You couldn't care less about what Lucifer's going to think if I don't round up the stipulated quota of doomed souls. He'll think I'm falling down on the job.'

'Well it's no use you sounding off at me –'

'Oh, I'm well aware of that, you self-satisfied bag of bones! You couldn't care less if I never ever got another doomed soul. The trouble with you is that you've got no soul.'

'A fat lot of grim reaping I'd be doing if I had!' Grimshaw yelped back with spirited indignation. 'Me with a soul? Thanks – but no thanks! I don't want to be stuck out there with Solly reading the riot act at me.'

'It would damn well serve you right,' came the vindictive retort, 'because you would be sent straight down to us, and I'd soon make those lilywhite bones creak!'

'Don't take on so, Scabwort,' murmured Grimshaw uneasily. The young demon's tantrums always made him nervous. 'He's nearly finished with this one. Perhaps the next soul will be the lucky one. A mass-murderer or a telesales caller.'

'I'd like to think so,' muttered Scabwort gloomily, peering past Grimshaw at the scene in the Auditorium, 'but it looks as if old Solly literally has found a soul-mate.'

Quite unaware of the seething discontent that smouldered within the temporal veils of the light lock, the Soul Searcher smiled down benignly at the mortal soul who stood before his desk. Professor Doyle, a comfortable-looking, elderly gentleman in a heathery tweed suit, enlivened by a red polka dotted tie.

'I don't think you have anything to worry about, Desmond,' he assured his latest client from the Limborium. 'In fact, I'm absolutely sure that you are A1 at Lords as we say up here.'

'I'm most gratified to hear it,' smiled the Professor, stroking his chin as he glanced around appreciatively at his surroundings. 'I must say that I am most impressed by your system. Highly efficient. Did the other, er, gentleman do all right – the nautical gentleman, if I may make so bold ...?'

'Neptune?' The Soul Searcher's smile became evasive. 'So-so. But he's gone now, thank goodness. May we be spared the rattling of tin gods. However, I feel it only fair to point out, Desmond, that we do not discuss other clients' cases. House rules, y'know. I'm sure you understand ...'

'My dear fellow, I do apologise,' replied Professor Doyle. 'I certainly never intended any breach of conduct. Er, where do I go now – if may so inquire?'

'We-ell ...' The Soul Searcher thoughtfully stroked his beard for a few seconds. 'According to your dossier you're doing very nicely. You will be reincarnated again a few more times, but by then you should be ready for promotion to higher things.'

'Really? How interesting. Might one make so bold as to inquire what the next reincarnation is to be?'

The Soul Searcher laughed uneasily as he steered the amiable old soul towards the light lock. 'I'm sorry, but that would be another of the house rules. But just to make amends – well, we do have a few moments to spare, so why don't I show you around the place before we send you on your way for another threescore years and ten? It's several millennia since I had an intelligent conversation with someone like yourself who would appreciate how the system works.'

'That would be splendid,' Doyle responded enthusiastically. 'I confess that there is much I would like to see while I am able. After that strange business at the observatory when that eye appeared on the glactoscope screen I have often wondered. As you doubtless know the whole system overloaded and blew up so there was no proof to substantiate what I saw. Of course, poor Frank Raven, being an atheist –'

'Language, Desmond,' winced the Soul Searcher.

'Oh, I do beg your pardon. Well, unbeliever then – he put it all down to mass hallucination.' The Professor leaned confidingly towards the Soul Searcher. 'But tell me, sir ... that eye. Was it really the eye of ...?'

Once again the Soul Searcher shook his white-maned head. 'Sorry, old chap. Classified information. I'd lose my job straight away if I was to give the slightest hint, and be demoted to something like guardian angel of lemmings. And you can take it from me that particular post is extremely hard and thankless work.'

Disappointment showed on the Professor's mild face. 'But surely it wouldn't hurt? After all, when I am reincarnated I would automatically forget all this.'

'That's what usually happens,' sighed the Soul Searcher, 'but every once in a while there's a screw-up. The last one happened when my predecessor became too talkative with a certain soul who was reincarnated as Nostradamus. That wretched mortal had almost total recall and his prophecies caused no end of embarrassment. He had what you would call a telescopic memory.'

'Surely you mean photographic?'

'No – telescopic. He was a prophet and could see into the future.' The Soul Searcher studied the crestfallen expression on his companion's face. 'Cheer up, Desmond. There's still plenty of things I can show you. Just follow me through the light lock.'

Professor Doyle stared at the whirling vortex of colour and hesitated nervously. 'Light lock?' he echoed. 'I've heard of airlocks – waterlocks, too. But never light locks.'

'How else would we gain access to different dimensions?' replied the Soul Searcher. 'Just follow me through. It won't bite you.'

He led the way through the rainbow whirlpool and peered ahead into the distant ultra-violet. There was a furtive movement on the far side of the indigo. Two flitting shapes. Grimshaw and Scabwort, he thought. Showing some tact and making themselves scarce.

Grimshaw had nimbly slipped out of sight, but Scabwort, with the insatiable curiosity of all youthful demons, paused to glance over his bat-winged shoulder at the favoured mortal soul.

'I say!' exclaimed the Professor, adjusting his spectacles. 'That fellow looks just like milkman! Is he dead, too? He looked quite healthy when he collected his money last Saturday.'

The Soul Searcher gritted his teeth. 'No, Desmond, it is merely one of our, er, boiler room staff. Never mind him. He's gone now anyway. Well, what do you think of our lock?'

'Remarkable – most remarkable,' remarked the Professor, the 'milkman' now completely forgotten. 'It's really kind of you to go to all this trouble on my behalf.'

'Not at all,' the Soul Searcher smiled. 'Now here we are at the ultra-violet. Mind the step.'

Professor Doyle gazed about him in astonishment. Glorious nothingness on all sides. Above, below and around him – absolutely nothing. A momentary spasm of vertigo swept through him and he clutched at the Soul Searcher's sleeve to steady himself. 'This is incredible!' he gasped. 'We are standing on nothing and yet we are not falling!'

'That is because there is nowhere to fall to,' the Soul Searcher explained. 'We are at the centre of All Things. Now do you see that silvery band of light?'

'Why, yes,' murmured the Professor, peering at the diffused mysterious emptiness around then. At first he had not noticed it, so indistinct was its luminosity. It looked like cotton wool with odd little glowing bits in it. 'Is that the Milky Way?'

'You've got milk on the brain,' chuckled the Soul Searcher. 'No, it's what you mortals call Time. And please don't ask me to explain the physics involved. Your psyche has not undergone sufficient incarnations to grasp the fundamentals.'

Doyle drank the spectacle with childlike rapture. Somehow – he couldn't even explain it to himself – it all made sense. Without thinking he fished in his jacket pocket and withdrew his pipe and tobacco pouch. Then halfway through filling the bowl, he glanced somewhat guiltily at the Soul Searcher. 'I say, old fellow, is it all right if I smoke?'

'Of course, Desmond. It won't hurt you. You're dead already.'

'Why, so I am,' chuckled the Professor, contentedly applying a match to the blackened bowl and puffing out a veritable smoke-screen. 'I keep forgetting. By the by, I've been meaning to ask, how did I, er, die?'

'Through smoking,' came the off-hand reply. 'Now if you would be so kind as to follow me I think I can show you something that will really open your eyes.'

Surreptitiously tapping out his pipe and replacing it in his pocket, Professor Doyle followed his celestial guide. They passed quite close to the Time Zone and he distinctly heard someone shout 'Eureka!' followed by what sounded like bathwater running away. Then the Soul Searcher halted, reached forward with one hand and opened up an invisible hole. 'Just take a look through there, Desmond,' he proudly invited. 'This is one of the marvels that I can show you.'

The Professor eagerly craned his neck and peered through the intensified square of nothing in nowhere. To his amazement a young lady who, to put it delicately, would have been somewhat more respectable if she had been wearing a bikini, skipped across his restricted field of vision. 'Good gracious!' he exclaimed, his voice a whisper of shocked modesty. 'I would never have expected to find a "what the butler saw" machine here of all places!'

The Soul Searcher glanced at him reproachfully, not a little disappointed that his surprise should be misinterpreted. 'It is not a "what the butler saw" machine, what you saw was a random residual image on the subliminal plane.'

The Professor had got his head trapped in the 'nowhere' hole in his efforts to see where the astonishing vision had disappeared. 'It didn't look very random to me,' he retorted, his voice muffled by one-and-a-half dimensional levels. 'She reminded me of someone long ago ...'

The Soul Searcher gently but firmly eased his head from the aperture. 'Please don't tell me that it was your milkman again. But perhaps I am being a little unfair on you. It was unfortunate that you happened to chance upon that particular type of manifesta-tion, although it's always a bit of a gamble. Even we don't know for sure who or what is on call in there.'

'Well I'm sure I would be the last one to criticise,' replied the Professor. 'You are so wonderfully organised up here. You man-aged to materialise my spectacles and pipe – even my false teeth!'

The Soul Searcher permitted himself a complacent smirk. 'Every detail is attended to, Desmond. They are, of course, astral den-tures, but in your present astral state you doubtless feel quite at home with them. But I digress. What I intend to show you is that part of Shadowshine which actually impinges on your own quaint little three dimensional universe – the Dream Zone.'

'But I thought dreams were just so much mental residue working out of the system,' objected the Professor. 'It has been scientifically proven be the case.'

'Only because it suits us for you to believe that,' came the smug reply. 'And it has been so for countless centuries, my dear mortal, to use one of your rustic misconceptions of time, thus avoiding a lot of tiresome adjustments to the natural order of things.'

'Please don't misunderstand me,' Professor Doyle hastened to assure him. 'I was merely thinking aloud. This is incredible. Would a visit be in order?'

'You could,' mused the Soul Searcher after a moment's pause, 'but it would only fog up the system. Someone would dream about you and might wake up with the knowledge of what things are like up here. Anyway, it would upset the system because there already are an infinite number of persons, places and things, all specially trained to be dreamed about.'

'This is truly fascinating,' the Professor sighed wistfully. 'I never dreamed that such a place –'

'I like it!' crowed the Soul Searcher with a sudden guffaw, clapping the Professor on the shoulder. 'We don't often get jokes up here. Now it's my turn to make you laugh so you just take another peep through into the Dream Zone and see what's going on. I assure you, Desmond, you'll never have seen anything like it before ...'

WE'LL SEE YOU IN YOUR DREAMS

The old crone sat cross-legged, mumbling to herself in the eternal twilight before her blackened cauldron. Bleak, stony landscape surrounded her, falling away to the dark shores of a grey, tideless sea. A sea on which the sun had never shone. Some distance to her right, stretching away to the misty, mountain-girt horizon, a serpentine labyrinth coiled and twisted its convoluted ways and byways like a jumble of stone entrails. Nobody had ever been known to emerge from that labyrinth. Indeed, nobody was particularly keen to venture in there in the first place. Only Trevor seemed at home there. In fact, he never came out of it.

Aggie Runnicles gnashed her tooth in vexation, her nose and chin forming a crescent moon profile. 'Young idiot,' she muttered, glaring at a neat hole in the bottom of her cauldron. 'Zapped a hole clean through it, he did. Lost all my newts' eyes and fenny snake fillets.'

Aggie glanced over her shoulder and saw, just to the left of her hump, a tall, flaxen-haired young man, sauntering along the shore, whistling. A dark blue cape billowed out from his shoulders, beneath this he wore a colourful uniform that looked as if it had been hired from *The Prisoner of Zenda*. A sword and holster hung from his belt. No trace of guilt showed on the Greek god profile as he casually ambled towards her.

'You've gotta helluva cheek!' Aggie exploded, 'showin' your face around here after what you did to my pot! Look at it! Ruined!'

Flash Gordon, hero of the old Saturday matinees, glanced across. 'Not my fault, Aggie. You weren't supposed to be in last night's dream. You've only got yourself to blame for being nosey.'

'It's not fair,' wailed Aggie, her thin fingers raking agitatedly through her grey and stringy hair. 'Nobody dreams about witches anymore. It's all sex and science nowadays.'

Flash raised an eyebrow in admonition. 'Don't let Dale hear you talking like that. She's a very well brought up all-American girl.'

'Like some I've heard about,' sniggered Aggie. Then a gleam of suspicion crept into her watery, red-rimmed eyes. 'What are you doin' here anyway? Are you on call again?'

'I have indeed received the Etheric Summons.'

'It's not fair!' raged Aggie, jumping up and waving her gnarled fists in the air, scattering wings of bats and tongues of dogs in all directions. I haven't had an Etheric Summons since the MacArthy witch hunt! Nobody dreams about witches anymore,' she ended with a sad croak.

Flash Gordon looked embarrassed. This was nothing new. Even in the old days his most loyal fans declared that he often looked embarrassed. Something to do with the terrible scripts. 'Well that's hardly my fault, Aggie.'

'Don't call me Aggie!'

'All right, sorry, Dame Runnicles. But like I said, it's not my fault. I don't get as many Etheric Summonses as I used to – not since *Star Wars* and the Soap Operas.'

'But it didn't prevent you from showing off to that bottle blonde little piece of nonsense. She was dreaming about you last night!' Aggie snapped maliciously. 'Zappin' the backside clean outa my pot – just to impress her. Target practice was the last thing she was hopin' for.'

Flash shrugged his shoulders resignedly. 'We don't get a briefing of what's expected of us. We just have to play it by ear. Anyway, Dale wouldn't have approved.'

Aggie fixed him with a gimlet eye. 'All this talk ain't gettin' my pot fixed. What are you gonna do about it, "Hero of the Universe"?'

'Honest, Ag – Dame Runnicles, I just don't seem to get the time to help. I'm busy every dreaming moment. Why, I haven't had a decent game of polo for ages.'

Then being an honest all-American boy, he relented – but only slightly. 'Look, if this next dreamer gets woken up early and I have some spare time, I'll fix that cauldron.'

Aggie squinted up at him shrewdly. 'Is that a deal?'

Flash struck an heroic pose. 'Flash Gordon always keeps his word. You ask Dr Zarkov.'

'He ain't around anymore.'

Flash frowned. 'So he isn't. Don't see much of him at all nowadays. Brilliant man and fine friend. But who wants to dream about elderly scientists?'

Aggie sniffed. 'I might, except for his habit o' tryin' to mess up my spells with new-fangled scientific clap-trap. But he's real dishy, an' I just love that tickly beard.'

'Then you should hit it off with Ming the Merciless. The kids all loved him in the serials. He was the baddie they loved to hate.'

'Fat chance I've got with that slinky Dale Arden girl sashayin' about the place,' fretted Aggie. 'He's always chasin' after her. But he's a lovely man,' she sighed. 'He looks just like Old Nick with that fork beard. Is he on call, too?'

Flash glanced around. 'He might be. I saw him down by the shore with his shrimping net.'

Conversation flagged. Aggie poked her fingers through the hole in her cauldron and grumbled, 'Don't look like your client's gonna show. You might just as well fill in the waitin' time fixin' my pot.'

'People take longer to get to sleep nowadays,' Flash told her, 'what with late night TV shows and noisy traffic.'

A figure appeared out of thin air only a short distance away. His scant hair was awry and his round face bore a look of bewilderment as he gazed at his strange surroundings.

'So, you've sleepened up at last!' Aggie yelled at him. 'Took your time, didn't you!'

'Quiet!' Flash sternly told her. 'You're not in this dream. You can watch – but you're not to interfere.'

Aggie cackled softly into her hand. 'Oh, my hat! Just look at those pyjamas! Blue-striped winceyette – and with a cord! Not even an elasticated waistband. Your fans sure do go back a long way, Flash.'

Flash Gordon swirled his cloak in a theatrical gesture, glancing down at her coldly. 'Don't be repugnant. He's a perfectly respectable mortal.'

'He's gotta be! Those pyjamas! I didn't think folks wore 'em nowadays. Not with central heatin'.'

But Flash was preparing to play out his part in the new arrival's dream. 'Welcome to the planet Mongo,' he called out. 'I am Flash Gordon.'

'The planet Mongo!' guffawed Aggie. 'This there-when is as much the planet Mongo as Peckham Rye tube station!'

'I-I'm Arnold Clutterbuck stammered the dreamer. 'I-I've come to help you save the beautiful Dale Arden from the evil clutches of Ming the Merciless.'

Flash handed him his ray gun and dealt him a hearty slap on the shoulder. Then, with the theatrical swirl of his cloak, the 'Hero of the Universe' unsheathed his sword with a flourish that had raised a million juvenile cheers. 'Stout fellow!' he cried. 'The time has come to put the Emperor Ming to the test of cold steel!'

'Where is he?' murmured Arnold, staring around.

'Here, puny Earthling!' snarled a harsh voice as Ming, dead on cue, leapt from behind a convenient boulder. In his crimson robes and black skull cap, his twitching fork beard freshly waxed, he looked like the devil incarnate. In one hand he clutched the wrist of a suitably frightened-looking and scantily clad blonde. In the other a shrimping net which he cast aside as he leered at the two men before him.

'Let her go, you fiend!' cried Flash. 'Face me like a man – if you dare!'

Arnold was struggling to aim his gun and secure his pyjama cord at the same time. 'Don't fire,' Flash warned him. 'You might hit Dale.'

'I have you all in my power,' cackled Ming. 'You shall both die in the disintegration room – but not before you have seen me wed to Dale Arden in the Temple of Tao!'

Then Arnold, who was too preoccupied with his pyjama trousers to notice, accidentally fired his ray gun. White fire beamed out and zapped Ming's shrimping net to ashes, only inches from his feet.

'My shrimping net!' roared Ming in terrible fury. 'You vandal! Where will get another one now? Who dreams about Pedro the Fisherman in this era?'

Dale, seizing her chance, broke free and bolted towards the labyrinth. Screeching with rage, Ming set off after her. 'Not that way, Dale!' shouted Flash, pelting after her with Arnold close on his heels. 'You're doing it all wrong!'

'But she'll be safe in there,' panted Arnold, stumbling along barefooted. He'll never be able to find her.'

'And neither will we! Try to head her off.'

But complications have a nasty habit of giving birth to other complications. Ming tripped over the hem of his robe and went headlong to the ground. Flash, who was about to grab him by the collar, tripped over him and went flying. He was dimly aware of Aggie dancing about and gleefully clapping her boney hands together. Her thin cackles sounded particularly devoid of any sense of occasion.

Dale, seeing the downfall of hero and villain alike, paused, wondering what to do next. However, she did remember to assume the classic pose and stand in the shadow of the labyrinth, one dainty hand raised in dread to her throat.

But poor, well-meaning little Arnold got it all wrong. Assuming that Dale had entered the labyrinth, he recklessly dashed in to find her, getting himself hopelessly lost after no more than ten paces. Only Flash saw him vanish into the twisting stone maze. 'Arnold!' he yelled, clambering up and treading on Ming's head in the process. 'Come out! It's not safe!'

But he was too late. Arnold heard an ominous bellowing somewhere behind him in the darkness as heavy footfalls rapidly approached. He risked a glance behind him – and promptly wished he hadn't bothered. For bearing down on him along the gloomy passage was that massive dark haunter of nightmares – the Terrifyingly Revolting Evil and Vicious Organic Ripper – more familiarly known as TREVOR – Arnold squealed in panic and woke up.

Outside the labyrinth a glum trio listened to an equally glum 'Trevor' cheated of his prey. 'Well, we've lost him,' sighed Flash. 'He's woken up.'

'Damnable waste of time,' snorted Ming, wiping Flash's muddy footprint from his face with the hem of his robe, 'and I've lost a perfectly good net, too.' Still grumbling to himself he stamped off towards the shore, quite possibly intending to go after shrimps barehanded.

'My face is in a terrible mess,' Dale pouted, 'and I've laddered my nylons. I sure don't want another Etheric Summons like that again in a hurry.'

Flash watched her depart. 'You and me both,' he sighed. 'What a complete and utter waste of dream-time.'

'Yoo-hoo, Flash Gordon.' It was Aggie, a grin of triumph transforming her face into a Halloween mask. 'Looks like you're at a loose end. Now about this pot of mine that you zapped ...'

Flash Gordon groaned. 'Okay, Dame Runnicles, I'll see what can do.'

SHADOWSHINE NINE

'Not one off our most successful sessions,' the Soul Searcher apologised as he led Professor Doyle back to the light lock. 'I shall have to have a word with the Sandman about his employees. That Runnicles woman will have to be brought into line. She quite ruined that dream sequence.'

Desmond Doyle hung back, casting a regretful glance at the Dream Zone. 'Most interesting,' he murmured. 'I wish I were able to have a closer look, though. That young lady we saw before the session started – I'm sure I've seen her somewhere before.'

The Soul Searcher smiled a sardonic smile. 'That's what they all say, Desmond, but you probably just dreamed about her during your, er, salad days.'

'But even so –'

'Now, now.' The Soul Searcher wagged an admonishing finger and grinned roguishly at Professor Doyle. 'It wouldn't do you any good at all. In fact it could well set you back several incarnations, and that would be a shame as you've been doing very nicely for the past few centuries. A paragon of virtue. Truly a credit to Shadowshine and its enviably high moral standards. And just think of the scandal! Here of all places! No, no, Desmond. It just won't do, you know.'

'Perhaps you're right,' sighed Doyle with one final, vain glance over his shoulder as he followed the Soul Searcher into the light lock. 'I'm past that sort of tomfoolery anyway.'

'I'll say you are,' chuckled the Soul Searcher. 'You're dead.'

Professor Doyle fiddled with his glasses as he waddled his blundering way over a springy patch of purple. 'I suppose I am, but I keep forgetting. How silly of me. Alice always said I was absent-minded. By the way, sir, how is my wife? She died some years before me. Is she well?'

'She was the last time I looked, Desmond,' came the confident reply. 'She is, of course, reincarnated again – has been within a short while of her latest demise.'

'Oh, er, good,' nodded the Professor. 'I trust she is happy?'

'Rest assured she is quite happy,' the Soul Searcher retorted, ducking his head to avoid a knobbly lump of orange projecting from the light lock tunnel. 'She was reincarnated again as your brother-in-law's uncle's grandson's cousin's daughter.'

Doyle's tranquil expression broke into a beaming smile as he made a few hurried mental calculations. 'Really? That must be little Agatha. I gave her a rattle last Christmas.'

'We prefer to keep things in the family where deserving cases are concerned,' the Soul Searcher acknowledged with a superior smile. 'Also it helps to keep the records in order.'

They soon arrived back the Shadowshine Auditorium in all its cloudy white and misty blue splendour. 'Most impressive, most impressive,' commented Doyle. 'I found the Dream Zone extremely fascinating.'

'Just our usual high standard,' the Soul Searcher remarked with a complacent smirk. 'Of course, you appreciate that the security precautions are of the most stringent order. The whole area is vigilantly guarded by squads of crack troops of the Seraphic Security Brigade. I personally have always regarded the Dream Zone as an unnecessary weak point in Shadowshine's organisation, as any unusually perceptive mortal dreamer might well, upon awakening, recall certain items of prohibited classified information regarding the Dream Zone and its environs. Then there is always the constant threat of marauding teenage imps from Down Below sneaking through the security cordon and causing havoc and dismay among the unsuspecting visiting dreamers. This deplorable situation occurs all too frequently, resulting in what you, Desmond, would term as nightmares. Believe me, the SSB guards have their work cut out to keep the little devils out of the way. But, they're grand lads and they do a good job. You should see them on parade – a fine sight they are, swooping overhead with their gleaming thunderbolt bandoliers freshly blancoed and strapped around their shoulders between their wings. It really stirs the ectoplasm.'

'I do wish I could see it,' the Professor sighed wistfully. 'I always did like parades and brass bands.'

'Brass!' snorted the Soul Searcher. 'Brass is for that centrally-heated rabble Downstairs. Our troops have gold. There's none to match the Shadowshine Flying Gold Band.'

'Shadowshine?' echoed Professor Doyle. 'What a lovely name.'

'Yes, isn't it?' The Soul Searcher led the way across the Auditorium towards a shimmering portal of nothingness, Doyle trotting obediently at his heels until they emerged on a pinnacle of sharply-pointed, reinforced ether that twinkled with tiny motes of crystal, all colours of the rainbow.

'Where are we now?' Professor Doyle eagerly enquired, gazing about at the infinite blue spaces in rapt wonder.

'Departure Point,' the Soul Searcher informed him. 'But before you depart for your next incarnation you might be interested in how this incomparably splendid realm came to be known as Shadowshine?'

Doyle regarded his austere guide and host with owlish surprise. 'Why, hasn't it always been called that?'

'Gracious goodness, no!' chuckled the Soul Searcher. 'It was only as recently as your Seventeenth Century that it came to be known as Shadowshine. Your Bard of Avon, William Shakespeare himself, coined the name when he died and came here. He was so entranced with the place, he wrote what could only be termed as his truly immortal lines –

'Where silence is golden and water is wine,
And even the darkest shadow shine,'

Professor Doyle gulped, sniffed and blew his nose loudly. 'Truly beautiful, sir, truly beautiful. The Immortal Bard bestowed the blessings of his genius on those before and after the grave.'

The Soul Searcher examined his fingernails with affected nonchalance. 'That's what he thought, too, but it didn't do him much good. Due to his most unsavoury conduct involving a weasel-catcher's wife from Potters Bar, he was duly sentenced to a brief period of correction for his sins in the, er, Downstairs department. One can sympathise to an extent with the outrage which the Bard must have felt – and no doubt vented – after dedicating his poetic arts to the praise of the after-life, but the law must be upheld.'

'Dear me,' murmured the Professor. 'It does seem something of a shame, though.'

The Soul Searcher sniffed. 'That was the general impression he gave us when he came up for parole. He seemed particularly put out about something concerning the copyright. In fact he made so much fuss that he lost his good conduct remission.'

The Professor looked most distressed. 'Most distressing,' he said. 'Is he still, er, down there?'

'No, not anymore. After a few more eternities of wailing and gnashing his teeth, Shakespeare was up before the parole board again and duly reincarnated into a new life on Earth where he grew up to be a rather spiteful-tongued and waspish television critic.'

Professor Doyle shook his head in amazement. 'Wonders will never cease,' he mused, half to himself.

The Soul Searcher looked at him sharply. 'Of course not, and least of all up here. Has anyone told you otherwise? But now it is time for you to depart for your next incarnation, Desmond. It has been very pleasant for me to have such an appreciative and intelligent audience, but you really must be on your way now.'

'Must I go?' Professor Doyle pleaded. 'It's so nice here. Surely there must be some minor post in the administrative section where you could fit me in?'

The Soul Searcher shook his white-bearded head, but his smile was gentle. 'I'm sorry, but you really must be on your way. We had this very same conversation before on your last visit between incarnations. Take comfort that you will be here again.'

'You're right, of course,' Doyle smiled back. 'All good things must come to an end.'

'Not up here they don't. Farewell, Desmond Doyle. Enjoy your next incarnation and dine well but wisely on the fruits of life.'

The tweed-suited figure began to fade from view and dwindle until it was no more than a mere wisp of thought. Then it sank to the pinnacle of Departure Point, condensed to a gleaming pinpoint of silver light. 'Live in peace, good mortal,' whispered the Soul Searcher, gazing down fondly at the mote of light. 'Live in peace for another threescore-years-and-ten in the fantasy and illusion which you believe to be reality.'

Then he snapped his fingers to a passing Cherub. 'Here, boy. See to this delivery at once.'

The Cherub duly about-turned in mid-ether and came to attention before the Soul Searcher, fluffy wings poised for flight. 'How do you want me to send it, sir?' he piped, gathering up the glowing microcosm that had been Doyle. 'Temporal Transport or Ether Mail?'

'Ether Mail, I think. It's a promising soul, a well-matured psyche. Now here is the destination.' The Soul Searcher fished in the folds of his white robes and withdrew a scroll of snowy white vellum, edged in pale blue and covered in copperplate writing in gold ink. 'Miss Claudia Gossage, 31 The Pines, Fligwhich, Manchester, England, Earth. Got that?'

'I think so, sir,' the Cherub hesitantly replied, 'but surely you mean Mrs?'

I know what I mean, boy. Now you're too young and innocent to understand, but it's a hard world and Miss Gossage will only have herself to blame.'

The Cherub blushed a bright pink and scanned the scroll. 'But there isn't any postcode, sir.'

'And there never will be!' thundered the Soul Searcher with such violence that the poor little Cherub shed wing feathers with the shock of it. 'You'll never catch me subscribing to that accursed, bureaucratic, suburban rubbish! The day we have to depend on postcodes is the day I'll hand in my halo! Now run along, laddie – and don't mess about!'

Not wishing to risk another outburst the Cherub soared aloft on trembling wings, executed a double loop and vanished through a lock located just above Departure Point. 'Whippersnapper,' muttered the Soul Searcher. 'Always questioning their betters. Who do they think they are?'

Grimshaw and Scabwort were waiting for him in the Auditorium. Having long since become bored with standing around and doing nothing, they had sought a diversion and were deeply engrossed in an arm-wrestling contest across the Soul Searcher's tall desk. The Recorder Book had been knocked flying and lay on the cloudy floor, its pages bent and crumpled.

'I just can't leave this place for a moment without you two disrupting everything!' howled the Soul Searcher. 'Look what you've done to the Recorder Book! What are the Celestial Beaks going to think when it gets sent back in that state?'

The Grim Reaper started back guiltily, giving Scabwort the opportunity he was waiting for. 'Gotcha!' crowed the young demon, forcing Grimshaw's boney arm back across the desk top. 'C'mon, I'll give you another chance. The best of three.'

'Come away from there this instant,' snapped the Soul Searcher, shoving Grimshaw aside and retrieving the precious tome from the floor and batting him over the skull with it. 'Irresponsible numbskull! You're old and ugly enough to know better!' He swung round on Scabwort, intent on serving him the same but refrained from doing so on account of the demon's stubby horns possibly damaging the binding.

Grimshaw slunk back out of striking range, rubbing his aching skull, but Scabwort stood his ground, his piggy little eyes fixed defiantly on the Soul Searcher. 'There isn't much else to do around here,' he retorted. 'You go swanning off with that old codger and leave us hanging around here with nothing to do but waste our time. Grimshaw here was all for having a crack at a bit of soul-searching –'

'Don't say it!' screamed the Soul Searcher, tearing at his beard. 'Don't even think it! He would have the rest of the souls down in the fiery pits at the first chance, be they good, bad or indifferent!'

'That's not fair,' whined Grimshaw but the others took no notice of him.

'And why not?' challenged Scabwort, threshing his fork tail aggressively. 'The odds are that they would all be due for the chop, so what's the difference?'

'That's for me to decide,' came the pompous retort. 'You are merely on stand-by in the event that you just might be needed. And as for you, Grimshaw, officially you really have no business here at all.'

'Are you telling me to clear off?' Grimshaw demanded, fixing the Soul Searcher with an accusing eye-socket.

'In so many words – yes.'

Grimshaw about-turned, his raggy old hooded shroud swirling about his skeletal frame. 'That does it!' he snapped clicking his teeth angrily. 'I'm not one to stay where I'm not wanted. I'm handing my notice here and now!'

The Soul Searcher slumped against his desk, goggle-eyed and ashen-faced. 'But – but you can't!' he blustered. 'You are the Grim Reaper – Death! The whole system would break down if you left!'

Grimshaw paused at the light lock. 'That's your problem, Solly. I've had a sound offer from Fifteenth Century Transylvania to take the post of Troopmaster to the Ghoul Guides. At least I'll be appreciated there.'

'I'm slinging my hook, too,' added Scabwort. 'There's been nothing for me since that yobbo with the technicolour hair-do, and if I stay up here much longer I might find myself getting into non-bad ways.'

The Soul Searcher knew when he was beaten. 'All right, you've both made your point. You can both stay.'

Grimshaw preened himself and grinned complacently, but Scabwort was not, so easily satisfied. 'Just as long as I'm not wasting my time, squire. Like I said, I can only take so much this place.'

'Oh, you won't be disappointed,' the Soul Searcher hastened to assure him after a quick glance at the Recorder Book as he placed it dead centre on his desk. 'There's a couple of real stinkers due to come through. In fact they are both very desperate and dangerous souls, and I think it would be just as well if you had some help.'

Scabwort stared at him incredulously. 'Are they that bad?'

'Oh, yes – quite that bad.'

'In that case I'll see if I can find Rubbish-Legs,' offered Grimshaw, heading towards the fireproof escalator. 'I'm not not much good at the strong-arm stuff and I loathe violence.'

'You could have fooled me,' sniggered Scabwort.

The Soul Searcher moved over to the inner light lock that overlooked the Limborium and beckoned to Scabwort. 'How about that one?' he said, indicating one of the waiting souls within.

'Does that soul look rotten, evil and utterly nasty enough for you?'

Peter Calvert tossed the much-thumbed *Reader's Digest* back number onto the table in the centre of the gloomy waiting room. A faint but rhythmic buzzing sounded in the otherwise silent room. It was the African gentleman, deeply slumbering within the colourful swathes of his tribal blanket. Elvira Spratt, the traffic warden, had completed her 'hit list' of motoring offences and was deeply engrossed in a magazine which appeared to be something to do with bloodsports.

Calvert glanced at the window and the gentle eddies of mist that swirled outside, masking the world beyond in its autumnal folds. The 'world beyond'? Autumnal folds? What world beyond, and was it Autumn, anyway? Try as he may, Calvert could not recall anything prior to his entering the waiting room. Perhaps the old fellow was right and we are all dead, he mused. Oddly enough he felt no dread at the thought. If he was dead then that was that. On the contrary, the thought amused him.

Fatalism. He must be a latent Hindu – or was it a Moslem?

A wordless, typically English phlegmatic throat sound drew him from his reverie. It was Horace Hapgood, looking anything but Hindu or Moslem. In fact he looked completely scared out of his wits. 'I say, Calvert,' he murmured hoarsely. 'D'you think there's anything in what that old fella said – about us being, er, dead?'

'I was just contemplating the same line of thought,' Calvert admitted. 'But one thing I am sure of, is that when we go through into the doctor's surgery or whatever it is, we'll know for certain … one way or the other.'

'What preposterous rubbish you men talk!' snapped the unexpected voice of Elvira Spratt. 'Of course we aren't dead! I distinctly recall coming off duty earlier on account of a mild stomach upset. There were no blackouts – no shining tunnels of light. I simply handed over my round and came straight here. And that's the end of it!'

'Well, Miss Spratt,' replied Calvert, 'how do you account for the rest of us having no memory of why we are here – or for that matter – how we came to be here?'

Elvira's face glared across the waiting room in accusing triumph. To Calvert her visage had something of Fingal's Cave about it, while Horace Hapgood thought she reminded him of one of the characters out of an old western movie. One of the cattle rustlers … or was it one of the cattle?

'Because you are probably drunk!' came the sharp retort. 'All you men ever think about is drinking. It's either that or you are quite insane.'

Calvert winked at her and grinned. 'There's more to life than drinking, beautiful. Don't be so modest, you shy, blushing rose.'

Elvira's face was certainly red but it was questionable as to whether or not it was a maidenly blush or, more likely, blazing anger. But before she could give voice to her seething emotions, be they affectionate or homicidal, the disembodied voice boomed forth yet again.

'Zamba!'

And in response, the sleeping African gentleman suddenly stirred awake, and clutching his gaudy tribal blanket closely about his naked shoulders, scuttled from the waiting room and vanished through the doorway ...

THE NIGHT OF THE DOLL

'You're a fool if you stay!' Karl Dobkin spat the words out angrily, almost fearfully. 'You may think you know it all and what can't be seen under a microscope doesn't exist – but you're wrong!'

Roy Jordan shook his head and said nothing. He had said it all, over and over again. Six months of his life he had sweated away in this hot stinking jungle, and he was damned if he was going to give up everything now, all because of some superstitious clap-trap! He had achieved much, and up until a few hours ago, had won the confidence – and even the friendship – of the locals. Now all that had changed and they had gone slinking back to their verminous mud huts, afraid to come near the medical post. Even the local helpers had deserted then. All who were left were his wife, Ann, and their eight year old son, Kenny.

'I thought you too hard-headed to believe in all those ghost stories, Karl,' Roy lamely fought back. 'Just because some crazy old fanatic comes on the scene and puts the fear of God into the locals –'

'The fear of the devil more likely,' Dobkin cut in. His square-jawed face held no trace of humour. 'I've been in the African badlands for more years than I care to remember. Zamba has passed this way before, and he left behind a lot of terror ... and a lot of death.'

Roy shook his head again. It seemed the only gesture he was capable of. This change of attitude in the locals towards him had, at first, hurt him. Now he felt the outer limits of something deeper, some ageless fear which had its roots in the beginning of time. It had become worse when that strange, black-skinned skeletal figure had appeared on his veranda just before noon.

Zamba. The Dread Lord of Darkness – or so he was called by the houseboys before they took off into the wide blue yonder with their bulging white eyes rolling fearfully.

'So you're staying put then?' Dobkin summed up the whole argument in that terse question. 'Guess you think you know best.' He fished in the pocket of his bush jacket for a cigarette. 'All the same, when I get back to the trading post I'll wire the Commissioner and let him know that Zamba's come down from the hills. He's got more sense. Like as not he'll have all three of you flown out of here. For your own sakes, I hope so.'

He strolled out onto the veranda. Roy followed in silence and watched as Dobkin climbed into his battered jeep. The older man settled himself behind the wheel and studied the tall, fair-haired young doctor critically. 'All I hope is that you live to know what a damned fool you are, Jordan. I know you don't think much of me – come to that, I don't myself – but I've had my trading post by the river for too many years not to know trouble when I see it. And Zamba's trouble with a capital T. I told you about that missionary like you, who wouldn't be warned. Found cold, stiff and dead the next day, and judging by the expression on his face it weren't no cute little jungle chick paid him a visit that night. Zamba worked the old ju-ju on him. Reckon he's done the same to you.'

'Karl, you're talking rubbish!' Roy angrily snapped. 'I've got a couple of hunting rifles if the worst comes to the worst and –'

'Hunting rifles!' Dobkin's mirthless bellow was half-drowned by the racket of the jeep's engine revving up. 'It just ain't that simple. Guess you're like that missionary guy – you gotta learn the hard way. Remember me to that cute little wife of yours – and the kid. Poor little –' The rest of his words were lost as he angrily hurled the jeep away, along the rutted track that led through the clearing and skirted the fringe of the jungle, back to the river.

Roy turned gloomily back towards the wooden shack that was his home. His wife stood in the doorway, watching him strangely. He returned her stare blankly and leant his arms wearily on the veranda rail. 'Looks like we're on our own, sweetheart,' he smiled crookedly. 'Where's Kenny?'

Ann Jordan studied her husband with tired eyes. Like him she was tall and fair-haired which showed up becomingly against the healthy sun tan of her face. Now gaunt stress lines and shadows marred her attractive features.

'He's in bed. Scared out of his wits, too. Your drunken friend, Dobkin, talks too much – and too loud!'

'Easy on!' Roy protested. 'Karl was just trying to help. He's been out here a long time. These loners get a bit eccentric after the first few years.'

'After the first few whiskey bottles, you mean!' Ann flared up. 'We must have been crazy to bring Kenny out here with us. This is no place for a child.'

Roy felt inadequate. He just couldn't think of the right things to say. 'When we came out here things were different. This was a scientifically-run centre. We couldn't have foreseen this happening. It's like a return to the Dark Ages, all this voodoo rubbish!'

Something in Ann's expression caused a chill to skitter down his spine, despite the sultry dusk. 'Surely you don't believe in all that nonsense, Ann? Not you, too, for God's sake!'

Her impassiveness crumbled. When tears came there was no stemming them. Clumsily, Roy gathered her to him in his arms, murmuring endearments and vague words of comfort.

'I don't know what to believe,' she sobbed. 'That filthy, terrible old creature coming here with his curses and talk of death! I know I shouldn't believe it but I've heard of this sort of thing before. Magic or whatever it is – they do have some sort of power and they can kill us without so much as laying a finger on us.'

She was on the verge of hysteria. Brusquely, Roy hustled her inside the house, sat her in a creaky old cane chair and poured her a large brandy. After a moment's thought, he poured himself one as well and perched himself on the arm of her chair. 'I didn't know that you saw him,' he murmured.

She choked on the fiery, amber spirit, but after a few seconds some shards of her natural composure returned to her. 'I was just outside the door,' she began. 'I heard what he said to you and saw that hideous-looking doll thing he had clutched in his hand. Made out of straw, soaked in lion's blood.'

Roy forced a laugh into his words. 'Just window dressing for his big act.'

'You think so?' Ann challenged him, her voice brittle. 'He was too full of himself for my liking. If he was a fake he would have made more of a song and dance. But he was so quiet ... so certain of things.'

'You think we should clear out then?'

'It's a bit late for that now, isn't it?' The houseboys took our truck when they left. The only hope of getting out of here is if Dobkin persuades the Commissioner to fetch us out.'

Roy's face was pale. 'You really do believe in this witchcraft stuff, don't you?'

'I heard what was said when that – that creature was here. He was going to send the Brain Eater to destroy us at midnight. It's obscene, Roy! The Brain Eater! What horrible thing can that be?'

Roy forced a smile to his dry Lips. 'Not to be taken too literally, darling. Karl mentioned it to me. It's a local evil god or demon. It kills by striking its victims dead with terror. It "eats" away their mental reason by the sheer horror of its appearance – hence the name.'

Ann shuddered. 'And that's the monstrosity he's called down on us!'

'He may think so,' Roy told her, trying to convince himself as much as anyone, 'but it won't wash. I threw that filthy straw effigy right back in his face when I saw him off.'

Ann gazed up at him and sadly. 'You really don't know anything about anything, Roy. Do you honestly believe that he meekly trotted back to the village with the straw doll? He's hidden it here in some place where we wouldn't think of looking for it, to act as a focus for his demon.'

Roy began to protest, but something stopped him. A sound that he had never heard before, but even so, recognised. The devil drums in the village were beating! He glanced at his wristwatch. Eleven-thirty. Whether or not it was the drums or his wife's earnest conviction of the dreadful fate that lay store for them, he did not know. All that he was aware of was a desperate sense of urgency which told him that he must find and destroy that blood-soaked doll within the next half hour. 'Let's find the darn thing and be done with it!' he muttered harshly.

Frantically they searched the place, room by room. Even the outhouses were not forgotten. Every cupboard was cleared out – all to no avail. In the darkened kitchen they faced each other. 'Fifteen minutes left,' Ann murmured with a catch in her voice. 'We've searched everywhere.'

'No we haven't,' said Roy, clutching at one final straw. 'We haven't looked in Kenny's room.'

Ann placed a restraining hand on his arm. 'Must we disturb him?' she pleaded. 'Kenny was absolutely terrified by that dreadful old man. He cried himself to sleep. Let him rest, and if – if the worst happens, perhaps he won't know about it.'

Roy pulled his arm away and brushed past her to the door of their son's room. His face was a glistening, fearful mask of sweat. 'We must find it!' he muttered, fumbling with the door handle. 'We daren't leave anything to chance!'

He flung the door wide open. Kenny's bed was empty. He had disappeared.

Ann choked back a scream of anguish. 'God, they've taken him already!'

'Steady on!' Roy snapped. 'He can't be far away.'

They blundered outside, stumbling in the darkness of the African night. Desperately, frantically they called his name, but the only reply was the eerie chirping of the crickets ... and the ceaseless, diabolical drums. It was now ten minutes to midnight.

'Where is he?' Ann cried hysterically. 'What have they done with him?'

Roy mustered his scattered wits. 'He wouldn't have gone along the track towards the river. He must have been taken to the village. Get the rifles – quick! We might just catch up with them before it's too late!'

They wasted no more time and were soon stumbling blindly through the dense jungle, unheeding of the rough branches and sharp thorns that tore clothing and skin. Against his will, Roy found his eyes drawn to his watch, as if by a magnet. It was but a few seconds to midnight! Even as the icy shock clutched at his heart, a denser patch of shadow in their path swayed towards them.

Then the hideous screams which rent the night could be heard even as far away as the river settlement ...

The next morning was as hot as ever. Infernally so. Karl Dobkin and a young police sergeant, in his crisp khaki uniform, sat on the veranda of the medical post. 'You were damned lucky to get through last night,' announced Dobkin, leaning back in the rickety old cane chair. 'I reckon you must have used up a whole lifetime of luck.'

Roy Jordan, sitting with his wife on the veranda rail, smiled as he put an arm around her shoulders. 'You don't have tell us that, Karl. I'm sorry I doubted you. I said some pretty harsh things –'

Dobkin eloquently dismissed the apology as unnecessary with a sweeping gesture of his brawny arm and a brief, unprintable word which caused Ann to blush with gracious embarrassment. 'You got through and that's all that matters. Very soon now your *brave* little houseboys will come creeping back with their tails between their legs – and it'll be business as usual, eh, doc?'

'It's all going to look remarkably odd in my report,' sighed the young police sergeant. 'What happened after you discovered that your son was missing?'

He nodded towards the sturdy little fair-haired youngster who sat, some short distance away in the clearing, apparently none the worse for the previous night's experience. He was engaged in a rather one-sided conversation with a pair of monkeys that were frolicking in the branches of a nearby tree.

'We both nearly went out of our minds,' Ann replied with a laugh which was due more to tension than anything else. 'Everything seemed to happen so quickly, but Roy saw most of it, didn't you, Roy.'

'More than I ever want to see again,' nodded her husband. 'We were halfway to the village when I looked at my watch and saw that, it was midnight. We both nearly died of fright because, at that very moment, something came at us out of the undergrowth. We thought it was, er, you know … the worst.'

'The Brain Eater,' supplied Dobkin, laconic as ever. 'Don't be ashamed about it, man. I spent most of yesterday trying to convince you.'

Roy had the good grace to look somewhat abashed. 'As it was, it turned out to be Kenny, alone and unharmed.'

'And scared out of his wits and covered in mud and mosquito bites,' Ann added. 'Thankfully he seems to have got over his fright now.'

'But why had he taken himself off into the jungle?' asked the sergeant, mystified.

'That's the crux of the whole matter,' explained Roy. 'He heard Zamba the witch doctor threatening us yesterday, and while he didn't understand most of what he was on about, he knew well enough that the old wretch wanted us out of the way. It seems that when I slung Zamba out he must have hidden that straw doll under the verandah steps to draw the evil spirit to us. Anyway, Kenny found it and said nothing about it to us. When he was put to bed he waited a few minutes, got dressed and climbed out of the window, taking the doll with him – back to the native village!'

Dobkin guffawed in brutal humour but the young sergeant looked decidedly pale about the lips. 'Why should he do that, Dr Jordan?' he asked.

'For the most simple, innocent and child-like reason imaginable,' Roy told him, beaming proudly. 'He reckoned that Zamba had accidentally dropped the straw doll here and if he took it back to him he might feel grateful to us for returning it and not cause us any more trouble. Somehow he sneaked into the village without being seen and slipped the doll into Zamba's hut. And we all know what happened then!'

'I'll say we do,' Dobkin grinned. 'We could hear the old swine screaming across the jungle. Your kid neatly boomeranged the curse right back to his own front door! That's rich – it really is!'

But the police sergeant was completely out of his depth. There was nothing to cover this in the police manual. 'Let me get this straight, Dr Jordan. You claim that this doll being returned to the witch doctor caused the curse to be visited upon him, so that the evil spirit claimed his life?'

Roy nodded. 'That's about the size of it.'

The sergeant looked worried. 'I just don't know how I'm going to explain all this to the Commissioner,' he murmured. Did you see the, er, deceased, Dr Jordan?'

'I went to the village at sun-up,' Roy answered, 'and the natives were in a fine old flap, too. They won't be causing us anymore trouble now that Zamba's dead. I was unable to examine the body as he had been cremated, as is the local custom, at dawn, along with the doll. All that was left when I arrived was a smouldering ruin that had been his hut. Obviously the "locals" decided he was bad medicine and thought it best to get rid of his mortal remains, along with his mumbo-jumbo paraphernalia as soon as they could.

'Anyway, I've written up an official report of the death, just for the record. In short, it states that he died of fright, which is probably quite true. You could say that death was brought on by autosuggestion. Finding the doll in his own hut at the stroke of

116

midnight psychologically threw the switch on him and he died in a fit of sheer terror. Speaking as a medical man, that's my report.'

'And what about the doll?' ventured the sergeant. 'Do you really believe it possessed occult powers? It's something of a pity that you didn't bring it back. It would have been a very interesting piece of evidence.'

'Roy made sure that it was completely destroyed,' Ann laughed, hugging her rather sheepish-faced husband tightly. 'He may be a scientist, but, he does have some very human reservations, too.'

SHADOWSHINE TEN

'Not a very pleasant record, is it sir?' commented the Soul Searcher, frowning down from his lofty desk at the blanket-wrapped, spindly figure of Zamba the witch doctor. 'I believe the expression is "being hoist with one's own petard".'

The Grim Reaper and Scabwort watched the interview with gleeful anticipation from the coloured shadows of the light lock. There could not be the slightest doubt about this one, and Grimshaw said as much, too. 'Your luck's in, Scab,' he chortled, clicking his toothless gums in merriment. 'He looks the meanest one of the whole session.'

'That wouldn't be difficult,' retorted Scabwort, biting his talons and toying nervously with his pitchfork. 'You could hardly call that yobbo, Eric Dodds, much of a catch.' He glanced over his shoulder and glared at the gangling, acne-spotted young demon who was hand-jiving by himself further down in the green zone. 'Why I had to call up Rubbish-Legs for this assignment I'll never know. He's worse than useless. I can manage this client on my own quite easily. Just look at him, Grim! Have you ever seen a more pathetic – more soulful – soul? Even Rubbish-Legs could handle this one without any trouble. It's almost an insult – me being on Soulwatch Duty – to look after that pint-sized mortal. Just think of all the really big bad and beastly ones I've dealt with.

Real bloody-minded rottens like Nero, the Marquis de Sade and that unspeakable disc, jockey – it's really not unbad enough!'

Grimshaw looked hurt. 'That's not being fair on Rubbish-Legs. After all, he did stand in for you.'

'And look what happened. He got lucky straight away and left me with this mob of no-hopers and do-gooders.'

'Well that's gratitude, I must say!' sniffed Grimshaw with a petulant wriggle of his shoulder blades. 'I'm down there, working my pelvis off to knock together a good batch – even including this one especially for you, too! And he was not at all popular on Earth so he must be sufficiently evil to bump up your commission, not to mention earning you a few more pit points.'

'No offence, Grimmo baby,' Scabwort hastily apologised with a friendly nudge in his companion's rib cage. 'I appreciate the thought – I really do,'

'Even so,' Grimshaw reminded him, 'you want to go easy on poor old Rubbish-Legs. I know he's a bit slow, but it's hardly his fault. Ever since his pin-up girl was burned at the stake in the Salem witch trials, he's been out of sorts. If she really had been a witch she would have been sent to Hell and they could have settled down in a nice little semi-detached pit and looked forward to hearing the pounding of little cloven hooves. But as it was, she was innocent and sent back to Earth again for another incarnation.'

'I guess you're right,' Scabwort nodded sympathetically. 'It was something of a tragedy. She became a manageress of a charity shop. And a fat chance of her ever going to Hell after that.'

Grimshaw waved a frantic fingerbone for Scabwort to be silent. 'Never mind all that now. Old Solly's nearly finished reading the riot act to your next customer, you had better be ready for your cue. You mark my words – this one will earn you a bonus. All I ask is that you remember your old pal Grimshaw who set it up for you.'

The Soul Searcher was just concluding what had been, in his personal opinion, one of the finest pronouncements of doom that it had ever been his pleasure to deliver to a deserving soul. 'You are found guilty of witchcraft, harassment, and causing the death of no fewer than forty-one of your tribesmen, killing a cockerel, stamping on a cat and frightening to death one missionary when he wasn't looking. It was only fitting that your earthly incarnation should be terminated by the same evil power which you wielded with such malevolence over your fellows. I thereby condemn you to the torments of Hell for a period of seven years. He's all yours, Scabwort!'

In response, Scabwort skipped eagerly out of the light lock, brandishing his pitchfork. 'Game, set and match!' he crowed. 'C'mon, laughing-boy. We've got an appointment Downstairs with my boss. Get the lead outa your pants and get moving!'

Zamba, who had remained aloofly silent during the entire session, merely stirred himself sufficiently to blow his nose on the corner of his tribal blanket. Then he turned to stare at Scabwort. 'Get lost, brother,' he retorted disdainfully. 'You're out of order.'

Scabwort skidded to a halt, his cloven hooves gouging little puffs of vapour out of the cloudy floor. Tears welled in his eyes. Never before had a doomed soul spoken to him in such a rude manner. 'I thought this was too non-evil to be true!' he wailed, turning his distraught countenance towards the Soul Searcher. 'What's happened now, Solly? Surely this one is dead and not just visiting?'

'Of course, he's dead, Scabwort,' the Soul Searcher frantically reassured him as he riffled through the pages of the Recorder Book for confirmation. 'He was struck down when his curse was turned back on him.'

'Utter nonsense,' snorted Zamba. 'My hernia strangulated unexpectedly.' He produced a white card from the folds of his tribal blanket. 'And as I said earlier, brothers, you are out of order – all of you. And I quote Item 4, Paragraph 9 of the AWFUL.'

Grimshaw popped his skull out of the light, lock. 'The – the what?' he squeaked.

'AWFUL,' Zamba repeated, his black and wrinkled face smirking, 'or to give it its full title – the Association of Witches and Foul and Uncanny Legislators, of which I am a card-carrying, fully paid-up member, brothers. In short, you cannot send me to Hell as a doomed soul for the simple reason that I am one of Prince Lucifer's field agents.'

With a deafening screech Scabwort hurled his pitchfork to the floor, stamped on it, then hurled himself to the floor, too. 'I can't, take anymore of this!' he sobbed, drumming his little red fists on the wall-to-wall clouds. 'It's too much! I really did think I had got the break I had been waiting for. And now this has to happen!'

Grimshaw clattered out of the light lock, his skull wrought with concern for his little chum's distress. 'There, there, Scabby,' he crooned, patting the quivering bat-wings. 'Don't take on so. Grimmy's here.'

'Well you can shove off!' came the muffled reply. 'I wish I'd stayed on as an elemental. I was so happy, throwing Ming vases around stately homes and table-turning. I want my Mum ...' His voice trailed off in a series of glutinous and sobs.

'Get him out of here, Grimshaw,' snapped the Soul Searcher, clearly embarrassed by the scene. 'There's been some sort of administrative cock-up –'

'I'll say there has, brother,' Zamba declared as Grimshaw helped Scabwort to his hooves and steered him towards the light lock. 'You want, to get your facts sorted out before you have a strike on your hands.'

The Soul Searcher glared up at the soft folds of clouds directly overhead where he glimpsed a knot of eavesdropping Cherubs sniggering to themselves at the confusion. 'And you lot can clear off!' he shouted up at them. 'I know what you're thinking. The old codger's not up to it anymore! He's losing his grip! Well you're wrong – so clear off!'

'What about my rights?' chimed in Zamba, planting himself obstinately before the Soul Searcher's desk, his arms folded aggressively. 'As a fully paid-up, card-carrying member of AWFUL I expect due consideration as a Union member, brother –'

'I'm not your bloody brother!' the Soul Searcher thundered, causing the clouds directly overhead to darken ominously.

Zamba gripped the edge of the desk with his gnarled little hands and thrust his prune-wrinkled face forward. 'Don't you take that tone with me, you – you celestial capitalist! I'll report you to the Father of the Chapel!'

The Soul Searcher screwed his eyes tight and took a deep breath. 'Rubbish-Legs!' he bawled out. 'Come here and take this – this person to your chief so that he can be re-allocated to another assignment.

Rubbish-Legs bounded out of the light lock, cannoning into Grimshaw and Scabwort. 'All systems go!' he sang out, ignoring Grimshaw's soft but vicious swearing. 'Who's for the chop?'

'No one is "for the chop",' the Soul Searcher answered with studied patience. 'You are to escort Brother Zamba to your Master. Is it conceivably possible that you can undertake just that small thing without making a mess of it?'

Rubbish-Legs, being of a less sensitive disposition than Scabwort, as far as personal insults were concerned, waved his fork tail in a cheery gesture. 'Consider it done, boss. Okay, Brother Zamba, just follow me down the fireproof escalator.'

'Thank Hereabouts we've got that settled,' muttered the Soul Searcher. 'I'll get one of my people to notify Prince Lucifer on the hot-line so that he'll be expecting you.'

At the top of the escalator Rubbish-Legs paused, one talon on the asbestos handrail. 'Oh, one other thing, Solly,' he called out, 'There's someone in the light lock who wants to see you.'

'To see me? Who?'

'Sandy,' the reply floated back as the young demon and his charge disappeared into the fiery depths.

The Soul Searcher stared at the light lock through which Grimshaw and Scabwort had just disappeared. A tall figure drifted into view. Owing to the incredibly long red flannelette nightshirt that completely hid his feet, he could have hopped, skipped or jumped out of the light lock and it would still have looked as if he had drifted. A pair of hexagonal-shaped spectacles adorned his long, pointed nose and a tasselled nightcap of the same material as his nightshirt was pulled down around his narrow, bewhiskered face.

'There was a young demon called Scabwort,' he sang,

Who had a raw deal – or so he thought.

The warlock dilletante

Was a Union militante,

Which made Scabwort, old sport, just one soul short.'

'Great steaming seraphims! Groaned the Soul Searcher, covering his face with his hands. 'The Sandman! What are you doing here?'

'I thought you wanted to speak to me about something or other,' smiled the Sandman, depositing a large blue sack on the floor. 'Something about a complaint concerning one of my dreamees.'

'Yes, that's right.' The Soul Searcher regarded the pleasantly sleepy-looking old man sourly. 'A most disgusting display – and be careful with that sack of sleepy dust. We don't want the damn stuff floating around up here. You'll put all Shadowshine to sleep.'

'Tut, tut,' chuckled the Sandman. 'You do worry so, dear boy. Now what's all this about a complaint?'

With an effort the Soul Searcher composed himself, reforming the nebulous bits of vapour at his extremities where he had lost concentration and lapsed into his natural formless form. 'I was showing a particularly promising soul around Shadowshine and all went well until we got to the Dream Zone – your Dream Zone, Sandy. It was then that this unclothed blonde appeared –'

'Ah, that would be Beryl. A pleasant child. Most industrious, too.'

'That's as may be,' the Soul Searcher retorted coldly. 'But she appeared out of thin air without warning – without anything at all! – utterly stark naked, and ran across the Dream Zone as fast as she could.'

'Oh, I see,' murmured the Sandman, his placid face lighting up with understanding. 'You mean you couldn't catch her.'

'I wasn't trying to!' exploded the Soul Searcher. 'I am merely complaining about her state of undress! It creates an entirely false impression of Shadowshine in front of the mortal visitors.'

The Sandman waved the matter aside. 'Well you really should have given me fair warning that you were on the prowl, er, I mean visiting. I could have laid on a special dream sequence for you and your guest.'

'I'll bear it in mind, the Soul Searcher gruffly replied. He never felt quite at ease with the Sandman. He was a pleasant enough old entity, but it was a spooky sort of pleasantness. 'Anyway, I've said my piece, Sandy. Good of you to pop in.'

But the Sandman showed no inclination whatsoever to depart. Instead, he loitered around the Soul Searcher's desk, poking his long, inquisitive nose into the open pages of the Recorder Book. 'What are you doing, Solly, my dear fellow?' he politely enquired.

'What d'you think?' growled the Soul Searcher, moving the tome from the prying nose and eyes. 'I'm tied up in the middle of a soul session. And kindly keep your nose out of this book. It's classified information.'

'Any royalty?' the Sandman asked in a hopeful little voice.

'No there isn't. Just clear off.'

But the Sandman ignored the rebuff. Neither did he appear to be in the least offended by the curt dismissal. 'Oh, what a pity. It always adds a touch of class – romance even – when you have a royal soul here. How well I remember King Arthur's visit. What times he lived in! The colour! The pageantry!'

And he began to hum a little ditty.

'When Arthur of Pendragon reigned,
He made sure that his knights were trained
In jousting, duelling, courtly dance and manners.

And handsome, bold sir Lancelot
Would often sing and dance a lot
Around Queen Guinevere's heraldic banners.

'Please, Sandy, I've got a job to do!' protested the Soul Searcher. 'Come to that, so have you. What about all those poor insomniac mortals trying to get to sleep? Don't you owe them some sort of responsibility?'

The Sandman pursed his lips and made a soft 'pum-pumming' sound, then executed a few graceful steps of a gavotte. 'Not so you would notice, dear chap. A great many people are on sleeping pills there on Earth. And as for the rest – well I've got my loyal minions to help me out there.'

'Minions? What loyal minions?'

The Sandman came to a halt before the lofty white desk, his long fingers laced together before him in a sinew steeple. 'Oh, the televised party political broadcasts, of course. They never fail to do the trick. Now what can I do to help? You do seem to be rather short-handed, what with young Scabwort retiring with a fit of the vapours and dear Grimshaw playing nursemaid. What can I do to make myself useful? Oh, do tell!'

The Soul Searcher cradled his head in his hands. There was just no getting shot of the fellow! He began to harbour wild ideas such as re-siting Hell in the Dream Zone ...

'There was a young lady from Aberystwyth –' piped the Sandman.

'Enough!' bellowed the Soul Searcher. He knew when he was beaten. 'Very well. You can be on stand-by just in case someone is needed. But I don't think we'll have any trouble with the next soul so it's just as well that Scabwort isn't here to deal with things. If he knew who was to be next it would utterly destroy his faith in inhumanity.'

'Ooh, goody!' chirped the Sandman as the Soul Searcher descended from his high stool and made his way towards the inner light lock that overlooked the Limborium. Who's going to be next?'

The Soul Searcher peered through the boiling rainbow of colour that spiralled endlessly from There to Then. Finally he pointed a fateful finger at one of the microscopic trio within. 'That one,' he decided firmly.

Elvira Spratt glared across the waiting room at the auburn-haired young man. 'In my opinion, Mr Calvert, you should be seeing a psychiatrist, not a doctor. All this talk of us being dead! It's morbid – unhealthy!'

'Death is only unhealthy to the living,' Peter Calvert responded. 'It's all relative. When you're dead – you're dead. Healthily so.'

'Sorry old chap, you've lost me,' chipped in Horace Hapgood with a nervous laugh. 'I only feel dead on Monday mornings, but manage to come to life by Friday.'

Calvert smiled. 'A chronic case of the humdrums. What line are you in, Hapgood?'

'It was accountancy, but I inherited some valuable family property and was able to retire early. My hobby is gardening and Aunt Amanda's house – that's the property I inherited – has a sizeable garden to keep me amused ...' Horace paused, frowning. 'Funny I should remember that. There's something I should have done before I came here, but I can't remember what it was for the life of me.'

'Or the death?' murmured Calvert. 'Could that be why you're seeing the doc?'

Horace looked plainly scared. 'What d'you mean, Calvert? What possible connection could there be between my garden and me visiting the doctor?'

Calvert shrugged. 'Don't ask me, chum. It's your garden.'

Elvira sniffed contemptuously. 'What drivel you men talk! I shall certainly speak to the doctor about both of you when I see him.'

Calvert studied her robust physique and lantern-jawed countenance. 'Wa-al,' he drawled, 'a man's gotta do what a man's gotta do.'

'You are an extremely rude young man!' snorted Elvira, 'and I sincerely hope that one day I will have the satisfaction of giving you a parking ticket.'

'I doubt it, Miss Spratt,' chuckled Calvert. 'Not unless the traffic wardens have a river patrol. You see, I live on a canal barge.'

Elvira's piggy little eyes glowed with red vindictiveness.

'And pity your poor wife, having to endure her existence with such an arrogant, heartless person!'

It was as if Calvert had become a different man. 'You will not mention Erica again,' he retorted with icy softness.

Horace could stand no more. 'What's happened to us?' he bleat-
ed. 'Why are we – three people who have never met before –
trapped in some stupid argument? A meaningless duel of words!
Let's just each grab a magazine and ignore each other, just like
normal, dull people do in any other normal, dull waiting room.'

And suiting his words he snatched up a magazine from the table
– a back number of *Mothercraft* – and surprised himself by becoming absorbed in pre-natal exercises.

A chair creaked as they are wont to do when the changing
temperature of the closing day affects their wooden limbs, and
Horace Hapgood started nervously. That Spratt woman was right
after all, he thought. Even if she was a traffic warden, she was
right. Calvert was definitely weird. He hoped it would be his own
name called out when the doctor was ready to see the next patient.
His name or Calvert's. He desperately hoped that he wouldn't be
left to share the dusk-wrapped waiting room with this strange
young man who was displaying such unnerving characteristics as
well as such disturbing thoughts.

Then his heart rose as he heard the brief crackle of 'white noise'
that immediately preceded the next patient's name – only to sink
again as the voice boomed out, 'Elvira Spratt!'

THE DOWNFALL OF ELVIRA SPRATT

Storm clouds loomed darkly as the figure paced its slow, relentless
way down Pike Lane. The general air of the gathering storm
created a backdrop for the stern, stocky figure in the severe black
uniform – one large thumb hooked in the tunic belt, and the
sinister black cap set squarely on the scowling block of a head.
Below the shiny peak the black brows merged as one above the
broken-bridged nose, and the thin, bloodless lips were pursed
across a lantern jaw. Elvira Spratt, the traffic warden, was a
formidable person to behold. Here was a face that had stopped a
thousand cars. A face which resembled a landslide.

Elvira felt disgruntled with life for two reasons. She had not
booked a single car all day, and as if that was not bad enough, she

had doubts as to the state and age of that sausage she had lunched on while sitting on the park bench where she was able to watch the yellow lines beyond.

What she needed was a victim! Someone to take her mind off her grumbling, rumbling indigestion. Pike Lane was a little-used road – one-way traffic only – and she had hopes of catching some unwary motorist risking its fifty yards short cut up Pike Lane the wrong way and that some had reckoned without the vigilant Elvira Spratt and had lived to regret it.

A shattering clap of thunder – a sizzling explosion of lightning too close for comfort – and Elvira was thrown face down in the mud, squawking with fear. She scrambled up, struggling to regain her dignity, glancing around to see if she had been observed, and it was in this covert glance that she first noticed that something was amiss. The whole lane had taken on a different aspect.

For one thing it was noticeably darker – almost dusk. And the trees seemed denser, so dense, in fact, that Elvira could not even see the high rise flats that stood beyond them ... or did they?

'Who goes there?' a cracked and ancient voice challenged her.

Elvira peered into the deeper gloom of the lane. A hunched form, swathed in a long, shapeless cloak and equally shapeless hat, was waving a lantern and peering intently at her.

'Who wants to know?' she gruffly retorted, though there was more than a slight squeak in her voice as it emerged. Then she noticed the gate – a five-barred affair – across the road. A traffic diversion? Surely the gas main hadn't burst again!

'It be Ezra Higgins, the turnpike attendant,' called back the stranger, still holding the lamp aloft. 'State your business, woman. What be you a-doing here at this hour when most Christian folk are abed?'

Lost for words, Elvira glanced at her wristwatch. It said twelve. Noon or midnight? But it was nearer midnight if the darkness was anything to go by. 'Who authorised that gate?' she demanded, desperately clutching at officialdom 'Unless you can produce the correct authorization, you are guilty of contravening ...'

She paused in mid-sentence. A vehicle was approaching along the lane on the far side of the gate. And travelling the wrong way! This was something she could deal with. She was on surer ground here. Marching briskly forward she swung the gate wide open and shoved the turnpike attendant to one side with a sweep of her brawny arm. The old man shrilled out a yelp of indignation and fell backwards into the bushes.

But Elvira had forgotten him already. Standing with legs firmly astride, she withdrew her notebook from her satchel and her pencil from her pocket. Her pale tongue licked its point in exquisite anticipation, flicking from between her thin lips like the tongue of a serpent.

Then her jaw dropped. Four horses were drawing a stagecoach and seated up on the driver's box were two men clad in caped cloaks and tricorne hats! Elvia's mind reeled. What had happened to her? Had that bolt of lightning somehow transported her through time to the Eighteenth Century when Pike Lane had had a turnpike gate?

But even as these thoughts raced through her brain she acted purely by reflex, and stepping forward with one commanding hand raised aloft, called out in a stentorian voice, 'halt! I wish to inspect your driving licence!'

True, the driver reined in his horses, slowing down the coach, but he also bellowed out a warning to his companion. 'Footpad, Barney! It be Turpin most likely!'

And Barney acted promptly. Before Elvira could comprehend what was happening, he raised an ancient, bell-mouthed blunderbuss to his shoulder, took aim, and fired with deadly accuracy, discharging a rotten sausage which hit her fair and square in the mouth!

And fell Elvira fell ... fell heavily from the park bench where she had succumbed to a fitful sleep in the midday sun, a victim of her own dreams and indigestion.

SHADOWSHINE ELEVEN

'Where's the doctor?' demanded Elvira Spratt, surveying the Shadowshine Auditorium with narrowed eyes beneath furrowed brows. 'I've been kept waiting long enough in that squalid little waiting room and don't intend to wait any longer. I've got a job to do.'

'A lady of Traffic Control
Ate a dubious sausage roll
The result was quite toxic
And made the old ox sick,
Unfit to continue patrol.'

Elvira's crag-browed eyes swung in the direction of the chanting voice, but all she could see was a strange swirling patch of something in the air on the far side of the cumulus-floored Auditorium. It appeared to be a multi-coloured hole in ... nothing. But that was impossible, she told herself. You couldn't have a hole in nothing. And anyway, who was it chanting that insolent poetry?

A dry cough somewhere to her left caught her attention. A tall, doddery old man with long white beard and wearing what appeared to be a bedsheet, sat at a lofty white and gold desk. 'Please, Sandy,' the old man called out peevishly to the unseen rhymer, 'I'm having a session and I don't think the iambic metre was quite right either.'

Elvira's cauliflower ears pricked up at this – cauliflower on account of her losing an argument with a vicar who had parked his BMX on a zebra crossing – and she glared at the white-haired old gentleman. 'The metre's not quite right?' she echoed. 'If anyone has been tampering with a parking meter I'll have something to say about that. It is an offence to tamper with or damage a parking meter.'

'Oh, do shut up, you stupid woman!' retorted the white-bearded man. 'I don't want any trouble from you. It's been bad enough with the others –'

'And it won't get any better when you see those two idiots in your waiting room. If you're any sort of a doctor you'll have them both certified.'

'That's a good one, Solly,' chirped the voice of the hidden lyricist from the shimmering blob of colours, and a lanky figure in a red flannelette nightshirt and matching nightcap, popped into view. 'Using the waiting room syndrome, eh? That's one way of keeping them quiet.'

'Is this or is this not a doctor's surgery?' Elvira loudly demanded to know, 'and are you or are you not a doctor?'

The apparition in red shook his head and chuckled. 'Oh, dear me, no. I'm not even a nurse.' He pointed a pale finger which resembled a bleached twig at the old man at the desk. 'He's the one you want.'

Elvira strode towards the desk. 'I've come about my stomach –' she began but was interrupted yet again by another merry chuckle from the garrulous presence in red.

'I'd be careful if I were you, Solly,' he piped. 'She's out for trouble. I know body language and this one's ready for battle – physical or verbal. So take your pick.'

Elvira paused to favour the odd-looking man with a basilisk glare of contempt. 'I don't know who you are!' she snapped, 'but if your body language is anything to go by, you've got a distinct stutter. And now,' she added, turning again to the venerable-looking figure at the desk, 'what have you got to say about my stomach?'

'It's fat,' came the bleak response.

'W-what!' Elvira goggled furiously, her lantern jaw dropping like a crane scoop. 'What sort of a doctor are you? I've come about my stomach and all you can do is insult me! You're no better than those two clowns in the waiting room!'

'I am not a doctor, I am the Soul Searcher,' answered the Soul Searcher. 'I am most certainly not the Stomach Searcher. And while we are on the subject of what is and what is not, this is not a doctor's surgery. It is the Shadowshine Clearing House. And that cavorting fool by the light lock is the Sandman.'

Elvira went white beneath her stubble. 'What am I doing here?' she croaked.

'You are about to be celestially cleared,' sniggered the Sandman.

'Sandy!' barked the Soul Searcher. 'Shut up!'

'I must be dreaming,' protested Elvira, clutching at the desk for support, 'or else I've gone mad. This can't be happening to me!'

'Well you certainly are not dreaming,' the Soul Searcher assured her. 'The Sandman hasn't been near you. And you haven't gone mad either. You haven't got the mental capacity to go mad. A certain amount of intelligence is required.'

At last that prehensile organ which served as Elvira Spratt's brain began to accept the enormity of the situation in which she now found herself. 'Then I must be dead!' she squeaked.

'Wrong again, mortal!' the Soul Searcher announced amiably. 'To be dead you would have had to have been alive in the first place – and that, Elvira Spratt – you never really were. Not in all the years of your adulthood were you ever truly alive. You were just a self-centred, dull, unimaginative little blot of sentient life. The fine and fiery senses of true awareness were never yours. The nearest you ever came to experiencing any sort of emotion approaching happiness was when you slapped a parking ticket on someone's chariot –'

'Wrong era, dear man,' the Sandman tactfully prompted from the light lock. 'Car – not chariot.'

'– car,' continued the Soul Searcher as if there had been no interruption, 'and even then it wasn't a true, red-blooded emotion. It was more in the category of an amoeba feeding off plankton.'

Elvira staggered, seeming on the point of collapse, and at a brief summons from the Soul Searcher, two plump little Cherubs flew down from somewhere beyond the pillars that ringed the Auditorium, and gently steadied her. Even so, fourteen stone of Elvira Spratt – astral or otherwise – took some supporting, and their downy little wings were flapping nineteen to the dozen in the effort to steady her and keep themselves aloft.

'I think there is something that you should see, Miss Spratt,' murmured the Soul Searcher, climbing down from his desk and moving towards the light lock. He glanced at the two puffy cheeked Cherubs. 'Help her along, laddies. The poor mortal has suffered a nasty shock.'

'Where are you taking me?' quavered Elvira as she waddled along between the two solicitous Cherubs, following the Soul Searcher into the yawning mouth of the light lock.

'Just something I think you should see, my dear,' the reply floated back over the white-robed shoulder.

'Blast you, Sandy!' the Soul Searcher exclaimed in a more positive tone as he sprawled headlong. 'Why do you have to leave your sack of sleepy dust right where people are going to fall over it?'

'Sorry about that,' the Sandman at once apologised as he nimbly slipped past Elvira and her escort to retrieve his sack, treading on the back of the Soul Searcher's neck in the process. 'I hope you haven't spilt any.'

'Gory purgatory!' swore the Soul Searcher, threshing about like a windmill as he tried to dodge the Sandman's dancing carpet slippers. 'However you manage to lull the laziest mortal to sleep is far beyond my comprehension. Get out of the way! How am I expected to preserve the slightest vestige of dignity with you trampling all over me?'

Burbling effusive apologies, the Sandman swung his sack on his shoulder, clouting the side of the light lock such force that a wide patch of red went pale pink. Still muttering, the Soul Searcher clambered wheezingly to his feet and stamped off along the light lock, the dazed Elvira still following behind, hardly aware of the slight hitch in proceedings.

At last they emerged where the purple sizzled out to near-invisible strands of zapping bursts of ultra-violet. So great was the awesome of absolute black nothingness above, below and around her, Elvira was stirred from her torpor. 'Now where are we?' she demanded warily.

The Soul Searcher waved his arm in a grandiose gesture, the sleeve of his toga falling back to reveal a tattooed anchor on his forearm and the words 'I Love Ruby', which somewhat detracted from his air of dignity. 'Behold, mortal woman,' he proudly declared. 'The Time Zone.'

'I didn't know you went in for tattooing,' chirped the Sandman gleefully.

The Soul Searcher regarded him with a haughty and distant glance. 'We all have our little foibles,' he stiffly defended himself. 'Now be quiet and let me get on with the job in hand.'

    'The Soul Searcher had a tattoo, (warbled the Sandman)
    Of an anchor with words "I Love You"
    He had got another
    which said, "Hello Mother"
    Tattooed just above his left shoe.'

'Shut your face!' hissed the crimson-faced Soul Searcher. 'Ignore him, Miss Spratt,' he added in Elvirat's direction. 'He's having one of his stupid days. Now you just follow me out onto the Time Walk and we will see what there is to see.'

'Now who's being stupid!' the Sandman called after them in a rare burst of uncharacteristic indignation. 'She's hardly likely to see anything else ...' His voice thankfully tailed off as the Soul Searcher made his aloof way across the fragile-looking promenade of glittering black heavenly concrete that stretched out through the endless abyss.

Elvira was entranced by it all. Even the tough, beefy expression which was the usual state of her countenance in repose had mellowed to that of processed pork. 'What's that faint silver cloud rolling around us?' she asked, gazing at the luminous mass of opacity that coiled in frozen spirals on all sides of the vast Time Zone.

'That, my dear woman,' responded the Soul Searcher, 'is what you call Time. You're the second mortal to ask me about that on this session. I suppose it is quite impressive,' he added, cocking his head on one side.

Elvira just blinked dumbly. It was all far beyond her. One of the two Cherubs steadying her, quipped, 'So now you know that when someone says they haven't got time, they're speaking the truth. It's all up here.'

'Solly does the jokes here, laddie,' the Soul Searcher sternly rebuked his winged minion, 'so watch out – or it's back to modelling Christmas displays for you.' He glanced along the endless roll of Time. 'Now let me see if can find the place without using the Temporal Direction Indicator,' he mused.

For several seconds he stared at one particular area which glittered with countless points of multi-coloured light. Then from that particular spot a voice called out, 'sorry about that, Guy, thought you would be bringing the matches.'

'Wrong place, wrong place,' mumbled the Soul Searcher, shuffling along the diaphanous time cloud. 'Aha! Here we are.'

'What's he on about?' muttered Elvira with a questioning glance at the two Cherubs, but they just shrugged their wings.

'Nothing to do with us, ma'am,' said one. 'We're only the hired help around here.'

'Miss Spratt, come and look at this!' The Soul Searcher seemed quite excited and was beckoning urgently to Elvira. 'This is what I wanted you to see!'

Not knowing quite what to expect, Elvira allowed her Cherubic escort to steer her across the Time Walk to where the Soul Searcher was peering intently at a puce-coloured fragment in the fabric of Time. 'Here – look here. Tell me what you see,' he urged her.

Elvira peered at the mote, and as she did so it seemed to spread, to open out like some sort of cosmic window. She was looking down on a familiar scene. Her doctor's surgery. And as she looked she saw her mortal self emerge into the street, resplendent in her black uniform with the familiar yellow trim. A slip of paper that could have been a prescription for some sort of purgative jollop was clutched in her rough-casted paw. But even as she stepped onto the pavement with her familiar Teutonic tread, a hapless motorist paused for a millisecond on a yellow line. She pounced at once – an allegorical act which symbolised the hunter and its prey – and the luckless motorist stood no chance and was left with the lethal poisoned ticket buried under his windscreen wiper and his carcass to decay in the sun until it was nothing but a bleached pedestrian. Her bloodlust satisfied along with her digestive problems, Elvira Spratt, the Scourge of the Back Doubles, Stalker of the Hatchbacks, proceeded on her way in search of other victims.

Elvira tore her gaze from the vision and stared at the Soul Searcher in wondering amazement. 'But that was me down there,' she croaked. 'I was coming out of Dr Patel's surgery. This is all so confusing. I thought that was where I was when I turned out to be here instead. And if I am here and not there, what am I doing here when I'm there?'

The Soul Searcher shook his head sadly. 'You still don't understand, do you? Your mortal self exists in such a narrow, humdrum mode of life that it does not need a soul. It is as much use to you as an appendix. In fact, the soul of Elvira Spratt fossilised soon after adolescence and never really came to life at all, with the exception of that Rumanian stoker you met in the Odeon cinema in Newcastle.'

A large and oily-looking tear coursed its way down Elvira's dry and leathery cheek. 'I can't even remember his name,' she sniffed.

The Soul Searcher patted her bicep in a comforting, fatherly manner. 'Elvira Spratt cannot remember his name, but the soul of Elvira Spratt can – if you try. You see, dear, your mortal body is still alive and going about its dull life, even though you – its soul – are here. You are a sinecure as far as your corporeal form is concerned, and Elvira Spratt will go about her day-by-day routine until, at the age of sixty-three, she will abruptly depart from the world of the living when she accidentally falls into the penguin pool at Regent's Park Zoo and contracts pneumonia.'

'But that's me you're talking about,' wailed Elvira as she was escorted back to the light lock by the Cherubs.

'Not anymore it isn't,' the Soul Searcher told her, following along closely behind. 'The mortal shell of Elvira Spratt no longer needs a soul – which is why you are here. It is now time – if you will pardon the expression – for you to move on to another incarnation.'

At the entrance of the light lock Elvira paused to dab away her tears. 'Will it hurt?' she snivelled, blowing her nose on a crumpled parking ticket.

'Not at all, my dear,' the soul searcher smiled benignly. 'You just come with me. All is under control. It always is up here.'

Back they went, traversing the colourful pageant of the after-life. Through the velvet-smelling purples and violets, the brine-tanged indigo, tangy oranges and yellows to the rose-scented reds ... and the Shadowshine Auditorium. Apart from a few aproned Cherubs, treating the cloudy floor with moisturizer sprays, the place was deserted, although the Soul Searcher observed that the Sandman's sack was propped up against the fireproof 'down' escalator. But there was no sign of its owner.

'It's all so very sad,' Elvira sobbed. 'I never realised that I was such a non-entity.'

'There, there. Don't take on so, you poor, pathetic and most uninteresting creature,' the Soul Searcher murmured soothingly. 'If it's of any consolation there are plenty more like you – and just because you aren't yet ready for higher things doesn't mean you are wicked and condemned to the fires of torment. Oh, no, not at all. In a sense you are a sort of "don't know".'

He moved over to his desk, and taking up a small silver hand bell, rang it three times. In response a plump female angel wafted down from the pillared heights on widely spread wings, to alight before the Soul Searcher who had resumed his customary seat at the desk. 'You rang, sir?' she politely inquired.

Despite her own problems Elvira could only gape at the new arrival in utter astonishment. The 'angel-ess' was somewhat more rotund than those depicted in all the stained glass windows she had seen, and furthermore she was dressed in a pale blue smock, over which she wore a white apron. And encircled by her halo was a freshly-starched nurse's cap with a red motif on the front, enclosing a symbol which looked like a stork in flight carrying a pudding cloth in its beak.

'Ah, prompt as usual, Matron,' smiled the Soul Searcher. 'This is the case I sent you the memo about. Would you see that she is suitably incarnated?'

'I'll see to it at once,' Matron announced briskly. She turned to Elvira. 'Now come along with me, my girl. It's time for your injection.'

Elvira, who had a lifelong dread of hospitals and anything pertaining to them, shrank back in horror. The stern but homely face with the hair worn in a severe bun was so typical of the popular image of a hospital matron. But what was a hospital matron doing in this unearthly place? Was this all some sort of hallucination?

The Soul Searcher dismissed the Cherubic escort and watched them wing their way aloft in the wake of the nattering Cherubs, their celestial gold mops and buckets and clattering into the upper distance. 'Nothing to worry about, Miss Spratt,' he assured her. 'This is Matron Birtha who is in charge of all premature incarnations.'

Elvira nervously pulled up the cuff of her traffic warden tunic. 'Will it hurt?' she asked in a small voice.

Brandishing a rather larger than usual hypodermic syringe, matron Birtha loomed over her. 'Not at all, you silly girl. Now let's get it over and done with.'

Elvira closed her eyes and gritted her teeth. 'I'll try not to faint,' she squeaked as she bravely extended her wrist.

'Don't you play the fool with me, madam,' admonished Matron Birtha. 'Bend over.'

'Bend …?' Elvira's eyes blinked wide open and her teeth ungritted. She stared imploringly at the Soul Searcher. 'Can't I just go back to my old body? I don't even mind the penguin pool bit.'

The Soul Searcher discreetly averted his gaze. 'Best do as she says, dear. Matron knows best.'

Elvira shut her eyes again, re-gritted her teeth and bent over, one hand against the front of the desk and the other clutching at her traffic warden's cap to keep it in place. Matron Birtha uttered a 'humph!' of triumph and the hypodermic needle was plunged home like a harpoon. And as the plunger was drawn back the etherised soul of Elvira Spratt began to metamorphose back into glittering, coagulated thought and vanish as it was sucked up the needle and into the syringe.

Five seconds later and it was all over. The spiritual essences that comprised the true soul of Elvira Spratt were in the syringe, twinkling like liquid starlight. 'This patient's soul has responded successfully to treatment,' Matron Birtha announced with professional smugness. 'Will that be all, sir?'

'It will, thank you, Matron,' nodded the Soul Searcher, settling back on his high stool and watching the Matron soar aloft on a flutter of wings. A most efficient surgical spirit, he thought.

He was rudely brought down to paradise by the sound of raucous voices in the light lock. Scabwort and Rubbish-Legs, and interspersed with their carousing was the stupid giggling, piping voice of the Sandman. The Soul Searcher grasped the thunderbolt paperweight on his desk, his fingers clenching spasmodically around its pitted surface. 'I just can't let them loose for a second without something happening,' he muttered. 'They're all stoned rotten by the sound of them.'

Two pot-bellied demons rolled from the light lock, tripping over their cloven hooves. Behind them the pipestem figure of the Sandman reeled into view, flapping his nightcap about like a semaphore flag in one hand, while in the other he flourished a large bottle labelled Hellbore and Witch Hazel Wine.

'We been cheerin' up pore ol' Scabwort,' hiccoughed the Sandman as his legs gave way, allowing him to slide to the clouds in a limp heap of red flannelette. 'Feelin' a lot better now, eh, Scabby, ol' chum?'

'Lots and lots,' burbled Scabwort, rolling over on his back and hurling his pitchfork at an inquisitive Cherub. 'I feel great.'

But Rubbish-Legs appeared to have become rather maudlin in his cups, for he just sat propped up against a pillar, crooning 'Stardirt' and snuffling with self-pity about some obscure and imaginary wrong that had been done to him by someone who didn't exist.

The Soul Searcher completely lost control of himself and his Olympian mode. Before even he realised it, he had reverted back to a near-invisible cloud of nervous energy and then progressed – or retrogressed – to hysterical energy. At last he mastered himself and resumed his humanoid form. 'Pack it up, you lot!' he screamed. 'Where the Heaven do you think you are? I've still got two more souls to search!'

Then the cloaked and skeletal figure of the Grim Reaper emerged from the light lock, picking his way fastidiously between the swearing and rolling revellers. At least he appears to be sober, observed the Soul Searcher thankfully.

'C'mere, Grimshaw, an' 'ave a drink,' slurred the Sandman, tugging at the Grim Reaper's tattered shroud. 'C'mon, Grimmo baby. It's great. You'll love it.'

Grimshaw stared at the proffered bottle, his skull set in prim disapproval. 'I'm not drinking that rot-gut,' he snapped. 'It makes my bones shine like cheap plastic. Anyway, it goes straight through me.'

'Tell you what,' wheezed the Sandman, grabbing hold of Grimshaw's femur and hauling himself to his feet. 'Why not come to my place? I gotta couple of bottles of Deadly Lampshade stashed away –'

'Will you stop pawing me!' Grimshaw cried out shrilly. 'You know I don't like to be pawed! Anyway, you mean Deadly Nightshade – not Lampshade.'

The Sandman scratched his gingery side whiskers and sniggered. 'I know what I mean, dear boy. It's Deadly Lampshade. Two glasses and the lights go out!'

'That does it,' the Soul Searcher announced. 'Unless you shape up by the time I count to ten, I'm going to get straight on the hot-line to Lucifer and tell him that two of his demons are displaying distinct tendencies of goodness and have been trying haloes on.'

It did the trick much quicker than an ocean of black coffee would have done. It even surprised the Soul Searcher – the three of them – the Sandman, Scabwort and Rubbish-Legs – all lined up as quiet and meek as any bunch of first term Cherub Cadets.

'That's more like it,' the Soul Searcher nodded approvingly. 'And now we'll bring in the next customer ...'

The gloom of the gathering dusk that pervaded in the waiting room seemed to be intensified by a sense of menace which was almost tangible. At least that was how it seemed to Horace Hapgood as he sat behind the glossy barricade of *Mothercraft*. Across the room from him Peter Calvert sat smoking his pipe and humming to himself.

'My God, he is mad,' thought Horace. Nobody normal would smoke a pipe and sing in a doctor's waiting room.

But, was he in a doctor's waiting room? All the disquieting speculations put forth by Calvert came flooding back. The inability to recall anything other than being in this room ... the Martian ... the peculiar scaly gentleman with the nautical smell ... the watches, all stopped at different times – because we have all died at different times ...?

Without thinking, Horace dropped the magazine to his lap and groaned. Calvert stared at him and smiled. 'I wonder how she got on?' he remarked.

'Wh–who got on what?'

'La belle Spratt. I wonder how she got on in the doctor's surgery?'

'I neither nor care,' Horace retorted. 'I just hope they hurry up and get around to my turn.'

Calvert stared at him fixedly. 'Is that what you really want, Mr Hapgood? Are you absolutely certain? Supposing that behind that door, instead of a doctor's surgery –'

'Shut up!' roared Horace. At least it started off as a roar, tapered slightly to a shout by the molars, then emerged as a squeak.

But neither man heard the squeak, for it was drowned by the mysterious voice against the background of white noise, summoning the next patient. 'Peter Calvert.'

'Well, well, chuckled the young man, tapping out his pipe and rising from his chair. I would have put money on you next, Hapgood. Just as well I didn't. Cheerio.'

And Horace Hapgood was left utterly alone in the waiting room. Alone with his own doubts, fears ... and memories ...

ERICA

If Jill had not decided to take the short cut home through the park she would never have run into Peter. It was such a fine afternoon – especially for February – with the cloudless blue sky and the dazzling winter sunshine taking the edge off the little gusts of north-easterly wind that nipped at fingers and nose. But Jill, with thoughts of spring and finer weather and an impulse to escape from the street's monotonous traffic drone, took the opportunity of more pastoral surroundings – and so ran into Peter.

At first she didn't recognise him, this tall, athletic young man whose whole being radiated health and vitality. She remembered Peter as a pallid, rather sickly youth, and had it not been for the distinctive mane of auburn hair and the quirky grin she would have passed him by. As it was, she paused, smiling. 'It is Peter, isn't it? Peter Calvert?'

The young man halted in his stride and smiled back. In one hand he clutched a bouquet of roses, their brilliance intensified by the drabness of his khaki anorak. 'That's right,' he grinned. 'And you're Jill Fenton if my memory is correct.'

'Your memory is,' chuckled Jill, 'but it's just plain Smith now. I got married last year.'

'Belated congratulations, Mrs Just Plain Smith,' Peter murmured, his eyes twinkling as he fell into step with her. 'I did hear it through the grapevine but it's years since I saw you. Must be –'

'It isn't gallant, to quote dates and ages,' Jill good-naturedly teased him. 'Anyway, how's the world been treating you, Peter?'

'Very well, indeed. I'm in commercial art now and I must say that I've had some very good breaks. It's certainly an improvement on that desk job I had before.'

Jill nodded. 'Oh, yes. I remember you were very keen on art but you used to treat it as more of a hobby than anything else.'

'I'll not deny it,' Peter agreed, 'but that was before I met Erica.'

'I might have known,' Jill exclaimed triumphantly. 'Behind every successful man there is a woman. I don't think I ever met her, did I?'

'You might have done. She used to work with Maureen Barr at the Health Centre. Erica Vale, receptionist to old Dr Beckett.'

Jill recalled her then. She had never actually met Erica but she remembered the tall, elegant and sophisticated young woman at the Health Centre. More striking than beautiful – as far as conventional beauty went at any rate. But she had heard something of her. A quiet but capable girl who kept herself very much to herself. What was termed a 'private person'. A more unlikely match than her and Peter she couldn't imagine. He was not at all sophisticated. In fact, he was always rather awkward and gangling. Far different to the healthy, confident young man who walked at her side now. She marvelled at how they could ever have become close friends.

Unable to contain her natural curiosity, she asked, 'how did you two get together then?'

'We were introduced at Maureen's birthday party about two years ago and I suppose I must have mentioned something about my interest in art. Anyway, she seemed quite taken up with it and asked to see some of my work. From then on I never looked back. She encouraged me to make something of myself and, well –' he smiled with boyish embarrassment – 'we became very close to each other.'

'That's marvellous, Peter,' Jill declared. 'And you mean to say you never swept her off her feet and made her your lawful wedded wife? Shame on you, sir!' she concluded in mock reproof. 'Faint heart ne'er won fair lady!'

'That's just it,' Peter replied with his characteristic lopsided grin. 'It was my faint heart that was literally the trouble. It used to be dodgy and was getting to a stage when it looked as if I would end up in a wheelchair. But that's all in the past now. I'm as fit as a fiddle.'

Jill glanced at him as they strolled past the ornamental lake with its winter-struck, stick-like reeds. 'I can see that Erica certainly seems to agree with you. I take it that those roses are her Valentine?'

Peter glanced down with masculine self-consciousness at the bouquet in his hand. 'That's right, he murmured, pausing in his stride. 'Look, I think I ought to tell you something about Erica before you hear it from someone else. There's a seat if you've got five minutes to spare.'

Whether or not Jill had five minutes to spare didn't enter into it. There was something interesting here and she was eager to hear what it was all about.

'Just about a year ago it happened,' began Peter when they were both seated on the rustic bench overlooking the calm lake. 'We had been out to a show in London and Erica was driving me back. It had been a grand evening, but then everything seemed to happen at once – everything wrong, that is. I had this sudden heart attack, and as is always the case, hadn't got my tablets with me. Erica knew that I had to have medical treatment and put her foot down to get me to the nearest hospital. What happened next I'm not sure, but the car went out of control and crashed. The next thing I knew I was waking up in hospital several days later. Erica died from her injuries and if it had not been for the skill of the surgeons I would have done so, too.'

Jill was appalled. 'My God, Peter,' she whispered. 'I'm so sorry ...'

'Erica knew the score – knew that she was dying and she signed the consent form before she ... Well, I found out that it was her idea. The heart transplant was carried out immediately and since that very moment my health improved and I made a complete recovery.'

'You mean it was Erica's ...?' began Jill, but Peter smiled gently and placed a finger to his lips.

'Yes it was, Jill. Erica died and I began my new life on February 14th. Now don't pull such a long face,' he softly chided her. 'Look at it this way. I'll always have part of her with me, and also her strength. A wonderful legacy.'

He stood up and playfully nudged Jill's averted face with his knuckles. 'I must hurry now, Jill. The cemetery closes soon – especially at this time of the year. Thanks for listening and – well – see you around.'

He strode off towards the park, a tall, strong figure in the afternoon sunshine, aglow with health and the joy of life. And as Jill watched him depart, the blurred vision of her moist eyes made it seem for a brief second that another shadow walked at his side, alongside his own.

SHADOWSHINE TWELVE

The Shadowshine Auditorium looked reasonably tidy – which was something of a miracle in itself, considering what had gone on before. The Sandman had been on a binge with the Grim Reaper and the two young demons on Soulwatch Duty, Scabwort and Rubbish-begs. With the exception of Grimshaw – who abstained from drinking on the grounds that it made him merry, and whoever heard of a Merry Reaper – they had all got roaring drunk and behaved in a most unseemly manner. Scabwort had been sick on the Soul Searcher's best cloud and the latter had packed them all off down the light lock to sober up while an emergency squad of Cherubs got to work and cleaned the place up, with Silver Lining sprays and Ether Fresheners.

Only the Grim Reaper had displayed any degree of contrition and had offered to stay and help. But his shroud was so dusty with cobwebs and mould, he left almost as much of a mess as he cleared up. Anyway, Grimshaw's presence had a disturbing effect on the cleaning staff, especially the young and impressionable Cherubs, so the Soul Searcher had sent him packing with the other three.

But now the cleaning was done and the Soul Searcher could relax and snatch a bite to eat before the next soul came up for review. He had just finished reading up on his case but had kept the soul in stasis during his lunch break. 'No sense in getting myself an ulcer,' he told the canteen Angel as she served up his plate of angel fish and chips on the neat white tablecloth draped over his desk top. 'That's the trouble when you have to assume these mortal modes. You automatically take on all the attendant defects.'

The canteen Angel, whose name was Evangeline, smiled at him sympathetically. 'It's not been the easiest of sessions for you, has it, sir? Why don't you apply for a holiday?'

'Holiday!' snorted the Soul Searcher, liberally dousing his lunch with vinegar. 'Fat chance I have of that! Mortals are always dying, no matter whether it's Earth or some other planet. Until they all discover suspended animation there won't be any let-up. Besides, where would I go for a holiday?'

'What about that nice place called Tunbridge Wells?' suggested Evangeline. 'They seem to be quite respectable people there. They're always writing letters to the papers saying how disgusted they are with everything.'

The Soul Searcher slammed down the vinegar bottle and attacked his meal with gusto. 'Too much of a busman's holiday. Though Pluto might be worth a visit,' he mused in mid-munch. 'There's a very placid-natured silicon life form there and I hear that they have a robot space probe that strayed in from the Magellanic Cloud Cluster which does very good female impersonations and water skiing acrobatics.'

'Don't you want any salt on your food, sir?'

'Do I not!' snapped the Soul Searcher, nearly choking on a fishbone. 'Not after that business with Lot's wife during the Sodom and Gomorrah sanction! You can't be sure where the damn stuff comes from!'

Evangeline looked offended. 'There's nothing wrong with our salt. It's got no human additives whatsoever.'

'I'm sure it hasn't,' the Soul Searcher replied in a more kindly tone, 'but I'd rather not. What's for pud?'

'Prunes and custard or Manna fritters.'

The Soul Searcher grimaced as he handed his empty plate to Evangeline and folded his tablecloth. 'Ugh! No thanks. I'll just settle for my usual mug of Ambrosia – and go easy on the sugar. All that fat makes it difficult for me to metamorphose into my disembodied state, and there's nothing quite so revolting-looking as an ectoplasmic cloud with a paunch.'

Evangeline fluttered off with the empty plate and soon returned with the steaming mug of Ambrosia. 'That's a good girl, the Soul Searcher grunted. 'I've been looking forward to this.'

A blissful moment to relax. The Soul Searcher contentedly quaffed his hot drink, taking care not to leave rings on the Recorder Book. Then a discreet 'ahem' caught his attention. A sheepish-looking Grim Reaper stood in the entrance of the light lock.

'Yes, Grimshaw, what is it?' the Soul Searcher enquired guardedly. A slight drop in the temperature tingled through his epidermis, warning him that things had been going too well – even for only fifteen minutes by Mortal Greenwich Time Standard.

'I just wondered if I could be of any help,' said Grimshaw in a pathetic little voice.

'Well, I don't know –' began the Soul Searcher, only to be seized by a violent coughing fit, spluttering Ambrosia to all points of the compass and beyond.

Grimshaw solicitously darted forward and thumped him hard on the back several times. 'It's all right, Grim,' croaked the Soul Searcher, gasping for breath. 'A blasted bone stuck in my throat. I distinctly asked for filleted angel fish.'

'Sorry about that, I'm sure,' Grimshaw replied huffily.

The Soul Searcher stared at him owlishly. 'What's it got to do with you, Grimshaw? You're not on the catering staff ... oh, I see,' he concluded in some embarrassment. He had forgotten just how sensitive Grimshaw could be about bones. He tended to take things too much to heart ... or thereabouts. 'No offence, Grimshaw,' he added. He had been a bit too hard on the poor fellow and after all, he had been the only one not to get drunk.

'Well, you could act as an observer. Quite an interesting case coming up – something of a novelty.'

Grimshaw looked uneasy. 'Solly, I think should mention that Scabwort and Rubbish-Legs are a bit, well ...'

'Inebriated, to use a polite term? Never mind. It's probably just as well. This next soul most certainly isn't a candidate for our two young worthies and judging by the way Scabwort has been carrying on it's just as well he's not here.'

Grimshaw's skull was alight with interest. 'Is it one I brought up?' he eagerly asked.

'Yes it is,' the Soul Searcher replied indulgently, 'and he's on his way through any moment.'

Dead on cue – in more ways than one – a form drifted from the inner light lock that led from the Limborium. At first Grimshaw thought he saw a tall, auburn-haired young man in casual attire. But was it? He rubbed his eye-sockets bemusedly. There seemed to be an odd shift in the form's etherised state that shimmered like a double image. One second it seemed to be the young man and the next it appeared to be that of a tall elegant young woman superimposed on the original. Must be a cock-up in the soul blending department when it was etherised on arrival, Grimshaw thought. Someone would be for the high jump, he reflected, thankful that it was nothing to do with him.

But the Soul Searcher did not seem to be in the least put out by the unstable appearance of his latest subject. 'You are Peter Calvert?' he asked, going through the usual formalised ritual.

'More or less,' responded the double image in a definitely masculine voice.

'Yes he is,' a clear, feminine voice endorsed.

Grimshaw backed towards the light lock, his patellas knocking. If he had possessed hair it would have stood on end. A fine film of ectoplasm had broken out on his marble brow and he was beginning to wish that he hadn't bothered to show up.

The Soul Searcher smiled benignly. 'And are you also Erica Vale?'

'Quite correct,' the feminine voice answered.

'That would certainly seem to be the case,' the young man smiled. 'I take it that – or rather we – are dead?'

The Soul Searcher nodded, smiling. 'In the mortal sense of the word you most certainly are, sir and madam. I must say that I am most gratified – most honoured – to meet you – the both of you – in your entirety.'

The dual soul seemed to be so unstable as to appear as a shimmering patch of human-shaped light which flickered alternately from the visage of a man to a woman. 'I thought it was something like that,' the man's voice remarked. 'I had this sort of gut feeling when I was in that waiting room of yours. I don't think my other companions were very happy, though. Especially that lady with the muscles.'

The Soul Searcher chuckled. 'Ah, yes. Poor Miss Spratt. Well, she doubtless asked for it – always leading with her chin.'

'And what a chin to lead with,' the woman's voice laughed.

It was too much for poor Grimshaw. Bleating with fear, he edged his way into the light lock's glowing portal. He needed a holiday. Somewhere nice and quiet like Dedham in Suffolk.

'And where do you think you are off to, Grimshaw?' the Soul Searcher's voice checked him. 'I thought you wanted to stay and observe?'

'I – I've observed all want to, thanks very much,' retorted Grimshaw through chattering teeth. 'You seem to be coping very nicely on your own – even if they aren't – on their own, I mean.'

'Oh, come on, you big booby!' the Soul Searcher laughingly admonished him. 'There's nothing to be afraid of. You read up on the case earlier, didn't you?'

'All I know is that this Peter Calvert mortal nearly qualified for collection when he had a heart attack, but was reprieved by a transplant. He died ten years later in a power boat accident. Though goodness knows what a mortal in his delicate condition was doing messing about in power boats –'

'Shut it, Grimshaw,' the Soul Searcher told him. 'Now if you had been paying attention to the Calvert/Vale dossier you wouldn't be in such confusion. Did you not think that there was an unusually strong bond between Peter Calvert and Erica Vale? Look how she turned him from a mediocre, little pen-pusher into a highly successful commercial artist. And what about the heart transplant, eh? It was more than a rapport – it was the same soul.'

Grimshaw waved a skeletal hand in weak protest. 'The same soul? Don't be daft –'

'Don't you call me daft!' thundered the Soul Searcher with such vehemence that a snooping Cherub was dislodged from the uppermost regions of a nearby pillar and thumped down on its bottom on the cloudy floor. 'Haven't you heard of an egg having a double yolk? That's how it is with *Peterica* – a double soul.'

'But they weren't laid by a hen!' Grimshaw squeaked.

'Idiot! Of course they weren't. But they have an affinity. In this celestial existence they are as one, but in their mortal existence they are two separate beings, mutually drawn to each other. No matter their rank or station, they have always been drawn together by psycho-magnetism.'

Grimshaw placed a boney talon to his brow. 'I've got the most awful skullache, Solly. Have you any migraine tablets handy?'

'In the fullness of time,' went on the Soul Searcher, ignoring his colleague's indisposition, 'they have shared many lives together. They were the original Adam and Eve and Antony and Cleopatra. They were Charles and Nell Gwynne, Burgess and Maclean –'

'I can't swallow that!' objected Grimshaw, mastering his reeling senses. 'They were of the same temporal era as this one – er, these two.'

'Dunderhead!' bellowed the Soul Searcher, intoxicated by his rhetoric. 'Have you never heard of peaceful co-existence? They were Horatio Nelson and Lady Hamilton. They were, er, they were ...'

'Marks and Spencer's?' suggested Grimshaw.

The dual soul image of *Peterica* looked at Grimshaw and smiled. 'Isn't that the Grim Reaper?' the voice of Peter Calvert said.

'He's shorter than I thought,' replied the voice of Erica Vale.

Grimshaw forgot his astonishment in a brief tinge of indignation. 'I'm five feet ten in my socks!' he snapped, drawing his shroud about his boney frame in a haughty gesture. I've never encountered such flippancy before – certainly not from mortal souls.'

The Soul Searcher erupted in majestic mirth. 'I've heard of a quick death and a slow death, but never before of a short death. Take no offence, Grimshaw. These are old friends who are approaching their final incarnation. And with each one they merge closer together. Ultimately, they will be one.'

The dual soul approached Grimshaw and held out a hand. 'You are Death, aren't you,' said Peter Calvert.

'We have met many times before and we think of you as an old friend,' added Erica Vale.

Grimshaw sniffed and blew his nose cartilage on the hem of his shroud. 'I've become all overcome,' he gulped. 'I don't believe this is happening,' he added as he numbly shook hands with *Peterica*. 'I must be dreaming. Pinch me, someone.'

'Then you had just better take our word for it, Grimshaw,' the Soul Searcher told him, 'for you have no flesh to pinch.'

'It's just as well Scabwort isn't here,' Grimshaw said. 'All this would have been too much for him.'

'Well you just make yourself useful and get back to being your normal, bad-tempered self,' the Soul Searcher advised him. 'And you can make a start by escorting this double yolk – er, dual soul – to Matron Birtha in the Reincarnation Wing.'

'Since when did we do guided tours?' challenged Grimshaw with a spirited return of his usual irascibility.

'Since now! And don't slouch!'

Grimshaw shrugged and slunk towards the light lock. 'Okay, okay,' he grunted. 'Keep your halo on. Just when I wanted to get back home early to see the kids in the Morass Dance Festival. I'd promised the wife, too. This way, sir and madam, to the high, wide and horrible. If you would be so kind as to follow me through the light lock. And watch out for the infra-red step. It's hot.'

Left alone once again the Soul Searcher dipped his quill pen in a bottle of golden ink and put his signature in the Recorder Book against 'Calvert P. and Vale E. 20th Incarnation' with a cheerful flourish. 'If only they were always as easy as that,' he sighed. But his tranquil muse was soon to pass as an all too familiar voice warbled from the deeper recesses of the light lock.

'There was a young lady from Twickenham
wore garters because she liked flicken 'em.
she didn't like tights
Because on moonlit nights
she complained that she always felt sick in 'em.'

The red-nightcapped and red-nightshirted figure of the Sandman popped out of the light lock and waved his blue enamel candlestick at the Soul Searcher in greeting. 'Good Eternity to you, Solly,' he called out, dumping his sack of sleepy dust down by the tall desk. 'Have I missed anything interesting?'

'After that bender you were on I doubt if you would have noticed, even if you had been here,' the Soul Searcher muttered, frowning over his book. 'Why on Paradise, are you always here? Haven't you got anything to do in your own department?'

'Not so's you'd noticed,' replied the sprightly old gentleman, peering about and rubbing his long hands together. 'How's business?'

'Dead.'

'There was an old man from Llanfairpwllgwngyllgogarchwyrnd-robwllltyailiogogogo ...' began the Sandman. Then he stopped abruptly and turned to stare at the Soul Searcher.

The latter gestured at him testily with his quill pen. 'Well get on with it, man. Drop the other boot.'

The Sandman looked embarrassed. 'You want me to go on? Is that what you said?'

'You've got ears, haven't you?' retorted the Soul Searcher.

Then a triumphant grin showed through his snowy-white beard. 'Caught you out at last! You can't! It's all bluff as suspected. You only do it so that I'll give in and allow you to hang around here.'

'You take all the fun out of everything,' moped the Sandman, his candlestick dripping hot wax on the cloudy floor. 'It gets so boring for me with all those mortals asleep and no one to talk to.'

'That's no excuse for getting personnel on Soulwatch Duty stinking drunk, Sandy. I know I don't care much for having such characters as Scabwort and Rubbish-Legs up here because they can be a bad influence on the Cherubs. Some of those youngsters are very impressionable. But demons on Soulwatch Duty are a necessary evil and I have to put up with it. However, I don't have to put up with you turning the place into a beer garden. Is that understood?'

The Sandman dashed away a tear with his nightcap tassel and then blew his nose on it. It was both a pathetic sight and sound. 'I know when I'm not wanted,' he sniffed forlornly. 'I'll be on my way.'

'Did I say that?' the Soul Searcher shouted after his departing figure. 'Did I say that you could go?'

The Sandman stopped in his tracks and peered uncertainly over his shoulder at the dignified personage. 'But I thought –'

'That'll be the day!' scoffed the Soul Searcher. 'Since you're here you might be able to make yourself useful. But only if you stand by quietly and don't get in the way.'

'It's a deal, Solly. Cross my heart and hope to incarnate.'

'Good. Then that's settled.' The Soul Searcher squinted hard at the Recorder Book. Now the first thing you can do is get those two demons sobered up and along here at the double.'

'Both of them?' queried the Sandman.

'That's what I said. And tell them to get kitted out with Mark IV pitchforks, crash helmets and riot shields.'

'Mark IV... crash ... riot?' echoed the Sandman, utterly perplexed.

'You heard me. And you had better get Grimshaw back, too. We'll need all the reinforcements we can lay our hands on – maybe even the Seraphic Security Brigade. This last soul is a real mean one.'

The gloom in the silent waiting room had intensified and Horace Hapgood, its sole occupant – to use an apt turn of phrase – harboured suitably grave doubts that the forty watt bulb was only a thirty-nine watt bulb. He was not sorry to see the back of Peter Calvert, for the young man had some decidedly unsettling theories. But now that he was left to his own thoughts Horace found these disturbing surmises coming back to prey on his mind. What sort of waiting room would be occupied by such odd people as that Martian, the little blanket-wrapped African and that peculiar tall green man with the scales who smelt of fish? And what about the watches which had all stopped at different times? Someone had made a most distasteful observation that it was because they had all died at different times. Was it that fat man, Square, or the old buffer, Professor Doyle, who had said that. Or had it been that young fellow, Calvert? In his present state of mind Horace wasn't even sure if Messrs Square, Doyle and Calvert had ever existed. In fact, he wasn't at all sure of anything.

In an attempt to quieten his jangling nerves Horace selected the most prosaic magazine from the pile on the table. Green lettering on a cheerful red and yellow cover informed him that it was called *The Kitchen Gardener*. He opened it and began to read, in an effort to entrench himself in the mystique of mulch and compost – and it seemed to work. Quite a fascinating subject, he told himself. Now what was this article about marrows? Marrows! For some awful yet unknown reason a spasm of sheer terror tap-danced down his spine. There was a photo of one of the brutes in all its hideous green and yellow-striped splendour! But why ...?

Then the white noise, followed by the portentous Voice ...

'Horace Hapgood!'

CHILLED TO THE MARROW

Horace Hapgood's inheritance came with all the suddenness of a bolt of lightning. It began when his Aunt Amanda took a fatal dive down her staircase and blossomed when it became apparent that Horace was her sole beneficiary. Aunt Amanda was a wealthy old lady and lucky Horace clicked for the large country house with its acres of surrounding gardens. Never mind how the poor old dear came to her unhappy end. Horace had carefully wiped the soap from the stair treads and nobody was any the wiser.

The fortunate if undeserving nephew soon moved out of his seedy little flat and into the palatial house. Also he retired from his office job and braced himself for a life of leisure. But it was on the third day of his new life that things unplanned became manifest.

Late one warm Autumn evening he was busy clearing out the old potting shed when he discovered three most unusual items. A corked bottle labelled 'Moon Wine', a tattered old notebook and a sack of peculiar, evil-smelling fertilizer which possessed a squirmy, almost fleshy texture.

After investigating the fertilizer, Horace turned his attention to the 'Moon Wine'. He eased his squat and chubby body down onto a packing case and studied the bottle dubiously. Then he tweaked out the cork, his pudgy snout executing an explorative sortie, ready to retreat at the first trace of any repugnant odour. But it lingered, savouring the aroma of sweet spices blended with the finest brandy and other rich essences which he was unable to identify. It certainly smelt most agreeable and there was only one way to find out. Horace raised the bottle to his mallow-soft lips and took a tentative sip. Excellent! By golly, the old lady knew how to make wine, even if she had been a bit cracked! He belched discreetly after the fourth swig and decided that enough was enough for the time being.

Then he picked up the notebook and thumbed through its pages which were covered with his aunt's familiar spidery handwriting. Horace could make out date references, notes on the moon's phases and the position of certain stars. It all smacked of some sort of mumbo-jumbo.

The he found a page headed 'Marrow Food'. There followed a bewildering list of herbs and chemicals, some of which he had never heard. On the facing page was another recipe which was of more immediate interest to him. 'Moon Wine'. Horace chuckled flatly. A good name, he congratulated his deceased Aunt Amanda, and one quite worthy of that elixir of joy. Unfortunately, some dampness from the floor of the potting shed had soaked through the page, half obliterating the list of ingredients. Horace softly mewed his displeasure. Stupid old woman! Fancy leaving the book to the mercy of the elements!

But one intriguing part was still legible, albeit a perplexing one. 'To establish the desired rapport one may partake of two drams of Moon Wine and spread three scoopfuls of the Marrow Food around the Marrow. This must only be done by the light of the full moon.'

The rest of the epistle was a mass of blotchy smudges and Horace could only make out a few disjointed sentences and phrases such as 'beware, for it is a cunning beast ...' and 'trust not its persuasive powers and abide strictly to the instructions.'

Horace sat back on the packing case, the notebook dangling limply from his fat fingers. What witless, superstitious, time-wasting rubbish had the old bat been fooling with? But was it rubbish? He shivered slightly. If it wasn't rubbish ...

It was dusk now and a full moon had risen, shining its pallid rays through the cracked and dusty panes of the potting shed's little window. His mind made up, Horace jammed the bottle of Moon Wine into his jacket pocket and, forcing himself to pick up the reeking sack of fertilizer, staggered outside with it and blundered his way to the as yet unexplored regions of the kitchen garden.

In the moonlight he could just make out the neat rows of onions, lettuces and other vegetables, all standing to attention. But, dominating all was the finest, largest, glossiest marrow that he had ever clapped eyes on. A giant! At least four feet long and no less than a foot in diameter at its widest point. It reclined in its bed of leaves like some splendid and yellow-striped dirigible, ready to float up into the clouds at any moment.

Horace gaped in astonishment. This Marrow Supreme was surely the King of the kitchen garden. These sparse little attendant weeds were only fit to pay homage to it!

'You're new here, aren't you, mate?' asked a voice.

Horace peered around owlishly, but there was nobody in sight. Odd sort of voice. Couldn't really tell where it came from. It was almost as it had spoken in his head.

'You done the old girl in?' the voice quizzed him again.

'Who ... who said that?' stammered Horace, whirling about.

'I did!' snapped the voice. 'And mind where you're putting your feet. You nearly flattened me then.'

Instantly Horace realised where the voice came from. The marrow! 'What!' he yelped. 'Who ... why ...?'

'Shut up and stop dancing around!' the voice in his head admonished him. 'I know the score. You done the old girl in and now you've found out about her little hobby – me. Now stop bleating and I'll give you the run-down. That Moon Wine you've been guzzling is a special formula which sensitises your dormant mental nerve-ends so that you can pick up my thoughts. Don't work in daylight though. Oh, no. All them noisy ultra-violet rays zapping through the air causes too much interference. Night time's the best – like now, with a full moon. Makes us both more receptive.

'But you're a vegetable!' squeaked Horace, clutching at his head with both hands. 'You haven't got a brain!'

'You watch your mouth!' the voice threatened. 'How the hell do you think I grow if I haven't got a brain? Answer me that, eh?'

Horace swept a trembling hand in a gesture that embraced the rest of the kitchen garden. 'You mean all these other vegetables as well –?'

'Them,' scoffed the Marrow. 'They're just a load of old scrubbers and layabouts. Not worth wasting your time on. I'm the one you should be concerned with, so get shovelling that gorgeous sackful around, just under my leaves. Then a good trench and tip the rest in.'

'But, it says only three scoopfuls in the book,' whined Horace.

'Blow the ruddy book! That old bird was too mean by half. I know what's best for me.'

'But the forecasters said it might rain tonight,' Horace weakly objected.

'The forecasters said it might rain tonight,' the Marrow mimicked him. 'What if it does? So much the better. It'll be easier to dig.'

'But all that Marrow Food in one go –'

'You just do as I say and never mind the damn book! This is the Twentieth Century and things have changed since that was first written.'

Despite the overwhelming influence of the wondrous marrow, Horace still possessed some vestiges of propriety. 'I can't do it now,' he objected. 'Someone might see me, and besides, I'll have to put my old gardening trousers on.'

'Okay, okay,' agreed the Marrow ill-humouredly. 'Have it your own way – but you make sure you're out here before midnight – or I'll come and drag you out!'

The mental picture of this threat sent, Horace scuttling back towards the house, knowing full well that to disobey was more than he dare.

As it happened, his fears had proved justified as far as unwanted spectators were concerned. There was Mrs Miggs, his housekeeper, to be disposed of – though not so drastically as his Aunt Amanda had been. Horace told her that she could have the evening off as he was going out to visit a friend, then watched her set off with nervous satisfaction, towards the Bingo hall.

The other obstacle was Mrs Skeggs, crony neighbour of his late aunt. Mrs Skeggs was inquisitive by nature and was forever popping in to see what changes Horace had wrought on the property. One could never be sure when she was likely to do her 'popping'. But once again fortune was on his side and he duly intercepted her halfway up the front garden path after seeing his housekeeper set off after the crock of gold.

Having headed off the only two problems before his nocturnal adventure, Horace set about preparing a meal. This was more to pass the time rather than to stave off any hunger pangs. Never had he felt less ready for food than he did now. In fact, all he could manage to force down were a few ginger nut biscuits and – less reluctantly – two large scotches.

What was this all about? How could a marrow – an ordinary vegetable – possibly converse with him, even to the point of intimidating him? But it had, and he had to see the business through. He glanced at the clock. Ten-thirty – and it was pouring cats and dogs outside. He poured himself another scotch, swigged it down and stumbled unsteadily upstairs to find his gardening trousers.

'Took your time, didn't you?' the Marrow greeted him out of the darkness.

Horace growled sullenly back and fumbled with the shovel that he had only just remembered to collect from the potting shed.

'None of your lip, sonny,' the Marrow warned him. 'You've been hitting the bottle by the look of you. You just make sure you dig that trench and pour the Marrow Food in before you pass out on me.'

Horace began to dig. He lost all sense of time as he toiled. He paused occasionally to take a swig of Moon Wine from the bottle still stowed away in his jacket pocket. Mixed with the whiskey and the ginger nuts, it had the most peculiar effect on him but not at all unpleasant. And as he dug deeper and deeper the Marrow sang rude vegetable songs, punctuated every so often by a snigger. And it rained. It rained hard, but Horace slaved away, now completely obsessed with the job in hand. When he had reached a depth of some five feet the Marrow told him to stop.

'I reckon that's deep enough. Why don't you finish the rest of that rot-gut instead of standing there puffing? You're a bigger twit than the old biddy ever was.'

Horace glared through the dark at the Marrow, gleaming in the faint light of the moon, obscured by heavy clouds. Glossy green tendrils coiled like ropes from beneath its bulk.

'For the luvva Mike! Get that drink down you and get on with emptying that sack in the hole, you fat old goat!'

Horace gulped the rest of the Moon Wine and cast the bottle into the trench. Emboldened by the liquid fire that coursed through his stomach and veins, he said, 'I must say you are quite a common-spoken fellow. I did hope – hic – that you would have better manners.'

'Yeah,' chortled the Marrow. 'Common or garden – that's me. What, did you expect? Oxford or Cambridge? You just get on with your work and don't get smart with me.'

'I don't see where all this is leading,' muttered Horace, dragging the sack of Marrow food to the edge of the trench.

'You just empty the sack and shovel all the soil back double-quick,' the Marrow retorted. 'You have got it all banked up ready, I suppose?'

'Of course I have!' snapped Horace irritably as he shook the fertilizer into the trench. 'Blowed if I know why I take orders from you –'

'Don't get stroppy with me, laddie, if you know what's good for you!'

'You'll do what?' declared Horace, hurling the empty sack and the shovel angrily into the trench as the rain cascaded down, soaking him to the skin. 'I've had enough of you and this blasted digging. I'm going to shut myself indoors, have a good bath and another double scotch – and you can go to the devil!'

Horace never had time to decide if he tripped over one of those green coiling tendrils or if it had actually wrapped itself around his ankle. Either way the result was the same. He tripped and sprawled across the waterlogged pit, his hands scrabbling vainly for a purchase in the bank of loose soil. They found none and he lunged headlong into the hole, too tanked up on Moon Wine and whiskey to fully comprehend what was happening to him. The bank of soil, dislodged by his clawings and by the incessant rain, poured in on top of him, filling the self-dug grave and burying Horace Hapgood forevermore from the world of light and life.

Mrs Miggs, his housekeeper, didn't call the next day, owing to a nasty head cold. In fact, she didn't show up until three days later. The house was like the *Marie Celeste*. There was no sign of Horace Hapgood anywhere. In due course the police were called in and the house was searched from attic to cellar – all to no avail. Horace had disappeared from the face of the earth. They didn't realise just how true this was.

Two policemen were poking around aimlessly in the garden, not really knowing what they were looking for, when one said, 'Cor! Take a look at that marrow, Charlie! There's a prize winner if ever there was!'

The other policeman stared at the super-size marrow – a gigantic six feet in length, nestling atop a mound of rich, dark soil, its broad leaves spread out to catch the sun. 'I've never seen one to equal that,' he solemnly declared. 'Whatever it's been fed on must have had plenty of body in it.'

SHADOWSHINE THIRTEEN

Horace Hapgood blundered through what had appeared to be the frosted glass of the light lock which still, more or less, bore a resemblance to a clinic extension. But it was not until he observed what had been a normal floor that had changed to a bluish-white with the consistency of meringue that he realised all was not as he had supposed it to be. Indeed, the surroundings in which he now found himself bore no resemblance whatsoever to Dr Patel's surgery. He was in a vast auditorium, enclosed by soaring white marble pillars that disappeared into serene and fleecy clouds high above. 'The Civic Centre,' he croaked.

'No, it is not the Civic Centre,' a stentorian voice corrected him. 'You have been summoned before the Eye of Truth in the Shadow-shine Auditorium so that your mortal deeds and misdeeds may be judged.'

Then Horace saw the tall desk with its Olympian occupant glaring down at him. He also saw the squat and scaly figures armed with pitchforks, riot shields, and wearing steel helmets. They crouched before the desk with their pitchforks held out menacingly before them. Also present was, to Horace's somewhat myopic vision, an anorexic-looking character in what appeared to be a tattered black plastic mac which hung on him so loosely that his diet really must have crash-dived. Next to him stood a spindly old weirdo with side whiskers and odd-looking six-sided spectacles, wearing a red flannelette nighshirt and cap. This latter person suddenly erupted in a warble of delight.

'Horace's auntie was a witch, and no excuse would pardon 'er. The spellbound marrow that she raised, ate up her nephew garden-er.'

'Shut up, Sandy!' shouted the white-bearded man at the desk. 'I shan't tell you again!'

So all the dreadful speculations were true then! He was dead after all! That Spratt woman, old Doyle, Calvert and Square ...! Horace would have died of shock there and then had he not been dead already. 'Wh-who are you?' he managed to squeak.

'I am the Soul Searcher who charts your immortal destiny,' thundered the presence at the high desk. 'You have been summoned before me to atone for your crimes – and black and evil they are, too.'

'He doesn't look all that dangerous to me, Solly,' said one of the squat and armoured figures. 'Can I take this helmet off? It's hurting my horns.'

'Silence, Scabwort!' retorted the Soul Searcher. 'This mortal is a desperate and dangerous character. He murdered his Aunt Amanda.'

'Who says so?' challenged Horace in defiance born of desperation.

'I say so, laddie!' bellowed the Soul Searcher, jabbing his finger repeatedly at the huge book on the desk before him, 'and so does this book! Oho, we've been reading up on your fun and games, Hapgood. Putting soap on the stairs so that your poor old auntie broke her neck. The Cherubs have got it all on video.'

Horace knew he was beaten. Now he remembered everything. 'She was old –' he weakly began.

'I'm no bloody spring chicken!' stormed the Soul Searcher threshing about angrily on his stool, 'but that doesn't give anyone the right to put soap on Jacob's Ladder while I'm on it! No – you bumped off the poor old duck and you'll face the music!'

Scabwort coughed politely – so politely that the Soul Searcher stared at him in surprise. 'There's something you oughta know, Solly,' he murmured in a loud whisper. 'Aunt Amanda –'

'Be quiet, Scabwort,' the Soul Searcher interrupted him. He turned his baleful countenance once again Horace. 'This poor lady in the evening of her years, without friends to give her solace and companionship – and you *croaked* her.'

'Old Mrs Skeggs used to pop over for coffee every Wednesday morning,' Horace pointed out defiantly.

'One or two hours out of an entire week – pah!' The Soul Searcher dismissed Mrs Skeggs with a disdainful wave of his hand. 'What comfort had she in her declining years? A lonely old house and her beloved back garden.'

'The old woman was loaded,' Horace objected indignantly, 'and that garden of hers was as big as a ruddy park! I know – I had to mow and weed the damn thing.'

'Hey, Chief,' Scabwort nervously interrupted again. 'Ain't you checked the files? The old biddy was a witch.'

'Witch-what-who?' gibbered the Soul Searcher through his twitching beard. 'Why wasn't this clarified? I don't know what the place is coming to these days.' Still gibbering to himself he riffled through the Recorder Book before him.

'I remember her,' remarked Grimshaw, snapping his finger bones. 'I brought her up on the last batch. A stroppy old woman in corsets.'

'That's right,' nodded Scabwort. 'Always sucking peppermints, wasn't she?'

'That's the one,' the Grim Reaper replied. 'I don't want too many like her, Scab. Bad tempered old crab, she was.'

The Soul Searcher slammed shut his Recorder Book. 'Will you two be silent!' He re-opened the book. 'Oh, yes ... well, I see. It does happen to say something about her dabbling in the Black Arts.'

'Oh, that one,' remarked Rubbish-Legs, emerging from his customary state of diabolical meditation and horn-scratching. 'Yeah, I remember her, too.'

'Rubbish-Legs remembers something!' applauded the Sandman, waving his skinny arms in the air. 'It's a miracle!'

'What else would you expect up here?' sniggered Grimshaw.

The two demons burst into raucous peals of mirth, much to the Soul Searcher's annoyance. 'I don't know what you two find so funny,' he snapped at them. 'In fact, you could both be in for a nasty shock.'

Scabwort stopped laughing at once and glared suspiciously at the Soul Searcher. 'Shock? What sort of shock?'

The Soul Searcher's voice was rich with honeyed sweetness. 'It would seem that what you say about the defendant's aunt is true. And that being the case it may well give rise to mitigating circumstances in Hapgood's favour and automatically cancel your claim to his soul.'

Scabwort's mouth worked in a spasm of dismay and his crimson, scaly face paled to a deathly pink. 'You can't mean it!' he croaked. 'Say it's not true!'

'Of course it's true,' chipped in Horace, seeing his chance of redemption. 'She was wicked and bad, and I did humanity a service by getting rid of her.'

'That's not fair,' protested Rubbish-Legs stamping a cloven hoof indignantly. 'She wasn't all that good at being bad. I saw her results. She took the Black Arts Open University Course. She got B Minus for Bad, absolute zilch for Positively Evil and she flunked out completely on her Morally Depraved paper. Her only high marks were for Advanced Naughtiness – B Plus.'

Soul Searcher was enjoying the situation immensely. He was now the actual fulcrum of the scales of justice. A freelance Cherub even flew down and took a stained glass photograph of him for a vicar in Strood to dream about for his new transept window. 'I have given this matter some careful thought,' the Soul Searcher finally deliberated, 'and I have at last come to a decision.'

'About time, too,' muttered Grimshaw. 'No wonder they call this place Eternity.'

'On one hand we have Hapgood's Aunt Amanda, who was a witch – and he most likely did do his society a favour by bumping her off. But, on the other hand his motives were prompted by personal gain. While on the other hand –'

'How many ruddy hands have you got?' Grimshaw grumbled impatiently.

'– While on the other hand,' the Soul Searcher continued, choosing to ignore his subordinate's whinging observations, 'when all is said and done, Hapgood murdered her. And that being the case I can see no reason why sentence should not be passed and the soul of Horace Hapgood consigned to the Nether Regions for an unspecified period of punishment.'

'Yippee!' screamed Scabwort, seizing Rubbish-Legs and dancing a merry little jig. 'A real live dead murderer – and he's all ours!'

'What about a plea for defence?' howled Horace, waving his fists in the air. 'Even if I did sort of help her on her way, didn't I give her a good funeral? I even fed her cat regularly. If you really want to find someone wicked, what about that damned marrow of hers? Now there's a murderer for you! The rotten thing got me smashed out of my skull on that Moon Wine rot-gut and then buried me alive in the kitchen garden! But I don't suppose that counts,' he added with bitter sarcasm. 'Who's ever heard of a marrow being charged with murder?'

The Sandman rubbed his wispy hands together and stood on one leg. 'I say,' he murmured, 'isn't it exciting?'

The Soul Searcher glanced questioningly at Scabwort who was still prancing around the Auditorium, waving his pitchfork jubilantly. 'That's an interesting point, Scabwort. What about that marrow?'

Put off his stroke, Scabwort caught Grimshaw a stinging clout on the side of his skull with the pitchfork. 'Watch out, you clumsy idiot!' yelped the Grim Reaper, rubbing his skull. 'You might have lifed me!'

'He's under psychiatric care in the Tartans Infirmary,' said Scabwort.

'Who is?' snapped Grimshaw.

'I was talking to Solly about the marrow,' Scabwort patiently explained. 'He's one of our field agents.'

'Garden agents would be more like it,' muttered Rubbish-Legs, sniggering at his own joke.

'Order, order,' the Soul Searcher called out, banging his fist on the desk top.

'Now then, Scabwort, what's all this about a marrow having psychiatric treatment?'

'Well, chief, he's not really a marrow,' Scabwort explained. 'He's an elemental called Nigel who took possession of the marrow when the defendant's auntie bewitched it. Lucifer's very pleased with him and as soon as Nigel is discharged from hospital he's going to be awarded the Despicable Order of Villainy for active service in the field – or garden in this case.'

'Very much merited, too, I'm sure,' pressed the Soul Searcher, fidgeting on his stool. 'But what is the fellow doing in hospital?'

'That's the sad part of it, Chief,' Scabwort sighed. 'When Hapgod's property was sold up, Nigel – still in his marrow form – was taken away by Mrs Miggs, the housekeeper, and served up for dinner in the hall canteen. Nigel then took possession of an elderly lollipop man who naturally ran amok and started trying to pole vault across a zebra crossing with his lollipop sign during the rush hour. When he was discharged from hospital, and after a few more similar pranks, he was exorcised by three dwarf Czechoslovakian vicars. And that's how poor old Nigel ended up in the Tartans Infirmary. He had been severely belled, booked and candled.'

'Serves him right,' sniffed the Soul Searcher. 'He should have got out while he had the chance. That's the trouble with your crowd, Scabwort – No wonder it's one of the seven Deadly Sins.'

During this exchange Horace had been standing to one side, staring incredulously at the group. His arms were sore where he had pinched himself several times to make sure that he wasn't dreaming. 'I don't believe it,' he whispered. 'I just don't believe it. This can't really be happening.'

'It most certainly is, Mr Horace Hapgood,' the Soul Searcher sternly assured him, 'and your hour of judgement is nigh. Take him away, Scabwort. He's all yours. Brandishing their pitchforks, the two demons converged on Horace, beaming from horn to horn. The latter did not share their holiday mood at all and then it seemed as if something inside him snapped. Considering his meringue-like fatness, he could move surprisingly fast, and when this speed was combined with a fury of desperation, he could become a force to be reckoned with. The pair of demons were quite unprepared for what happened next. Their quarry lowered his head like a bull and charged them, butting Scabwort in the stomach and kicking Rubbish-Legs in the teeth. Both demons fell to the floor screeching in terror while Horace seized their pitchforks and, virtually foaming at the mouth, hurled one of them at the Soul Searcher's desk with such force that, the sharp prongs split the white panelling.

'Run for it, Sandy!' bawled Grimshaw, gathering up his shroud and darting for the shelter of the light lock. 'He's dangerous!'

'There once was a mortal called Horace –' began the Sandman, but relinquished impromptu verse for survival as the second pitchfork whizzed past his nightcap and carved a great chunk of glittering green out of the light lock.

To his credit Scabwort was on his hooves in a second and attempted to bring Horace down with a rugby tackle. But all he got for his efforts was a sharp elbow jab in the eye.

'Tricky, ain't he,' remarked Rubbish-Legs, spitting out several loose fangs.

The Soul Searcher was almost hysterical with panic. 'Red alert!' he screamed, taking refuge behind his splintered desk. 'Someone send for the Seraphic Security Brigade! He'll wreck the place!'

Horace, frantically seeking some avenue of escape, darted towards the light lock. Grimshaw saw him coming and lost his skull completely. 'Leave me alone!' he shrieked in terror. 'I've a Night Hag and three Ghouls to support!'

'Out of my way, you – you dog's dinner!' yelled Horace, seizing the fallen pitchfork and making a threatening jab with it at the very Grim Reaper. 'You're not going to send me down to Hell – over my dead body you will!'

'But that's just the point –!' jabbered Grimshaw, cringing on the churned up clouds.

'Not another word!' Horace snarled, brandishing the pitch-fork over the cloaked skeletal form. 'Not another word or ... or I'll kill you!'

Grimshaw howled and threw his shroud over his skull in anguish. 'But that's what I'm trying to tell you, you twit! We're dead already – all of us!'

Several officers of the Seraphic Security Brigade in mottled blue and white camouflage battledress and armoured haloes, all armed with soul-suppressor hand guns, had appeared and grouped themselves around the Soul Searcher's wrecked desk.

'Halo, halo, halo,' remarked the officer in charge. 'And what's been a-goin' here?'

The Soul Searcher, having regained a few pathetic vestiges of his former composure, urged them forward. 'Subdue that soul!' he shrieked. 'He's been sentenced to Hell but refuses to go with his demoniac escort. He's turning the place into a battlefield!'

Somewhat uncertainly the angelic guardians of Light, Law and Order edged forward. The Sandman had quietly snuck off to the far side of the Auditorium where he could view the proceedings from a safer vantage point. But Scabwort and Rubbish-Legs, much to their credit, and taking into account their recent injuries, tried once again to pacify the renegade mortal soul. 'Now you just come along with us, sir,' cajoled Scabwort, edging forward, one hopeful talon extended for the pitchfork. 'It's not really all that bad there and you may even get to like it.'

'Oh yeah?' Horace retorted, still crouching by the light lock with the pitchfork held out menacingly before him. 'Penthouse suites and dolly birds, I suppose? Pull the other one – it's got bells on!'

'Take your punishment like a man!' bellowed the Soul Searcher, safely behind the ranks of Seraphic Security Troopers. 'You will roast forever in Hell, condemned to eating a never-ending supply of caraway seed cake baked by your wretched Aunt Amanda!'

Horace's response was a most eloquent string of profanities which surprised even himself.

'There you are!' declared Rubbish-Legs triumphantly. 'You speak the local dialect beautifully. You'll get on down there like a house on fire.'

With a howl of rage Horace hurled the pitchfork at the two demons, but fortunately it went wide and he turned and ducked into the multi-coloured shadows of the light lock. 'After him!' shouted the Soul Searcher. 'There's no telling what damage he may do if he gets loose in the Time Zone!'

Horace raced through the light lock, bumping into cross-sections of orange and yellow, unheeding of the bruises. At the far end he shoulder-charged the Time Seal, splashing dollops of ultra-violet in all directions. Wiping some of it from his fat and glaring face, he peered around for somewhere to hide. He seemed to be standing on nothing, in absolute nothing, but the vast and shimmering Clouds of Time that seethed around the abyss looked as if they might afford some sort of refuge.

The sound of the pursuers' voices some way behind him along the light lock spurred him into action. With a croak of rage he leapt onto the near-invisible Time Walk which skirted the Clouds of Time and hid himself behind a heap of moments that were packed ready to be loaded onto the temporal conveyor belt. He was only just in time, too. Approaching voices from some distance ahead prompted him to burrow even deeper under cover, but not enough to prevent him from observing the new-comers.

A scholarly-looking Seraph, wearing a mortar-board halo, was shepherding a class of junior Cherubs along the Time Walk, and as bad luck would have it, they paused only a short distance from Horace's hiding place. 'Now I want you all to pay careful attention to this,' the angelic tutor told his youthful gathering. 'We are now in the Time Zone and this endless wall of cloud which encloses the area is Time. Look through the portals and you will see what I mean.'

They all dutifully looked, Horace risked a peep, too. An endless line of goods trucks rolled and rattled by. On one was painted the word 'Wednesday' and on the next 'Thursday'. There was nothing particularly special about them except that they were all of varying colours, but even these assorted colours were dull and lacklustre. Slowly they trundled by – a never-ending, procession of trucks, all marked with the days of the week in faded grey paint. Week after week after week ...

'Please, sir,' piped up an earnest-looking Cherub. 'How many wagons are there?'

'As many as it takes to transport the stock of Time Godfrey Minor,' replied the tutor. 'In other words, they go on forever. Each one is a day of the week, making up a month and then a year – and so it goes on.'

'Who drives the train, sir?' asked another young spirit.

For a brief moment the Seraph looked perplexed – but only for a brief moment. 'That is something you may learn when you have graduated to the Higher Realms,' he replied. 'But I can assure you that the Time Train has been running ceaselessly since ... since Time began.'

A wild scheme was forming in Horace's mind but the sight of another figure approaching caused him to cringe down even further behind the shelter of the moments. The stranger was a tall, stoop-shouldered old man with a bald head and a long, long grey beard. He slouched along the Time Walk borne down by the weighty scythe he carried over one bent shoulder. In his hand he swung an hour-glass with casual nonchalance.

'Greetings, Father Time, the seraphic tutor hailed the aged, grey-robed figure. I was just showing these young Cherubs the wonders of the Time Zone. I trust that you have no objections?'

'Just as long as the sprogs don't meddle with anything,' grunted Father Time. 'One lot got to messing around and shunted an entire section of the Time Train into a parallel universe.'

The tutor looked mildly shocked. 'I can most certainly assure you, Father Time, that, my charges are most well-behaved.'

Father Time glared down at the upturned cherubic faces. 'Well, just you make sure they stay that way,' he snorted, and then stomped off into the temporal mists, muttering to himself.

'Time marches on,' the seraphic tutor observed brightly, 'and waits far no man.'

'So long, old timer,' called out one mischievous Cherub with an inky halo.

The Seraph clouted him in the mouth. 'Now hurry along, boys,' he chivvied them in decorous tones. 'I am now going to take you to see the Dream Zone. Hurry along now and don't dawdle, Optimus Minimus.'

Horace watched the crocodile of pinkly plump little Cherubs file away after their tutor. At last the coast was clear for him to make a break for it. The loud voices issuing from the light lock goaded him into action, sending him plunging through the outer mists of Time. Just then, Grimshaw, closely followed by Scabwort and Rubbish-Legs, tumbled out of the light lock with the Soul Searcher and the Seraphic Security Troopers close on his heels.

'He's trying to hide in the Time Zone!' shouted Grimshaw, tripping over the hem of his shroud and blundering into Scabwort. 'I just glimpsed his gardening wellies as he ducked into the cloud.'

In a body they plunged into the foggy temporal maelstrom in pursuit of the runaway mortal soul. Horace, risking a fleeting glance over his shoulder, realised that his pursuers were closing the gap and forced himself to make the final effort. The Train of Time rattled hollowly through the gloom before him. The never-ending montage of truck after truck, each painted with a day of the week, loomed out of the murk. Every so often a truck much larger would appear, marked with 'April' or 'May' and so forth.

Horace knew that it would be fatal – if it hadn't been already – to hesitate, and with one final and frantic effort he launched himself with hands outstretched at one of the trucks. The iron chain of seconds cut into his grasping fingers as he hauled himself up the side of a truck marked 'Wednesday'. But he had managed to get a foothold on one of the minutes that projected from the side of the vehicle. Then flinging one leg over the side and scrambling over a stack of hours, he tumbled down into the cargo of sun-shine, bus strikes, weddings, divorces, birthdays and early closing days which constitute a typical Wednesday.

He lay on the cold boards at the bottom of the truck, wedged between tea party conversations, slivers of suburban gossip and plastic bags inflated with party political broadcasts and speeches. Where he was bound he didn't know, but at least he was away from that celestial three-ring circus. Whatever happened, they wouldn't be able to send him to Hell now.

Overcome by exhaustion, Horace closed his eyes and sank into a deep sleep, oblivious of the Train of Time as it rattled with metallic echoes on its endless journey through the infinities of Is, Was, When, Where and Will Be …

'He's scarpered,' Grimshaw groaned, straining his eye-sockets after the truck marked 'Wednesday'. 'We've lost him.'

The Soul Searcher tore his beard in a frenzy. 'This is really terrible,' he fretted. 'Nothing like this has ever happened before. How is this going down in my report to Upstairs?'

'And how is it going to go up in my report to Downstairs, eh?' retorted Scabwort angrily. 'Lucifer will be in the very angel of a mood when he finds out about this.'

The officer in charge of the Seraphic Security Brigade reholstered his soul suppressor. 'I'll get my men to stop the train and make a search of the trucks,' he suggested. 'We'll soon have the fugitive back where he belongs.'

'You'll what?' screeched a new voice. It was Father Time, standing at the back of the group and trembling with such violent rage that the sand in his hour-glass had begun to fuse. 'A fine example you'll set the Cherubs if you do that! This is my province and I absolutely forbid it. Furthermore, I have sufficient authority placed in my hands by Upstairs to send you all packing! You're trespassing – so clear off!'

Grimshaw stepped forward, a pleading look on his skull. 'Be reasonable, Uncle. These are extenuating circumstances –'

'Don't you try to pull any strings with me, Nephew!' snapped Father Time, waving his scythe threateningly. 'Just because you are unfortunately related to me, Grimshaw, doesn't grant you any special privileges, you – you Nepotist!'

Grimshaw slunk back fearfully. 'He means it,' he muttered nervously. 'I reckon we'll just have to chalk this one up to experience.'

It was a disconsolate little group that gathered in the Shadowshine Auditorium. The Seraphic Security Troopers had departed, returning to their barracks, no doubt blancoeing their haloes and doing cloud drill. 'No luck, eh?' chirped a little voice from behind the pitchfork-impaled desk. Then the Sandman emerged into view from his haven where he had safely concealed himself out of harm's way.

'What does it look like, idiot?' growled the Soul Searcher as he prised the pitchfork from the front of his desk.

'Well someone's going to get blamed for this,' announced Grimshaw, folding his boney arms. 'But who is it going to be? Not me, I can assure you. My responsibility ended when I brought Hapgood's soul up from Earth.'

The Soul Searcher favoured him with a frosty look. 'It's at times like this when you find out who your friends are,' he remarked. 'And I can, tell you that it won't be me either. I had passed sentence on Hapgood and my side of the business finished then. So who's left?'

They all turned and stared at Scabwort and Rubbish-Legs.

'Now wait, a minute,' protested Scabwort nervously. 'He was still up here when he escaped. We hadn't even got him on the escalator.'

'That's right,' Rubbish-Legs hastily backed up his fellow demon. 'Your security was at fault.'

'I'm blessed if I'll stand for a pair of scrubby-faced imp cadets telling me how to run my show!' the Soul Searcher exploded. 'It's your fault and you know it! And that being the case, it's up to you to bring the soul of Horace Hapgood back!'

Both demons knew that it was no use arguing. Hapgood had officially been handed into their custody and had escaped from it. 'But where do we start looking for him?' wailed Rubbish-Legs, nervously chewing the end at his fork tail. 'He could be anywhere.'

'It's not so bad really,' Grimshaw consoled him. 'True he could be anywhere in the past, present or future. He could be back on Earth or even on another planet in a distant galaxy. For that matter he could be in an uncharted dimension – another parallel universe existing as a microcosmic star system. Come to that he –'

'Belt up!' Scabwort snapped. 'You don't have to paint a picture!'

'Every cloud has a silver lining,' Grimshaw continued his inane rhetoric, ignoring Rubbish-Legs who had just collapsed in tears to the cloudy floor, drumming his cloven hooves. 'But whatever, whenever or wherever he is, you can be sure of one thing.'

'And what's that?' gritted Scabwort.

'It'll be on a Wednesday.'

This was too much for poor Rubbish-Legs who began to gibber. Scabwort helped him to his hooves and glared murderously at the Reaper. 'Think yourself lucky you're dead already, Grim,' he snarled, 'otherwise I'd wring your rotten neck!'

Grimshaw petulantly tossed his skull and placed his hands on his pelvis. 'There's just no helping some people,' he sniffed.

The Soul Searcher, having taken a manna tablet, felt more or less his old organised self. 'Let's not beat about the bush,' he declared, ascending to his lofty desk and glaring down at his colleagues. 'Horace Hapgood must be returned to us, and that's the job of Scabwort and Rubbish-Legs. I suggest we all get on with what we are to be doing and get this place running properly again.' He rang a bell that rested on his desk. 'And the first thing I'm going to do is get this desk repaired. We can't have a new batch of souls seeing the place in such a deplorable state. It would quite undermine their confidence of the beliefs of a lifetime.'

'I suppose you're right,' sighed Scabwort as he stooped to help Rubbish-Legs gather up the helmets, shields and pitchforks which the earlier commotion had strewn about the Auditorium. 'Come on, Rubbish-Legs, you poor devil. We'll be on our way. Just try to regard it as a working holiday away from all the furnace stoking.'

'Well, if all the fun is over I'll get back to my Dream Zone,' said the Sandman, picking up his bulging sack of sleepy dust and swinging it up onto his shoulder.

Grimshaw collected his scythe from the stasis locker. 'The same goes for me,' he announced. 'I've got a deadline to meet.' He briskly shouldered the scythe, but in so doing, sliced the Sand-man's sack wide open.

'You calcium-ridden clown!' shrieked the Sandman as the twink-ling mass of sleepy dust billowed throughout the Auditorium. 'Look what you've done!'

'Someone switch on the extractor fans!' roared the Soul Searcher as the fine bluish mist seeped into every nook and cranny of the vast hall. 'No one's going to sleep on the job while I'm in charge!'

Grimshaw was the first to succumb. With the dense clouds of somnambulistic blue rising about him, his jawbone yammered in embarrassed stuttering and then stilled as his eye-sockets glazed over. Then he slumped to the floor with a cheap-sounding clatter.

Scabwort and Rubbish-Legs, on the point of entering the light lock, were next. Pitchforks, riot shields and helmets slipping from talons, they collapsed, already deep in slumber, no doubt dreaming of doomed souls jumping over electrified barbed wire fences.

The Soul Searcher glared frantically at the Sandman, standing in a rising cloud of the sleepy dust as it slowly welled up around his red flannelette nightshirt. 'Do something, Sandy!' he implored wildly. 'Heaven's Harps, this is your department! Surely you can do something?'

The Sandman grinned vacuously and yawned. 'Shall I send for Macbeth?' he giggled, obviously having lost whatever few wits he possessed. 'For did not the Bard of Avon write that "Macbeth hath murdered sleep"?' Then he yawned loudly, teetered back on the heels of his carpet slippers and sank from sight into the rising, slumberous mists, already sound asleep.

The Soul Searcher clutched in panic at the gilt-moulded edge of his desk and stared around wildly. They were all asleep somewhere beneath the coiling, roiling clouds of sleepy dust. Even as he watched from his lofty vantage point he could see eddies of the stuff swirling away in all directions. Gusting through the light locks, through to the Time Zone and the Dream Zone. Strands of it were seeping down the fireproof escalator and some – oh, no! – some was drifting upwards towards the Higher Realms!

A wave of weariness tugged at his drooping eyelids, but those eyelids were to open wide with alarm as he heard a loud plop not far away. Several more loud plops followed, and peering through the blue mist, the Soul Searcher saw Cherub after Cherub, all sound asleep, dropping like stones all over the floor of the Auditorium. They were falling thick and fast now and the Soul Searcher began counting them in an effort to combat the increasing torpor which was stealing over him.

'Eighteen, nineteen,' he murmured, staring glassily down at the cloud-carpeted floor, littered with Cherubs, pink, plump, naked and asleep. It looked like a mass of pink cobblestones. All Shadow-shine was sleeping!

And still he counted. 'Eighty-six ... eighty-seven ...'

Then the plops ceased. 'Eighty-seven and all for the count,' the Soul Searcher mumbled, slumping forward across his desk ...

EPILOGUE

'Eighty-seven and all out. Not bad, eh, Vicar?'

The Reverend Solomon Searchington blinked open his eyes and stared about him. Mellow evening sunshine garnished the pavilion and the crisp green cricket pitch before him. He stared owlishly at the elderly gentleman with dapper side whiskers adorning his narrow face who sat next to him, very relaxed and proper in blazer, cravat and flannels. Of course! Dr Sanderson, or Sandy as he personally knew him, ever since their boyhood days when they were school chums.

'Where am I?' murmured the Reverend Searchington staring bemusedly at the metal effigy of Father Time on the far side of the pitch.

'Why, Lords, of course, old man. Where the deuce did you think you were?'

The Vicar thought long and hard for a moment. 'Oh, that Lords,' he said at last.

Dr Sanderson regarded him quizzically. 'Where did you think you were then? You've missed the best of it, dropping off like that. You should have seen that young Scabworth – a real demon bowler. Got, Grimsdale out for a duck – leg before wicket.'

'Leg?' echoed the Vicar a faraway voice 'You must mean Rub-bish-Legs –'

'I say, are you all right, Solomon?' enquired Sanderson, peering closely at the pale, angular face of his companion. 'I must say you look a bit peaky about the gills. Spot of indigestion, I'd say. That caraway seed cake your housekeeper – what's her name? – Mrs Spratt packed up for your lunch – that's what I reckon has upset you. You don't eat properly – never give yourself time to digest your food –'

'That's right,' nodded the Reverend staring in a trance. 'There's never any Time. Hapgood rode off with it all ...'

'Snap out of it, Solomon,' laughed Sanderson uneasily. 'Are you still dreaming?'

The Reverend Solomon Searchington gazed at the cricket pitch before him with the rays of the setting sun languorously slanting across its emerald expanse. Diminutive, white-clad figures made their leisurely way across the turf towards the pavilion, their elongated shadows trailing along behind them like trains. 'Dreaming?' he echoed softly. 'Yes, Sandy, I do believe I have just started ...'

www.ingramcontent.com/pod-product-compliance
Lightning Source LLC
Chambersburg PA
CBHW051140020726
47501CB00005B/1602